L. BALLEW

His Spanish Rose

Second edition

ISBN (paperback): 979-8-9928281-2-2
ISBN (hardcover): 979-8-9928281-3-9

Editing by Nova Nox
Cover art by Aida Linnea

This book was professionally typeset on Reedsy.
Find out more at reedsy.com

To the Palestinian people who have been through hell and back. I see you, and I stand with you.

"The purpose of life, after all, is to live it, to taste experience to the utmost, to reach out eagerly and without fear for newer and richer experience."

— ELEANOR ROOSEVELT

Contents

Preface

Regarding Irish Lingo and the Spanish Language

While I am neither Irish nor Hispanic, I have traveled to Ireland, Mexico, and Texas. Along the way I picked up words and phrases that have been used in this book. All others were carefully researched. My goal is to always represent other people and cultures as accurately and respectfully as possible. If anything found within these pages is offensive, please know it was unintentionally done.

Chapter One

Teagan

"Where the hell is Kennedy going?" Rowan asks.

As soon as the final buzzer sounded, declaring the Seahawks' victory, Eamon Kennedy untangled himself from the pile of teammates and took off across the pitch toward his new mot, Norah. They recently started dating, and he's already head over heels for her.

"Isn't it obvious, Ro? Norah's here." I shrug.

I'll be honest. I'm a little jealous. My last relationship ended out of the blue at the end of last semester; we had met towards the end of our sophomore year at UNCW and instantly connected. I'd been with Ashley for over a year. The lass didn't know a stranger either. Everywhere we went, she knew someone or made friends with whoever just happened to be nearby. I loved that about her. She loved that I'm Irish but also said she loved me for so much more. Until, one day, she didn't.

"I'm sorry, Teags. I just can't do this anymore. I should have called it months ago, but I hated the idea of hurting you. I still want to be friends though," she says flippantly in the small kitchen of my apartment.

Laughing, I reach for her. "What are you talking about? Are you slagging me? Very funny, you."

Ashley steps away from my grasp and crosses her arms over her chest. "I'm not kidding. We've been drifting apart for a while now. Haven't you noticed?"

I am completely flummoxed. I thought we've been happy together. Yeah, we are always busy with school, jobs, and life in general, but I always make it a point to see her nearly every day.

"No, Ash, I haven't. I thought everything was fine. We've been up to ninety with finals, but I've done my best to connect with you."

"It's not that," she says hesitantly, running her hand through her golden tresses. "Our spark is gone."

"Our spark is gone? What the feck does that mean?" *I ask incredulously.* "Am I not pleasing ya in the bedroom, then? That was one area where I thought we excelled, love. Now yer tellin' me that my cock isn't keeping ya happy?" *I know my Irish accent thickens when I'm frustrated or overly emotional.*

"God, Teagan, that's not what I'm talking about. That's all our relationship had going for it, and I want more. I don't think..." She pauses, pressing her lips together in a thin line.

"You don't think what, Ashley?" *This is so out of left field that I'm making her spell it out for me.*

She takes a deep breath and squares her shoulders before looking me in the eyes. "I don't love you anymore. I haven't for a while now."

It feels like I've just taken a hit on the pitch. She doesn't love me? Hasn't loved me. I sink onto the bar stool behind me.

"I'm sorry," she continues softly. "I don't want to hurt you. I care about you, but I'm not in love with you. I can't keep dragging you along like this. It's not fair to either of us."

I just stare at her in utter disbelief for a moment before whispering, "When?"

"When what?" *Ashley questions.*

2

"When did you stop loving me?"

"Teagan..." she starts.

"No." I shrug. "You at least owe me that much, love. I've devoted myself to you and thought I was giving you everything, but at some point, it wasn't enough. I'd like to know when."

She wrings her hands in front of her and mutters, "Since February."

My head shoots up, eyes narrowing, "February? You haven't loved me since fucking February? Why didn't you say anything to me? I would have done anything to help fix this!"

"What was I supposed to say? 'Teagan, I'm feeling like I don't love you anymore'?" she asks, throwing her hands in the air.

"Yes!" I bellow, rising out of my chair and storming around the kitchen island. "You could have told me anything! Even a simple 'something doesn't feel right,' and then I would have explored that with you! I've always been open and honest with you, since the very beginning."

I stop in my tracks as a thought occurs to me.

"Wait..." I say, "February. That's when you did that internship in Texas."

Ashley's cheeks start to flush, and she refuses to look at me.

"Is there... Did you...meet someone else?"

"Teagan..." she pleads. "Can we just leave it? Please?"

My arms drop to my sides in defeat. She cheated on me. I should have known. Every time I called her while she was away, she either kept the conversation short or didn't answer. She would text me later, claiming that she had been in meetings all day and was exhausted. I wanted her to stay focused and be successful while she was there, so I never pressed the issue.

"Who is he?"

"Don't, Teag. All you need to know is that I'm moving to San Antonio this summer and finishing my degree there," she tells me, shame lacing her every word.

I blow out a rough breath and rake my fingers through my hair. "You're moving? You must really love him, then. I guess there's nothing left to say, is there? You didn't talk to me because you'd already made up your mind, didn't you?"

Ashley timidly closes the space between us, placing a kiss on my cheek. "I'm sorry. I really am. I never wanted to hurt you."

Then she walks out of my apartment and out of my life.

"Oi! O'Brien!" Rowan yells, pulling me from my thoughts.

"Right, sorry, mate. Yeah, I'll go get him."

I take off in a jog across the pitch to where my friend and teammate is kissing his girl passionately. It's pretty impressive actually. I'm about to make some smart-arse comment when I hear someone clear their throat. Turning, my gaze lands on the most luscious woman I've ever seen. Her long ebony hair hangs to the middle of her back in loose waves. The setting sun gilds her tawny skin and lights up the brightest pair of brown eyes I've ever had the pleasure of staring into.

"I didn't think they were going to come up for air; did you, lass?" I ask, peering up at the dark beauty from the sideline.

She giggles and shakes her head. Her cheeks darken with blush, and it makes me want to preen like a damned peacock.

"Oi! Kennedy! You can snog your girl later! Coach wants us in the locker room like five minutes ago!" Ro yells from across the field, clearly not trusting me to do my job.

All three of us are Irish, having transferred overseas at the same time. We didn't know each other at all until meeting on the field, but we bonded immediately and are usually referred to as the Irish trio. Eamon and I have similar personalities—both more reserved. Rowan Gallagher, however, is anything but reserved. I'm convinced it's due to the ginger hair.

While Eamon says goodbye to Norah, I keep my eyes on her friend. She has that voluptuous hourglass figure that makes me want to bite my knuckles and groan. She's an absolute smoke show, and I'm not leaving until I know her name.

"It's true," the girl says with a faint accent, remarking on something Norah just said. "She's an amazing baker too! I can blame every single one of these curves on her!"

She gestures toward her body with a sweeping hand motion.

"You say that like it's a problem," I say, climbing over the barrier to stand by Eamon. Eyeing her appreciatively, I watch as she blushes again. I thrust a hand in her direction and drawl, "Name's Teagan O'Brien. You are?"

"Uh...um. Layla. Layla Diaz." Her voice quavers nervously as she places a soft hand in mine.

"Pleasure, love. Now, excuse me while I take Romeo here before Coach blows a gasket." I wink at her. "See you around, Layla."

A grin spreads across my face as we jog back across the pitch and enter the locker rooms.

* * *

By the time I get home, I'm completely spent, having been up early to study for a test and then in class until about an hour before I had to be at the pitch. I used that hour to eat a late lunch and call my mum. I try to call her once every couple of weeks. After visiting for a few minutes and ascertaining that all is well back in Ireland, I made my way to the pitch to do warm-ups with the team. The game had gone spectacularly. We beat our rivals from Duke University, mostly thanks to Eamon's hat trick, but I'm pretty proud of the shots I blocked from entering the net. As the Seahawks' goalie, I make it my mission to defend that goal like a warrior defending a fortress.

Walking into my apartment complex, I stop to check the mail, finding a couple of bills, some junk mail, and a letter from the landlord. Christ, I hope the rent isn't going up. I'm doing okay financially, but I've been saving for a trip back home to see my family. Sliding a finger under the flap of the envelope, I trudge up the stairs to my second-floor flat. I've just reached the landing when I get to the point of the letter.

Attention Tenants:

I regret to inform you that the building will be under new management as of two weeks from today's date. The new management will be completely renovating the complex, requiring all current tenants to relocate indefinitely. If interested in keeping residence here, please visit the website listed below to fill out the inquiry form. Unfortunately, they will not be offering the completed units to current tenants before listing them to the public. It is strictly on a first come, first served basis. Due to these circumstances, I will be refunding everyone's original deposits and this month's rent. I will refer anyone to a new complex should they decide to pursue that route.

I apologize for any inconvenience this causes.

Sincerely,

Allen Roper

Rosewood Apartments Management

What the actual fuck? Is this a joke?

"Got your letter, I see," a withered voice says behind me.

I turn to find my elderly neighbor, Mrs. Bailey, standing in her doorway, leaning against her walker with the puff of white hair on her head illuminated by the fluorescent lights.

"Aye." I nod in greeting. "I'm hoping this is some sort of prank."

"I wish it were. Roper came to my door not two hours ago to tell me in person," she says with disdain.

"How can he do this? Is this even legal?" I'm dumbfounded.

"It's not him doing it. He didn't have a say in the matter. He's not the owner, only management. They're just making him do all the dirty work. The poor man was sick over the whole thing," Mrs. Bailey explains.

"How do they expect us all to not only pack up and move out but also find a new place to live?"

She wheezes a sardonic laugh. "They don't give two shits about us. Why would they when they know the new units will be bringing in three times what we're paying now?"

I gape at her. "Three times?! That's absolute bollocks is what that is! Something needs to be done to stop this."

Shaking her head, she turns to go back inside her apartment. "Too late, sonny boy. It's already done."

I stare after her until I hear the locks click into place, then enter my flat, kicking the door closed behind me and dropping my backpack and gym bag on the floor. Raking my fingers through my hair in frustration, I stalk towards the kitchen. What am I supposed to do? Two weeks isn't feasible at all. I yank a beer out of the fridge and twist the cap off. Taking a deep pull from the bottle, I make my way to the living area and sink onto the sofa, resting my head on the back of it and staring at the ceiling as I process all of this new information.

When I enrolled at UNCW, I knew I wanted to pursue a degree that would allow me to work with nonprofit organizations so I could do my part in making the world a better place. Receiving this bogus eviction notice only fuels that desire. I hate giant corporations that prey on small or local businesses. They don't care who they hurt as long as those zeros keep getting added to the end of their paycheck. Something needs to change. But for now, I need to figure out what the hell I'm going to do about finding a new place to live.

Chapter Two

Layla

"Earth to Layla! You're drooling."

My eyes snap to Norah's and widen. "He was... Did he just... I didn't imagine that, did I?" I'm stumbling over my words like I've just learned the English language.

"No, you definitely did not. If I've learned anything over the last week, these Irishmen don't have a problem expressing themselves." Norah says with a giggle.

"Holy hell, Norie. How do you stand it?"

She tilts her head to the side. "What do you mean?"

"I feel like I'm going to spontaneously combust after barely even speaking to him. I can't imagine being in a relationship with one of them."

This just makes Norah laugh harder.

"What?" I narrow my eyes at her. "I'm serious!"

"I know you are, Lay. Trust me, I get it. They're overwhelming in the best way." Norah sighs dreamily.

We make our way out of the stadium and head towards the parking lot where I hug Norah goodbye before getting in my car. Just as I start the engine, my cell starts ringing. It's my Mamá.

"*Hola, Mami.*" I greet her enthusiastically.

My mother, Raquel, is from Mexico originally but came to the States when she was fifteen. She met my father, Roberto, five years later, and it was love at first sight. They wasted no time starting their family. Mamá made it her mission to teach all of her children both Spanish and English, because being bilingual opens more doors in job fields.

"Hi, *mija!* How are you?" she croons.

"Good," I tell her. "I just left a soccer game that Norah invited me to."

"Oh, fun!" Her excitement is laced with a tinge of shock. "I didn't know you were such a big fan. Your brothers will be so proud."

I have a big family. Besides my parents, I have twin sisters and two brothers, of which I'm smack dab in the middle. It's chaos when we're all together, but I love it. My sisters are both ten years younger than I am, while my brothers are only one and two years older than me. I love to tease the twins about being surprise babies, which they definitely were. My parents were adamant that they were done having children, but a few weeks after returning home from a vacation to Tulum, Mexico, they learned she was pregnant. They were shocked at first but happy. Then when they discovered they were having twins, it took a while for them to come to terms with that.

"I'm sure they will be." I roll my eyes even though she can't see me. "I've always liked soccer, Mami; I've just never been to a game outside of Marcos' and Rafael's. Never had a reason to."

"I know, *hijita*, just teasing you! How is Norah?" She's only met Norah once but loved her from the get-go.

"She's good. She recently started dating one of the soccer players, which is why we were at the game." I wince. I won't lie to my Mami about anything, but I really regret saying that. She's constantly hounding me about dating.

"¡No me digas!" she says in disbelief. "Good for her! I didn't think she'd ever come out of her shell. Maybe she has a friend for you too, eh?"

I roll my eyes again.

"Mamá, stop," I beg.

"I was already married with babies at your age, *mija...*"

Pinching the bridge of my nose, I inhale deeply. The last thing I want to do is lash out at my mother, but this conversation is getting old.

"Yes, I'm aware. But that doesn't mean I have to be as well. Do you badger the boys like this? Neither one of them is married," I remind her.

"No, of course not. But that's because they're always bringing someone over to meet me, so I know there's hope for them. I just worry about you, Layla. I don't want you to be lonely," she says warmly.

"I'm not lonely. I have friends that I spend time with practically every day."

Finally at home, I get out of the car and climb the steps to my front door, peeking into the mailbox and finding only cobwebs.

"I didn't mean *that* kind of lonely. I meant the *other* kind of lonely. You know, the romantic kind..." Mamá hedges.

I drop my keys. "Are you talking about...no. Please no."

"I'm just saying," she starts before I cut her off.

"Nope. Not having this conversation. Also, why are you even thinking about that? What parents encourage their kids to have...*sex?*" I shudder as I fumble with my keys. Once I'm finally through the door, I set my purse on the small table next to it.

"The kind of parents that know their kids aren't kids anymore. You're a beautiful young woman. You should be experiencing life in *every way,* Layla."

My parents have never shied away from showing affection for each other in front of us. They're very passionate and proud of it.

"¡Por favor, Mami!" I grimace. "Okay, new topic. How are Cori and Jaz?"

I'm referring to my twin sisters, Corisande and Jazmina. Their names were inspired by flowers but could be a mouthful, so my brothers christened them Cori and Jaz.

Mamá lets out an amused snort. "They're both fine. Fully embracing being teenagers. You and your brothers were so much easier. These two—*ay ay ay*. They'll turn me gray before I turn fifty."

I laugh because she is absolutely ridiculous. She's only forty-six and beautiful—doesn't look her age at all. We're frequently mistaken for sisters whenever we're together, and Mami loves it.

"Papá will still love you with a little silver in there," I tease her.

She sighs wistfully. "It's true. I think he'd love me even if I went bald and wore a burlap sack everywhere."

"He absolutely would," I agree.

I'm not in any hurry to be in a relationship, but I do hope that, one day, my partner will love me the way my father loves my mother.

"Speaking of your Papá, he just walked in the door. Want to say hi to him?"

"Yeah, of course." It wouldn't matter if I wanted to or not. She'd still pass the phone to him.

"¡Hola, princesita!" His deep baritone voice greets me. "¿Cómo estas?"

"Hi, Papá. I'm good!"

Mami's voice sounds in the background, telling my father about me attending a soccer game.

"Is that right?" he exclaims. "How was it?"

"It was fun! Our team won. You would have enjoyed it. Maybe if you guys come up before the season ends, we can go to one together," I offer, knowing they won't.

"Or you could come home and watch your brothers," Papá barters.

I groan. If they're not hounding me about dating, they're constantly asking me to come home. They've only been to North Carolina once, and that was when I moved here from Texas. I've been home half a dozen times since then. Apparently, the whole "broke college kid thing" doesn't register with them. I have to be the one to travel—always.

"Papá, we've talked about this. I can't be the only one to make the trip. I've been here for over a year already, and you haven't come to visit since I moved here." I'm not trying to guilt them; I just want them to realize this is a two-way street.

"You're right. It's just so hard to take the time off right now. And your sisters can't miss school." He gives the same excuses every time.

"I know. It's fine," I say quickly. "Listen, I just got home and I need to finish up some homework. I have to open tomorrow at the store and then have class right after. Kiss Mamá for me and have her kiss you back."

"Happy to oblige," he teases.

"Gross," I say just to be a brat. "Okay, love you both! Adiós."

"Te amo, mija. Adiós."

Ending the call with my parents, I place my phone on the charger and flop down into my favorite cozy chair. I lean my head back, close my eyes, and blow out a deep breath. I know my parents love me as much as my siblings, but being the middle child comes with some unique challenges. For a long time, I was the youngest—and the only girl—so I was constantly doted on by my parents and brothers. I don't begrudge my sisters at all. It's not their fault. But once they arrived, I was either ignored or used as a babysitter. I never minded watching them. They were fun, and I was the first person to make them laugh—a fact I enjoy reminding the rest of my family of.

Once I started high school, my parents put immense pressure on me to get good grades so I could go to college. They wanted me to secure a degree in I.T., knowing that it would offer the most lucrative positions. I'm good with computers, but I don't love it. My passions consist of salsa dancing and makeup application. I love creating new looks and finding the best blend of colors for different skin tones. Norah's asked me more than once to do makeup for the Drama Department, but I always turn her down, hearing my parents' voices in my head keep telling me I'm wasting my time. So I continue to pursue my degree while working at a grocery store.

Feeling frustrated with my parents and with myself for letting their words get to me, I stand from my chair to turn on my favorite salsa playlist. I could easily eat my feelings, but my body needs to expel some negative energy. Pushing my coffee table out of the way, I hit play before getting into position. Once the song starts, I step backward with my right foot and lose myself to the music. Swaying my hips and letting the music flow through my arms, I release all of my frustrations. Dancing has been my outlet since I was a little girl. Mamá would salsa while holding me on her hip as a baby, so the steps have been ingrained since the beginning. I could probably do it in my sleep. I dance until my mind is clear and my shoulders are weightless.

* * *

After I finished my Monday classes, I headed straight to work. It was surprisingly busy, so my shift flew by. Normally, I'd rush home and stay there, distancing myself from people, but I'm feeling particularly social, so I call Norah.

"Hey, Lay Lay! What are you doing?" Norah answers, her voice full of excitement.

I scrunch my nose at the nickname. "Lay Lay? Really? Am I five?"

"What?" she asks. "I thought 'Hey, Lay' sounded too weird. Whatever. It doesn't matter. What's up?"

"I just got off work and was bored. Thought I'd come to see you if you're free," I hedge.

"Actually," she says. "I'm headed to the soccer field to wait for Eamon. They have practice for a couple of hours. Want to join?"

"Oh, uh..." That wasn't really what I had in mind when I called her.

"Teagan will be there...," Norah singsongs, and just as I perk up, I realize what she's up to.

"You're the devil. You know that, right?"

"I'd like to think I'm more angelic, bestowing blessings upon my friends. I'll see you soon! Kisses!" She hangs up before I can say another word.

* * *

Well, now that I'm here, I wish I'd been doing this for my entire college career. A group of sweaty soccer players running around is the most tantalizing thing I've ever seen. There's no denying that they all look good, but I can't take my eyes off Teagan. He's in the goalie's net, gloves on, crouched down, and waiting for one of his teammates to attempt to get the ball past him. His jaw is set with determination as he tracks Eamon and Rowan's movements on the field.

"Did you know that soccer players run an average of seven miles every game?" Norah asks suddenly, interrupting my ogling.

"That sounds like literal hell," I say in disgust. "Why do they subject themselves to this kind of torture?"

"I'm not complaining. God, look at him. It should be illegal to look that good. He makes me have very inappropriate thoughts." Norah sighs.

I throw my head back with a laugh. "Who are you, and what have you done with Norah Grady? I don't think I've ever even heard you talk about a man's body before!"

Norah sighs again. "I can't describe it, but Eamon makes me feel alive in ways I didn't know I could feel. He's not just the sexiest man alive, but he's kind and thoughtful. He hasn't even tried to pressure me into sleeping with him. Listen to me. I sound like a crazy person. We just met, and I already sound like…"

"You're in love!" The pang of jealousy I feel is quickly squashed by the joy I feel for my friend. Norah was raped in high school and, understandably, has been terrified of getting anywhere near men since. Meeting Eamon was one of the best things that could have happened to her.

Norah's cheeks flame, and she shakes her head. "No, that's not possible. People don't fall in love that fast in real life. I'm in lust, that's for sure, but every time things start to get heavy, my body locks up in fear. I'm not sure if we'll even be able to have a physical relationship."

"Hey," I say softly, squeezing her arm. "You're not always going to feel so scared. This is the first guy you've talked to in years, and if he's half as amazing as you say he is, then I'm sure he understands your hesitations. And if he doesn't, then he can take it up with me and the rest of the girls. You know we've always got your back."

Norah leans in to hug me tightly. "Thanks, Lay. I have the best of friends. Well maybe not Myra at the moment, but the rest of you are the best."

Any kind of conflict involving Myra is bound to be full of drama. Norah tells me how Myra barged into her house and accused Eamon of beating up her boyfriend, Mac. In the course of that story, she said some truly awful things to Norah, who is too sweet for her own good. She'd forgive and forget everything just to keep the friendship going. Norah is the *mom* of the group, always taking care of everyone and trying to keep the peace. Normally, I'm right there with her, but sometimes I wonder if some of the girls take advantage of that.

Chapter Three

Teagan

After the week I've had, I'm bound and determined to make the best of practice, so I'm laser focused on guarding the net. I can't control what's happening with my flat, but I *can* control what's coming into my net. Or rather what's *not* coming into the net. I haven't let a single ball past me for the entire practice. Ro keeps cursing me every time I block one of his shots, and Eamon is equal parts proud of and pissed at me.

When Coach finally blows the whistle ending practice, I'm relieved. I just want to go home and sleep. I make my way over to the bench where Eamon is downing a bottle of water and reach to grab my own when I feel a tap to my arm.

"Hey, mate, we have cheerleaders today," Eamon whispers.

My head snaps up, and I scan the bleachers. My eyes immediately land on

Layla Diaz, and I'm grinning ear to ear. Remembering how flustered she was at the game, I wink at her and am rewarded with that blush fanning her cheeks. Fuck, she's stunning. Norah is giggling next to her, then says something that causes Layla to whip her eyes to her friend in astonishment. She rolls her eyes before looking my way and wiggling her fingers at me.

"Hey, Norah and I are going to grab something to eat. Want to join?" Eamon asks after we enter the locker room.

"As your third wheel? No thanks, mate," I laugh as I pull a hoodie over my head.

"I think Layla is coming..."

"Well," I start, smiling broadly, "why didn't you stay that to begin with? Count me in."

"Not even going to play coy, are you?" Eamon chuckles, tossing his practice kit in his bag.

"Nah. You'd see right through that shite."

"Too right, I would," he jokes. "Come on. They're waiting by the exit."

As we exit the building, Ro comes *skipping* past us singing Galway Girl at the top of his lungs. He makes a beeline to where Layla and Norah are waiting.

"Fecking eejit," Eamon mutters when Ro grabs Norah's hand and twirls her. "Gallagher! If you place your lips anywhere near her, I will personally rip your bollocks from your body and shove them down your throat!"

I'm chuckling at his possessiveness until I watch Rowan move towards Layla.

"And is this the lovely Layla I've heard so much about?" he questions. "O'Brien said you were—"

"Oy Rowan!" I yell at him. "Shut yer bleedin' hole, you gobshite. I swear to God, you are more trouble than you're worth."

Shaking my head, I shove Ro playfully before stopping in front of Layla. "Sorry about the riff-raff, lass. He was dropped on his head as a wee baby, and he hasn't been right since. We only keep him around because we feel sorry for him."

"Oh, fuck off!" Ro yells from across the way.

Layla grins at me, and I just about drop to my knees. She's beautiful anyway, but her smile is radiant. I want nothing more than to coax that smile out of her every hour of every day.

"What brings you to the field today?" I ask, tilting my head to the side.

"Oh," she starts, twisting her hands together nervously. "Norah invited me to keep her company, and I was bored, so it worked out. I normally work the evening shift, but today, they scheduled me earlier."

Realizing that I have no idea where she works, I ask, "What do you do?"

"Just a grocery store clerk for now. Nothing exciting," she shrugs. "What about you?"

"I head up the children's department at the YMCA downtown," I tell her proudly. I love my job.

"That sounds like a blast!" Layla exclaims.

"Aye, it is," I confirm. "So, will you be joining us tonight so I'm not the third wheel with those two?" I jerk a thumb towards Eamon and Norah.

"Yeah, Norah invited me earlier. They're something, aren't they?"

I nod. "She's good for him. He needs someone like her in his life."

Layla peers up at me, pursing her lips. Those luscious lips. "He's good for her too, I think. Norah has had…some difficulties in life, and I think Eamon is finally helping her to overcome them. I've never seen her so happy."

Eamon is one of the best friends I've ever had. We didn't know each other when we lived in Ireland, even though we hadn't lived that far apart. I can always rely on Eamon to give me sound advice or be a listening ear. Although I don't know anything about Norah's past, there's no way Eamon wouldn't be good for her. He's solid and steadfast—as loyal as they come.

"Anyway," Layla says, nodding toward the couple, "we should join them before they leave without us."

"Aye. After you, love." I swing an arm in front of me dramatically, making her mouth tip up into a smirk. Not quite a grin, but I'll take what I can get.

We catch up just as Eamon says, "Ro's another story, though. Where is that eejit, anyway?"

"Probably going to bug Alicia," I answer. "He couldn't stay away if he tried."

"Alicia? Like, Pat's Alicia?" Norah asks, eyes wide with amusement.

"Aye, the one and only," I continue. "He's been after her since the moment he met her, but he doesn't have balls enough to actually ask her out. Which is probably a good thing. If he messes things up with her, which he no doubt will, we'll have to find a new pub."

"Or we could just keep going to Paddy's, and he can find a new pub?" Eamon suggests with a shrug of his shoulders. "I'm not changing pubs just because he fucks up."

"So, are you guys actually friends with him? " Layla cuts in, a doubtful look on her face. "Because it doesn't sound like it."

I chuckle. "Ah, we love the eejit, truly. It's just the Irish way. You give a good slagging to the ones you care about. Friends, family, significant others…" I pause to give her a meaningful look, one that has her blushing and avoiding my gaze. "If you ever come across an Irish couple that's not calling each other names, they're miserable together."

We decide to eat at a local pizza place on The River Walk. They have the best pizza, great beer, and outdoor seating. The hostess leads us to a table on the dock and promises the server will be right with us. Eamon and Norah naturally sit next to each other, which leaves Layla sitting next to me. Perfect.

"So," Norah begins, "Eamon says you're his new roommate."

"Aye," I nod, taking a drink of my beer before continuing. "He's a nice enough bloke that he wouldn't leave me stranded on the streets."

When I shared the news about my living situation, Eamon was quick to offer the spare room at his flat and wouldn't take no for an answer.

"What happened?" Layla asks, turning to me with concern on her face.

"Long story short, the property owner sold the building to a multi-million dollar corporation that plans on renovating them into some sort of executive suites. They evicted everyone. Told us we have two weeks to be out."

"That's insane!" she cries. "I'm so sorry."

"Aye, it's a mess."

"But look on the bright side," Norah interjects. "We'll all be able to hang out together more! Layla lives next door to me, and you live with Eamon. It will be fun!"

I grin at that but hear Layla mutter under her breath, "For fucks sake, Norie."

I turn, raising an eyebrow. "You don't think that sounds fun, lass?"

Her head whips towards me and that blush creeps across her cheeks. "No, I do! I just— I…" Norah giggles, which earns her a vicious glare from Layla. She turns back to me and says, "Sorry. Yes, I think that sounds fun. I'm more exasperated with Norah's poor attempt at subtlety."

"And what exactly is she *not* being subtle about? It sounds like she just wants four friends to spend more time together," I tease. I can't help it. The more I tease her, the more she blushes. This might have just become my new favorite hobby.

"*No manches!* You're all the worst." She's glaring, but laughs along with us.

The four of us spend the next couple of hours laughing and talking about everything from current majors to childhood stories to the state of the world. As attracted as I am to Layla, I think I'd be content just to have her as a friend. She's funny, kind, and full of so much life.

Layla

"I hate to end the fun, but I have a full day of classes tomorrow, starting bright and early," Norah announces, covering a yawn with the back of her hand.

Teagan nods and pushes away from the table. "Aye, we have practice before the sun is even awake, so we probably better head back too." He's stretching his arms over his head when suddenly he says, "Oh, shite. My car's still at the field."

"Do you need a ride?" I ask, attempting to hide the fact that I'm checking out the patch of his stomach that was bared while he was stretching. I had driven Norah originally, while Teagan rode with Eamon.

"You wouldn't mind?" he asks, raising his brows.

"It's on my way, and I'm guessing these two want some *alone* time," I nod towards Eamon and Norah.

Eamon quickly interjects, "You're right. We would. Teag, you have your key?"

"Aye"—he winks—"I won't wait up." He gestures for me to lead the way, grinning flirtatiously as he asks, "Shall we, Lovely?"

I love that he calls me *Lovely* all the time. I do *not* love that I blush every time he even looks at me.

"Text me when you get home, okay?" Norah says, hugging me goodbye. "Have fun!"

"Stop. I'm just dropping him off and heading back home," I say, rolling my eyes.

I watch Norah and Eamon stroll off hand in hand, thinking about how perfect they are together. Lost in thought, I don't notice that Teagan has sidled up next to me until he lightly touches my elbow. I glance over at him.

"Everything okay?" he asks.

"Yeah, sorry. Ready to go?"

"Aye," he says simply.

We amble down the sidewalk towards my car in companionable silence. As nervous as he makes me, he's also easy to be around. He doesn't seem to have any expectations other than to just enjoy the moment we're in. I could get used to that.

"I'm sorry if I made you uncomfortable at all tonight," he says suddenly.

Lifting a brow, I look at him. "What are you talking about?"

"Just all the teasing. I hope I didn't make you feel—"

"No!" I laugh, stopping Teagan from finishing that thought. "You didn't make me uncomfortable. I'm used to being teased; I just can't help but get flustered. And I have zero control of my blushing. I still blush over things I *used* to be embarrassed about as a kid that don't bother me at all anymore."

Teagan chuckles. "Now that's unfortunate. But I'm glad I didn't bother you."

"I have two older brothers who have made it their goal in life to tease me at all times. It will take a lot more than that to really upset me."

Settling into my car, I hand him my phone. "Here, put the address in the GPS for me."

21

"I can just direct you there," he offers.

"I don't like interrupting conversations with 'turn here' or 'at the next light turn left,'" I tell him.

"Huh. I never really thought about it like that," he says. "Now that you mention it, that does get rather annoying, doesn't it?"

"Yes," I laugh.

"So you have two older brothers. Are those the only siblings you have?" he asks me.

"No, I have two sisters. Twins. Ten years younger than me."

"Whoa. There are five of you?" he sounds astonished.

"Well no. Not five of *me*," I say slowly. "But my parents have five children together."

"Ach, you know what I mean! Smart arse."

I laugh again.

"That's quite the age gap between you and your sisters. How much older are your brothers?"

"My brothers and I are all stair-stepped. I'm twenty-three, Rafael is twenty-four, and Marcos is twenty-five. My sisters were a surprise," I explain.

"I'd say so," Teagan chuckles. "How'd your parents handle that? I think my Ma would have probably gone mental if she had been surprised with twins ten years after me."

"Well, they were definitely in shock when they found out they were pregnant again after so long, but they warmed up to the idea quickly. Until they had their first sonogram done and realized there were two in there. I don't think my Papá spoke for a full week, and Mami cried. A lot."

"But they were happy eventually, right?" he wonders.

"Oh, definitely. My parents have always had this amazing knack to roll with the punches and take everything in stride. They married really young and started their family right off the bat. My Mom is only forty-six, so it's not like she was past her prime child bearing years. And with three older kids to help out, it wasn't as daunting as it could have been."

"Your family sounds amazing, Layla."

I don't miss his melancholy tone. "Tell me about your family. Do you have any siblings?"

Following the prompts from the GPS, I turn into the parking lot of the apartment complex.

"Ach. It's not nearly as exciting as yours. I have an older sister and a younger brother."

"So we're both middle children. Guess that makes us trouble," I say with a grin.

"I don't know what you mean by *us*," Teagan says. "I'm an angel."

"Right." I snort. "I don't believe that for one second."

"You wound me, lass! How can you look at this face and think 'trouble'?" He turns towards me and smirks.

Damn.

I roll my eyes and say, "Easily. You're clearly nothing *but* trouble."

Teagan laughs loudly, then stops suddenly, "Ah, fuck."

I rear my head back and look around. "What? What is it?"

"I just realized that I had you bring me to Eamon's flat when my car is actually at the field. I'm a gowl and a half," he moans in frustration. "I'm so sorry."

"Oh," I whoosh out a breath. "You scared me there for a second. It's not a big deal. I can take you back to the field. It's not that far from here."

"No, I'll just ride with Eamon to practice tomorrow and get it then. Not to worry," he assures me. "Thank you for bringing me back, though."

"Yeah, of course. Not a problem." I wave a hand and look over at Teagan. The lights of the dash illuminate the sharp lines of his handsome face. I want to trace his jawline with my fingers.

He turns his gaze towards me and our eyes lock. The tension between us is thick with electricity. His green eyes flicker down to my mouth, and I unconsciously dart my tongue out to wet my lips. Teagan inhales deeply through his nose and shuts his eyes, breaking the hold he had on me.

"Well, I better let you get on, then," he says gruffly.

"Right." I clear my throat. "Well, have a good night, Teagan."

Grinning at me, he says, "You too, Lovely. Drive safe."

He gets out of the car, shuts the door, and saunters toward the apartment complex. I release the breath I'd been holding and stare after him. Teagan O'Brien is definitely trouble.

Chapter Four

Layla

"Mami, I can't come home for Thanksgiving *and* Christmas. You know that."

Didn't we just have this conversation a few weeks ago?

"I know, baby, but we miss you so much," Mami whines.

"Well, believe it or not," I tell her sarcastically, "there are these things called cars and airplanes that actually can go from Texas *to* North Carolina. Not just North Carolina to Texas. The road goes both ways."

"Don't you take a tone with me, young lady. It's harder for six people to travel than it is for one person. It just makes sense for you to come here. Plus, you know the holidays are more than just us. Abuelo and Abuela, the whole family…" Mami reminds me.

I roll my eyes so hard, I'm afraid they might just get stuck. She's being so unreasonable.

"Listen, I can come home for one or the other but not both. And I really want you guys to come here sometime soon. Can we please compromise on this?" I'm practically begging at this point.

"I hear you, mija." She sighs. "I'm sorry. It's been a long week with your sisters. I don't remember you being this much trouble at thirteen."

"That's because Marcos and Rafael paved the way for me. They were so awful at thirteen that anything I did was practically angelic." I grin thinking about Teagan claiming to be an angel.

"You're funny." She snorts. "Okay, listen, I have to get off of here. Let me know which holiday you want to come home for, and we'll buy your ticket, okay?"

"Well, I won't look a gift horse in the mouth," I tell her. "Thanks."

"Oh, I forgot to tell you!" Mami says suddenly. "Marcos and Rafael might be bringing their girlfriends to Christmas. Maybe you'll have a plus one this year?"

"Ugh. Mami. Please stop." I groan.

It's never going to end. Resisting the urge to bang my head against the wall, I flop onto my couch and stare at the ceiling. What would it take for Mami to understand that my worth doesn't depend on having a significant other? Sure, I'd love to find someone to share life with, but my goal in life isn't to marry and have a litter of kids. I love children and hope I'll be a mother someday, but I'm not in any rush. I'm twenty-three for crying out loud. I would have been finished with college already, but like Norah, I took some time off after high school to figure out exactly what I wanted to pursue. Why on earth would I want to add marriage and babies to the mix? Classes and day-to-day living are hard enough without extra mouths to feed.

"Okay, okay. I'll stop. For now." Mamá sighs heavily. "I'll talk to you soon, okay?"

"Yep," I say blandly. "Love you, Mami."

"Love you too, mija."

Growling loudly into the air, I rub the heels of my hands into my eyes. I'm exhausted. This last week of classes really took it out of me, and work

has been getting busier with the holidays around the corner. I actually have tonight off and don't plan on doing anything. My sweats and wine sound pretty good right now. Rising from the couch, I saunter into my small galley kitchen and take a wine glass from the cabinet. Before I can even open the bottle, my phone dings from the couch. I'm fully expecting it to be a message from my mother badgering me some more, but it's a group text.

Norah: *Hey, who's up for a slumber party at my house tonight? Wine and junk food? Girl talk?*

Amelia: *You KNOW I'm in! I'll bring beer!*

Charlie: *Yeah, girl, I'm down. I'll bring chips and dip!*

That actually sounds like a good time. And I won't have to change or worry about driving, since Norah lives right next door.

Layla: *Holy shit, I'm actually free tonight!*

Amelia: *Myra, cancel whatever plans you have going on and make it a point to be here! I WILL drag your ass here if I have to!*

Myra: *Okay, okay, calm your tits. I'll be there.*

I chuckle at Myra's response as I rummage through my fridge and cabinets to see what food and drink offerings I can provide tonight. I grab two bags of chips and decide to take the bottle of wine I was about to open. Setting them aside, I change into my favorite *Hocus Pocus* sweatpants and black hoodie. I could live in hoodies. After locking up, I walk the ten feet to Norah's house and knock once before stepping inside.

"Hey, it's me," I call out, not wanting to scare Norie.

"Coming!" I hear her call from the enclosed patio where she keeps all of her sewing stuff. Norah is the costume designer for the UNCW Drama Department and is insanely talented. The play they're currently working on is a modern retelling of Beauty and the Beast. Norah's designs are brilliant. She's been begging me to join the makeup team for ages, but I always find a reason not to do it. Honestly, I'd love to join. That's what I want to do with my future—be a makeup artist—and stage makeup is a ton of fun to do. But in the back of my mind, all I hear is my mother telling me how it's not a realistic or lucrative career choice.

"Hey, sorry," Norah says, walking into the room while putting her auburn curls in a messy bun on top of her head. "I was just putting the last of my supplies away."

"You're good," I tell her, giving her a quick hug. "I brought wine and chips!"

"Yay! Please tell me the chips are jalapeño Cheetos."

Laughing, I pull one of the bags out, revealing that I did, in fact, bring the goods. The two of us could put away a family-sized bag of jalapeño Cheetos in one sitting if we put our minds to it.

"You're so good to me." Norah beams. "I'm so glad you're off work tonight!"

"You and me both, sister. This week has been brutal. Apparently, old people like to stock up for the holidays starting in October. My manager has already set up a Christmas display. What is it with America and starting the Christmas frenzy so early?" I ask, scrunching my nose in disgust.

"Right?" Norah says, turning to pull random items out of her fridge. "Mom and I always gave Halloween and Thanksgiving their due diligence before bringing out the Christmas tree. Don't get me wrong, I *love* Christmas, but I love the others just as much. Speaking of, are you going home for the holidays?"

"Ugh, I guess." I sigh heavily. "My parents asked me to come home for *both* holidays this year, which is ridiculous. I've been begging them to come here, and they won't do it."

Norah scoffs. "That *is* ridiculous. I don't understand why they do that. You'd think they would want to come and see how you've settled in and stuff."

"Exactly," I say, pointing a finger at Norah. "But their excuse is always that it's easier for one person to travel than six of them. Which is true, but it's not like the twins are babies anymore. They're teenagers."

"Well, if you do end up here alone for the holidays, you know I'm free!"

"I know. And I love that," I tell her sincerely. "I'll probably go home for Christmas so I can stay longer. They did offer to buy my plane ticket, though, so that's a plus! And of course, my mother started asking if I was bringing anyone with me."

Norah cringes. "I'm sorry, Lay. Maybe you should find some random guy to go with you just to keep the conversation from constantly falling back on you."

"Ha!" I bark a laugh. "Tempting."

We chat until the rest of our friends arrive. There's an overabundance of junk food ranging from chips to charcuterie, soda to wine. Norah pushed all of the furniture back against the walls so we could all sit on the floor, surrounded by pillows and blankets.

"It was the worst day *ever!*" Amelia exclaims, recounting her day at work as she deftly winds her long, blonde hair into a bun on the top of her head. "Not only were we slammed but also short-staffed. I'm so glad I have the next few days off."

Myra has been uncharacteristically quiet, perched beside Amelia. I know there's been tension between her and Norah, but it isn't like her at all to not be a part of the conversation at all. She's been nursing a bottle of water and occasionally nibbling on a cracker. Out of everyone in the group, Myra is the one I spend the least amount of time with. Our personalities are just so different, and we have nothing in common other than being in the same friend group.

"Norah," Amelia continues, a sly grin spreading across her face, "has something she'd like to share with the class."

Norah throws her a glare and blushes so violently, her face is almost as red as her hair.

"I hate you," she says playfully before taking a deep breath. "So…Eamon might have spent the night last night."

The room goes silent for about half a second as we let that sink in, before everyone explodes into gasps and cheers.

"Our little Norah is all grown up now!" Charlie cheers, raising her glass of wine in a toast before downing it.

"Shut up," Norah says, burying her face in her hands. "I'm still me!"

"Of course you are, honey," Amelia cuts in. "But now you have a fine piece of man warming your bed!"

"Where is the man in question tonight?" I ask around a mouth full of chips.

"He had a paper to finish, so I'm assuming he's at his place," Norah says pointedly and tosses a grape at me. "With Teagan."

I blush furiously and glare at her.

"Wait, what's going on with Teagan?" Amelia blurts, shooting a wink at Norah. "Are you two a thing?"

"No!" I yell, just as Norah sings out, "Yes!"

"Norah Grady, I hate you with the fire of a million suns! *Nothing* is going on between me and Teagan!"

"Not yet, anyway!" She laughs. "But it's only a matter of time. You can cut that sexual tension with a knife!"

I roll my eyes. "Stop it. We've literally only been around each once."

"Yes," Norah agrees, "but there is absolutely no denying the attraction between the two of you."

"He's super hot, so good job, Layla!" Myra chimes in with a little more vigor.

Taking a sip from my wine glass, I nod. I can't, and won't, deny it. "Yeah, of course he's hot. But that doesn't mean anything is going on."

"Psh. Whatever you say. I've seen the way he looks at you, Lay. There's nothing but interest there," Norah says, waggling her eyebrows.

Rolling my eyes again, I say, "He's probably just a flirt like Rowan."

Norah laughs. "*Nobody* flirts like Rowan does. I've never seen Teagan flirt with anyone, actually."

My heart thrills at the thought of being singled out by him. I briefly entertain the idea of bringing him to my family's Christmas dinner and introducing him as my boyfriend, but I dismiss it just as quickly. Not only is he definitely *not* my boyfriend, but I'm not about to subject him, or any man, to a Diaz family Christmas.

Chapter Five

Teagan

"Hello? Earth to Kennedy." I wave my hand in front of Eamon's face. He's been staring into space for ages, with his lips tilted in a small smile.

"What? Sorry, mate. I was miles away," Eamon says, shaking his head.

"I'd say. What's got your head in the clouds?"

He grins then, and holy hell, is he *blushing?*

"Oh. You and Norah finally consummate the relationship, then?" I wag my eyebrows before slapping Eamon on the back in congratulations.

He shoves me away, a huge grin lighting up his face. "Fuck off. A gentleman doesn't kiss and tell."

"What about shag and tell? And I know for a fact you're no gentleman," I joke. If anyone is a gentleman, it's Eamon. He treats everyone, especially women, with the utmost respect.

"I'll tell you what," he starts. "When you and Layla finally seal the deal, we can swap stories over wine like a group of lasses at a hen party."

Eamon's words flood my mind with some very inappropriate thoughts of Layla. Winding her long dark hair around my hand and pulling it just enough to expose her throat. Kissing a path down her neck while tracing her luscious curves with my free hand.

Stopping those thoughts in their tracks, I quip, "Ooh, can we do each other's nails too? I quite fancy a new mani."

"Yeah, alright. Manis it is, but no waxing. I'm adopting a more natural look these days." Eamon chuckles as he says. "What *is* the deal with you and Layla? Have you seen her lately?"

I shake my head and grab the back of my neck. "I don't want to scare her off. I'm trying to let her know I'm into her without coming on too strong, yeah?"

"You know she's nervous, right?" Eamon asks. "Norah said she hasn't had a serious relationship before and doesn't sleep around, so she's probably completely out of her comfort zone. You may have to be more assertive."

"Aye, I figured that was the case. I'm fine with taking it slow. I'd like to build a friendship with her so she knows I'm not going to muck about with her. I'm not Ro." I grimace.

"Thank God for that. The world can only handle so much," Eamon jokes.

The last thing I want is a fling. I've never been one to indulge in one night stands. I've never snuck out before they woke up or blocked their numbers. In fact, the more I think about it, the more I realize I've never actually been the one to end any relationship. It's always been the other way around. The first night after Ashley left was a different story. I'd gotten completely banjaxed and hooked up with one of the girls in my apartment complex. I did sneak out then.

Falling back into silence, I should be focusing on my homework, but instead, I'm thinking about how to continue pursuing a friendship with Layla while also letting her know that I want more. Hanging out in a group is always a good time, but I want some one-on-one time with her. I want to know how her mind works and what she's passionate about. I also want to know how the hell a girl that gorgeous hasn't been in a serious relationship before. Either the men around her are blind, or she's blocked all their advances. It doesn't really matter, just as long as she doesn't block mine. Which, so far, doesn't seem to be the case.

I finally finished my classwork and am on my way to work. I'm looking forward to seeing the kids in the after school program. There are twelve of them currently, ranging from kindergarten to seventh grade. Since it's still soccer season, I've been mixing work with pleasure by teaching the kids some drills. Last week, we practiced footwork, and now they are ready to move on to blocking goals this week.

The doors to the gymnasium open, and the kids file in. The younger ones are talking excitedly to each other, while the older kids have their eyes glued to their phones. Shaking my head, I consider how lucky I was to have been raised without an electronic device at my beck and call. I'm thankful for today's technology, absolutely, but growing up on a farm and spending nearly every waking moment outside in the fresh air, getting dirty, kicking around a ball, or climbing trees, was far superior in my mind.

"Alright, you wans, put those buzzing boxes away! You know the rules!" I holler across the gym.

I don't have many rules for the kids, but the one I reinforce the most is no phones or tablets once they enter the gym. I want them up and active, engaging with me and other kids. They always grumble at me, but it doesn't last long.

"Mr. Teagan," a small voice says next to me.

Looking down, one of the little girls from the kindergarten class is staring up at me with wide eyes. I squat down to her level.

"Aye, what is it, Gabriela?" I can't help but smile at her. Her dark hair, big brown eyes, and caramel skin remind me of Layla.

"My mamá forgot to pack my tennis shoes in my bag today. Can I still play in these?" She motions to her small feet that are in flip flops.

"Unfortunately, no. That wouldn't be safe for you," I tell her, instantly feeling bad for the sadness in her eyes. "However, you *can* play barefoot if you like."

Gabriela's eyes widen with glee. "Really?!"

I chuckle and nod. "Aye, lass, really. Now, go on and put your stuff on the bleachers."

Once all of the kids are in and settled on the bleachers, I make my way over to greet them all. "How are we doing today, team?" I ask, clapping my hands in front of me.

A chorus of "good" sounds from the kids. I love this particular group. It's a diverse collection of kids in not just age but in ethnicity as well. I learn more from them than they do from me.

"Who wants to guess what we're starting on today?" I ask, gesturing to the small soccer goals scattered throughout the gym.

A flurry of hands start waving in the air. I point to one of the older boys, Gabriela's brother, José.

"Defending?" the boy guesses.

I grin and pick up the soccer ball sitting at my feet. "Close, José! We're going to be saving today. As you know, along with hanging out with you all, I'm also the goalie for the UNCW Seahawks..."

A few cheers ring out, filling me with pride.

"My job as the goalie, or keeper, is to keep this ball," I say, pointing from the ball in my hand to the goal closest to me, "from going into that net. To do that, the first thing we need to learn is how to pounce. Now, what I mean by that is this: Anytime a goalie has the ball in their hands and it drops, the first thing they need to do is pounce on the ball. Like a cat pounces on a mouse, yeah? So here's what that looks like."

I toss the ball onto the floor, drop to the ground, and immediately put both hands on it.

"Now, some of you might already be familiar with this, but we're going to start slow and work our way up, alright? Here in a minute, I'll have all of you spread out and you'll each get a ball. We'll start by standing on our knees behind it, like this"—I demonstrate—"then we'll carefully fall forward and grab the ball with both hands. Once we've all mastered that, we'll move on. Any questions?"

Gabriela's hand shoots up into the air.

"Yes, lass?"

"Can we pretend to be lions when we pounce?" she asks excitedly.

Laughing, I say, "Yeah, 'course you can. Goalies are a lot like lions. They have to be brave and fierce and fast in order to keep the other team from scoring a goal. Any other questions? No? Alright, everyone spread out."

I spend the next fifteen minutes carefully instructing each child on how to pounce. The youngest ones in the group make roaring noises as they fall onto their soccer balls. Once I'm satisfied that they all have the hang of it, I move to ankle rolls. I have them stand with their legs apart and the ball on the ground. While keeping both hands on the ball at all times, I instruct them to roll the ball around one ankle, then the next, then with their legs together, then in a figure eight between their legs, ensuring they use the tips of their fingers to roll the ball.

I continue with several more drills until they're eventually ready to start blocking. I demonstrate this by having the older students shoot the ball towards me while I save. I show them different techniques for getting to the ball and keeping it out of the goal while also showing them what *not* to do. Once I finish, I have them all practice blocking my shots. With the youngest ones, I keep the ball on the ground so they can perfect their pouncing. The older kids have the opportunity to block a ball in the air. By the end of the day, all of the kids have successfully managed to keep at least one ball from getting in their goals.

"Alright, team, good work today!" I call out as the kids round up the loose balls and put them away. "We'll do it again tomorrow. And, Gabriela? Don't forget your shoes, love!"

"Okay, Mr. Teagan!" She giggles as she runs after her brother.

Once I see all of the kids out safely, I head into my office to make sure I have everything in order for the rest of the week. Just as I'm finishing up, my phone rings. Pulling it from my pocket, I answer without looking at the caller.

"'Lo?" I say.

"Hey, Teag," the voice of my younger brother greets me.

"Tommy, how are ya, mate? Been a while." I'm closer to my brother than probably anyone in my family.

I love them all, of course, but my parents are difficult to talk to. My sister, Tarrah, is the golden child, and while we get along really well, her whole goal in life is to please our parents, which she does to a T. She's the light of their life, while I've always been their biggest disappointment. Not because I was shady as a kid; I was just your average boy. I got into the normal amount of mischief but never caused any real trouble, other than being adamant that I don't want to take over the family farm. I decided from an early age that I didn't want to spend my life tending sheep and crops. I wanted to go out into the world and do something bigger, make a difference to those around me. Yes, farming is important; I understand that, but it isn't what calls to me. My da, Martin, can't understand it and takes every opportunity to tell me so. My Mam, Siobhan, doesn't have the nerve to ever speak up on my behalf, so she sides with my father. As for my brother, he's the baby of the family that everyone dotes on.

"Aye, it has. How are ya getting on?" my brother asks.

"Grand. Been busy. You?"

"Grand, yeah. Started a new job last week," Tommy says.

"Oh yeah? Tell me about it."

Tommy proceeds to tell me about how he quit his dull delivery job and was hired on at a local pub working in the kitchen. Tommy never could hold down a steady job, which doesn't seem to bother him or our parents. Da doesn't think less of Tommy for not wanting to take over the farm someday. I listen to my brother drone on for a while before asking about the rest of the family.

"How's Tarrah? She still planning on marrying what's his name? Geoff? George?"

"Gerard," Tommy says with a laugh. "Yeah, they're thinking maybe next October? I don't know. I tend to zone out when she starts harping on about it. I can only take so much, ya know?"

"Yeah, mate, I hear you. How's your mot? Still seeing her?" My brother goes through girls faster than he goes through jobs. I gave up on even trying to remember their names. I think the last one was Angie?

"Kristina? Nah. We broke it off a few weeks ago. She was getting clingy. What about you? Have you moved on from what's her name?" Clearly remembering names is a family trait.

"Yeah, that's old news." I don't want to tell Tommy about Layla. One, there isn't really anything to tell, and two, I feel like voicing it out loud to my family might jinx me.

We talk for a few more minutes about our parents—still miserable—and if I'm coming back to Ireland anytime soon—I'm not. As much as I love my home country, the thought of going back just doesn't excite me. Probably because I know that no matter where in the country I live, it's still too close to the farm. I love the life I've created in North Carolina, not to mention the friends I've made along the way. Eamon and Rowan are more like family to me than my own.

Chapter Six

Layla

I've been sitting in Congdon Hall drinking coffee and studying for the better part of an hour when I decide to stretch my legs. Gathering my books, I shove them in my messenger bag, grab my cup, and head out the door. It's the perfect fall day. Beams of sunlight are peeking through passing clouds, and the air is crisp, blowing gold, red, and orange leaves along the sidewalk. I turn toward the amphitheater, choosing the scenic route over the quicker path. Just as I set foot on the small bridge that extends over the pond, I hear my name being called.

Whipping my head around, I see Teagan jogging towards me, grinning broadly. The dimple on the left side of his mouth makes him even more adorable than he already is, and the green Seahawks hoodie he's wearing accentuates his already brilliant emerald eyes. Sunlight brings out streaks of auburn in the chestnut hair peeking out from under his ball cap. Although he is certainly all man, his smile gives him a boyish quality. He jogs up to me, leaving less than a foot of space between us.

"Hiya," he breathes, making my heart race.

"Hi yourself," I say, grinning back at him.

"Fancy meeting you here," he says. "Just coming from Congdon?"

"Yeah," I reply. "Took a break to stretch my legs. Thought I'd take the long way to the library and back. Where are you headed?"

"I was heading to the library myself. I have a bit of a break before my next class. Mind if I join you?" Teagan gestures in the direction of the library.

"Not at all," I say, and we resume walking. "Haven't seen you in a while. How are you?"

"Grand! Been busy. Between classes, work, and games, I hardly know if I'm coming or going anymore," he says. "How are you, Lovely?"

Teagan lightly bumps his elbow into mine in a friendly gesture. He smells so good, like pine and clean laundry. I want to bury my face into his hoodie and never leave.

"Same," I reply. "Work has been ridiculously busy since someone in the universe declared it the start of the holiday season. I think I get asked ten times a day when we're going to start carrying turkeys."

A deep chuckle sounds from his throat. "Don't get me wrong, turkey can be delicious, but why is it the standard for holiday meals? Personally, I'd rather have a Sunday roast with all the fixings."

"What's the traditional Christmas meal in Ireland?" I ask, glancing sideways at him.

"Turkey." He winks at me, which only makes me blush. "What about your family? Do you follow Mexican customs or American?"

I laugh loudly. "Oh, definitely Mexican. Meals in general are a huge deal in our culture, but the holidays are an *event*. The amount of food made could feed an entire army, which is about the size of most Mexican family get-togethers. We always make tamales, which may not sound like much, but the *whole* family gets involved. It's one of the many traditions we don't skip out on."

"Don't laugh," Teagan starts, "but...what are tamales?"

I stop in my tracks and turn to gape at him in disbelief. "You don't know what tamales are?"

He shakes his head sheepishly.

A laugh bursts from me, and I quickly cover my mouth with both hands. "I'm sorry. You asked me not to laugh. But really? You've never even heard of them."

"Not from here, remember?" he says, pointing to his chest. "I was raised on a sheep farm. We ate mutton and potatoes."

"Oh, we're going to have to fix that," I state resolutely.

"Yeah?" I can feel his eyes on me. "Are you going to make them for me?"

Hijole. Did I just agree to cook for Teagan?

"Uh..." I begin.

"Or I can just buy some right?" he asks hurriedly. "Surely they can be found in the grocery store, yeah?"

My head snaps up. "You are absolutely *not* going to eat store-bought tamales for your first tamale experience. I imagine that would be the equivalent of me eating frozen fish sticks and saying I tried fish and chips."

Teagan grimaces. "Ach, you're right. So where does that leave us?"

I like being referred to as an *us.*

"Alright, O'Brien. I'll make some tamales."

The grin that spreads across his face is blinding.

"But," I add, not quite believing what I'm about to say, "you have to help make them."

"It's a date," he answers without hesitation. "Now, tell me what's in them."

Turning to resume walking, he motions for me to follow. I'm still trying to process how we went from discussing Christmas traditions to planning a...*date.* Like an actual date? Why is this so hard for me to wrap my brain around? I've dated before. The last one... When was the last one? Definitely before moving to North Carolina, and it hadn't gone well at all.

"You still with me, lass?" Teagan asks, concern knitting his brow.

"Yes! Sorry, just got lost in a thought," I admit. "What did you ask again?"

"I wanted to know what's in tamales," he says patiently.

40

"Right. Tamales."

I begin explaining the process as we stroll past the amphitheater and head towards the library. He's a great listener, asking questions when he doesn't understand something and repeating the process back to me, using his hands to mime the actions. By the time we reach our destination, he's convinced himself that he's already a professional tamale maker and is going to open up a food truck. My laughter only encourages his antics.

"I'm offended that you think my dreams of opening Teagan's Traveling Tamale Truck are so funny, love. This has been my life's work," he says, scowling playfully.

"*Tamal*. Just one is tamal. Plural is tamales," I correct him.

He glares at me, and I hold my hands up in surrender. "You're right; you're right. How thoughtless of me. I'm sure that your tamales will be just as authentic and delicious as my Abuela's family recipe."

"Abuela?" He tilts his head to the side questioningly.

Rather than going inside the library, we move to a shady section and lean against the wall. I pull my wavy hair over my shoulder and start twisting the strands around my fingers. "My Grandma. *Abuela* means grandma in Spanish. *Abuelo* is grandpa."

"Are your grandparents still alive?"

The thought of my grandparents brings a smile to my face. Abuela is a firecracker, always ready with a witty comeback, while Abuelo is reserved and as sweet as dulce de leche. "They are. Mami's parents, anyway. Papá's parents passed away before I was born. What about you?"

"Aye, both sets still alive and kicking last time I checked. My Da's parents live on our property, while my Mam's parents live in Belfast. Never saw them much growing up. They weren't happy that she married Da, so they only came around once every handful of years."

"That's so sad," I say. "Family is everything in our culture. Abuela and Abuelo live next door and were just as involved with my siblings and me as my parents were. And my cousins might as well have been siblings for all the time we spent together."

Teagan smiles warmly at me. "That's grand. I wish my family was as close as yours seems to be. I love the thought of making huge meals with the entire family and kids running around everywhere. That's why I love my job so much. I get to spend time with this great group of kids, and we just have a blast."

Before I can stop the thought, my mind fills with a vision of Teagan in my family home at Christmas. He's sitting at the table next to Abuela making her laugh while she teaches him how to make tamales. The vision shifts to him playing soccer in the yard with my brothers and cousins. I can see my sisters giggling and blushing every time he shows them the slightest bit of attention and Mami glowing with delight. Then I'm in the living room teaching him how to salsa. He wraps his arms around my waist and pulls me close...

Just as my thoughts start to take a heated turn, a group of rowdy freshmen come out of the library, jostling each other. One goes flying into Teagan, which sends him careening into me. One of his hands immediately grasps my waist, while the other hand braces against the wall next to my head. Instinctively, my hands land on his chest.

"Fucking eejit!" he barks at the student who is now on the ground. "Watch where yer goin', you bleedin' melter!"

The guy mumbles something and hurries off, laughing with his friends. Teagan turns his head back to me, our faces now inches apart. I suck in a breath at the proximity.

"Are ya alright, Lovely?" he asks, squeezing my hip gently.

"Fine." I nod, swallowing thickly. "Are you okay?"

Teagan's gaze flicks to my mouth briefly before coming back to rest on my eyes.

"Aye, grand. I didn't crush you, did I?"

He glances down at my body as if to check. Only then do I realize that in the course of the action, he's kept his upper half from crushing me, but his lower half is another story. His pelvis is flush against mine, and at that precise moment, I feel something twitch against me. *Dios mío.*

Teagan abruptly pulls his hips back and clears his throat loudly. He does not, however, remove his hand from my waist or from the wall beside my

42

head, but I also don't remove my hands from his chest. When his eyes meet mine again, they're no longer filled with concern but something heated. There's a promise in them that I'm very interested in finding out about. He slowly leans his head closer, his grip on my waist tightening. I can't breathe. He's going to kiss me. And I want it *badly.* It's been a long time since my last kiss, and it was awful. Somehow, I just know that kissing Teagan will be good. More than good. Curling my fingers into his hoodie, I raise my chin slightly, bringing our mouths closer.

"O'Brien!" a loud voice calls from behind us, making us jump apart like two teenagers caught making out by their parents.

Teagan

Fucking Rowan. I'm going to throttle him with my bare hands. Kissing Layla has been an ever-present thought in my head for a while now, but I didn't expect it today, like this. Being this close, with my hands on her body and the way she was looking at me, has me reconsidering. Expelling a sharp breath, I glance at Layla who's intentionally looking at her shoes.

Rowan saunters up to us with a shite-eating grin on his face. He claps a hand on my shoulder and looks back and forth between the two of us with wide, mischievous eyes. "Hope I wasn't interrupting anything, mate."

I glare at him and not so playfully punch his bicep. "Course not, *mate.* That's the last thing on your mind, yeah?"

Ro winces, rubbing his arm where I hit him before looking towards Layla.

"How's it cuttin', Layla Love?" he asks.

Layla's blushing but manages to raise a dubious eyebrow at him. "Todo bien, alborotador."

"Troublemaker?" he says aghast, shocking Layla and I both with his understanding of Spanish. "I'm hurt."

"Since when do you know Spanish?" I ask in disbelief.

"Ach, I've been taking a class every year. Surely I mentioned that." Rowan shrugs.

"Never. But *why* are you taking it?"

43

Ro looks at me like I'm the biggest eejit on the face of the planet. "Teagan O'Brien, in such a diverse world, don't you think it's important to learn more than one language? Look at yer wan here. She's clearly bilingual. Don't you want to know what she's saying when you're making her..."

"Stop. Stop right there, Gallagher." I cut him off before he can embarrass Layla further. "If you know what's good for you, you will not finish that sentence."

Ro raises his hands in defeat but winks at Layla, whose eyes are as wide as saucers. The nerve of him. I'll make sure to pelt him in the head with a ball at practice later. Gobshite.

"Well, I better be off. Saw the two of yous when I came out of the library and thought I better say hello. Carry on!" Ro grins before turning and jogging away.

"For fuck's sake," I murmur, looking back to Layla. "I'm so sorry, Layla. He's a royal pain in the arse."

She releases a nervous giggle. "It's fine. He reminds me of my brothers, honestly."

"God, I can't imagine having *two* Rowans around. You must be a saint to put up with that."

"I don't know about that. I've learned to dish it as well as I can take it. I'm just not as loud about it. My retaliation is more...calculated." She grins.

"Remind me never to get on your bad side, lass."

Chapter Seven

Layla

"Excuse me? Do you work here?" a middle-aged lady asks me.

It takes everything in me to *not* point at my name badge and the grocery store logo on my shirt and respond with an exaggerated eye roll. It's been a day from hell. Not only is it stupid busy, but I've been completely distracted since that almost kiss with Teagan the day before. That had been the hottest moment of my life, including the night I lost my virginity.

"Yes, ma'am, I do. How can I help you?" I answer, plastering a fake smile on my face.

"I was just wondering when you were going to get whole turkeys in."

Inhaling deeply through my nose, I silently count to five and explain to the lady that hopefully the turkeys will be available tomorrow. *Yes*, I'm aware that it's the middle of October and the holidays are just around the corner.

No, I don't know what time they'll be delivered, and *no*, I can't hold one for her.

"I'm sorry. There was an issue with the distributor, so it's out of our hands at the moment."

The lady huffs and walks away.

"Okay, you have a nice day too," I mutter under my breath.

It was six in the morning when I arrived at work, and I've been on my feet nonstop for the last seven hours. I haven't had a single thing to eat since before leaving my house and only one bathroom break. Thankfully, my shift ends soon, and then I can go home. I don't have class tonight, thank God. Even if I did, I'd probably skip it—attendance be damned. Going back to stocking the shelf in front of me, I let my mind wander back to Teagan and sigh. He's not only insanely good-looking but incredibly sweet. There's an undeniable attraction between us that I can't ignore any longer, especially after that moment at the library. But what does it mean? The anxiety of actually bringing the topic up to him is *real*, but I want him to know that I'm definitely interested in pursuing something if he is. And more than interested in continuing what Rowan interrupted. Freaking Rowan. I understand why Teagan and Eamon are always so exasperated by him. He's an absolute menace. A menace that apparently knows Spanish. I'll have to be more careful with what I say around him.

My phone buzzes in my pocket. I'm not supposed to have it on me at work, but not one of my fellow coworkers follows that rule. Glancing around, I make sure my manager and no customers are nearby before surreptitiously pulling my phone out and angling my body towards the shelves. There's a text from an unknown number. I grin broadly because I immediately know it's from Teagan. I have no idea how he got my number, but I'm not mad about it. I decide to play coy.

Unknown: *Hi, Lovely.*

Layla: *I'm sorry, who is this? I don't have your number saved.*

Unknown: *Oh. Right. It's Teagan.*

Layla: *Teagan who?*

I giggle to myself. As if I know any other Teagan.

Unknown: *Teagan O'Brien. How many Teagans do you know?*

Layla: *Oh, THAT Teagan. Sorry. There are so many I can't keep track of them.*

I quickly add him as a contact while I wait for his response.

Teagan: *Ouch. That stings, lass.*

Layla: *I'm kidding. You're the only one I know. Not that I mind, but how did you get my number?*

Teagan: *Ummm... I might have stolen it when you had me put my address in your GPS?*

I snort in amusement at how he worded it, like he wasn't sure if he did or not.

Layla: *That's an invasion of privacy. I'm not sure how to feel about that.*

Teagan: *Fuck. I'm sorry, I should have asked.*

Layla: *Kidding again! I really don't mind. Did you need something?*

Teagan: *Oh, good! No, I don't need anything. I was just sitting here zoning out in front of the TV when a commercial for tamales came on. Made me think of you.*

Layla: *I'm so glad that something wrapped in a corn husk made you think of me. How flattering.*

Teagan: *You're a bit of a smart arse aren't you, Lovely?*

Layla: *He's catching on. ;)*

Teagan: *I like it. What are you doing?*

Layla: *Working. I'm not supposed to be on my phone, but I'm off in half an hour.*

Teagan: *Can I call you then?*

My heart flops in my chest.

Layla: *Sure. Talk soon.*

With a new spring in my step, I put my phone away and quickly finish stocking the section I'm in so I can clock out on time. I don't want to miss Teagan's call. Why am I so nervous? The butterflies in my stomach remind me of the time in middle school when one of the boys I was crushing on asked me to couple skate at the Brownsville Roller Rink. I was so anxious, I hid in the bathroom for half of the skate.

As soon as my shift ends, I clock out and hurry to the car to plug my ancient phone into the charger. I really need an upgrade, but that requires money. The sun is nowhere to be seen, making the day colder than it has been recently. Starting the ignition, I crank the heat and rub my hands together for warmth. Teagan probably won't be calling right away, so I put the car in drive and head towards my house. What will we even talk about? Will he bring up yesterday? Will I mention it if he doesn't? Lost in my thoughts, I startle when my phone begins ringing loudly. Chuckling at myself for being so ridiculous, I answer, putting it on speaker.

"Hello?"

"Hello, Lovely," Teagan greets me, with what I know is a smile. I can *hear* it in his voice. "How was the rest of your shift?"

The way he calls me "Lovely" sends shivers up my spine.

"Uneventful," I tell him. "Which is more than I can say for the rest of the day."

"Another busy day? How many times did you get asked about turkeys?"

"Hmmm. Let's see," I ponder out loud. "I think today was only around half a dozen times, but people were less than friendly about it. I had one old man actually ask me why I didn't just go to the turkey farm myself and bring some to the store. That was a new one."

Teagan lets out a playful snort. "Did he want you to kill and dress them too? Or bring them alive?"

"That's a very good question. He didn't specify. I'll ask him next time I see him and let you know."

"Do that," he orders. "What are you doing now that you're free?"

"Heading home to do absolutely nothing for the rest of the day. How about you?"

There's a heavy sigh followed by the kind of groan someone stretching would make. "Shirking my responsibilities. I should be doing homework before work but made the mistake of turning on the TV."

"Ah, yes," I say seriously. "Those tamale commercials are quite riveting. I can see how distracting that would be."

"You have no idea. I've been thinking a lot about tamales since yesterday, actually. I've been thinking a lot about *yesterday* in general. Very distracting,

48

indeed."

I almost drop my keys while trying to unlock my front door.

"Oh yeah?"

"Yes, Layla," he says in a low voice. "I was thinking maybe we should… make tamales soon?"

I almost laugh out loud. Making tamales has never sounded so sexual.

"You want to…make tamales? When?" I ask him.

"Aye. I wanted to *make tamales* yesterday, but fucking Gallagher…" he growls.

Fucking Gallagher, indeed.

"When are you free next?" he asks.

"Well," I hedge, "making tamales can be a pretty lengthy process."

I almost choke. I was definitely talking about actually making tamales, but given the implied innuendo, I realize I probably should have reworded that.

"I mean—" I start to say before Teagan starts chuckling.

"You're right. We should definitely make sure we have enough *uninterrupted* time."

"Preferably where Rowan can't interfere?" I squeak out.

"Exactly," he replies. "So when, Layla? You name the time and place."

My heart is racing, and I can't figure out if he means making *actual* tamales or picking up where we left off. As much as I want him, I don't want to jump straight into bed before we've even talked about the attraction between us.

"Teagan, just to be clear, we're actually going to make tamales, right?"

He releases a breathy laugh. "Yes, Lovely. You promised to teach me, and I'm going to hold you to that. If we have extra time, we can…talk. Does that sound okay?"

Air whooshes from my mouth in relief. "Yeah, that sounds good. Let me take a look at my work and class schedules later, and I'll let you know."

"Grand," he says simply.

"Are you going to see Beauty and the Beast next week?" I ask, desperate for a subject change. "Norah's been working so hard on the costumes."

"That depends. Are you going?"

"Obviously," I say with more sass than intended. "She's my best friend."

"Well, then, I guess I'll be there. What showing?"

It takes a ridiculous amount of effort to keep from kicking my feet in excitement.

"Opening night. I want to be one of the first to see it all put together!"

"Fair point," he concedes. "Alright, where do we get tickets?"

"You're in luck. I actually purchased a couple of tickets yesterday. Charlie and I were going to go together, but then she found out she has to work opening night, so I have a spare." I'm going to kiss Charlie the next time I see her.

"Perfect! How much do I owe you?"

"Nothing. It's my treat," I tell him.

"I don't think so, Lovely. That doesn't sit right with me. Go on, tell me how much."

Why does that sound so dirty, and why do I like the idea of him bossing me around?

"Teagan, don't be chauvinistic," I say just to appease the feminist part of me that's shaking her head in disgust.

"Ach! I'm not! I just don't want you to be out the money. Was Charlie going to pay you for hers?" he asks, catching me off guard.

With a heavy sigh, I say, "Fine. I'll allow it." Tickets are only ten dollars, so it's not a huge deal.

"That wasn't so hard, was it? I'll give it to you when I see you next. That work?"

My thoughts turn dirty again. This is a problem. "Sure, sure," I say quickly, then change the subject again. "What are you doing with the kids at work right now? My brothers and I used to go to an after-school program like that in Texas."

Teagan's tone changes from soft and almost sultry to energetic and excited. "Yeah? Did you have a good experience with it?"

"Most of the time. Being a predominantly Hispanic town meant a lot of soccer was played. That's part of the reason my brothers still play."

"Did you play too?" he asks curiously.

"Meh. I'd kick the ball around a bit when I was younger, but when I hit middle school, I switched to the dance classes offered."

"Dance classes? We don't offer those, not that I'd stand a chance at teaching them," he jokes.

I'd like to teach him some moves.

"Salsa dancing. I've been doing it since I could walk, but the classes were more formal. Also, again, Hispanic community, so it's a given."

"Hmmm. I'm going to have to research this. I've been doing soccer with the kids since it's in season. We've been working on goal-keeping this week," Teagan says proudly.

"They have a good teacher! I bet they love it."

"Aye, they're a great group." The pride and affection in his voice melts me. "We've had a good time. I wish you could meet Gabriela and her brother. She reminds me of you, actually."

"Why's that? Because she's Hispanic?" I can't help but tease him.

"Ach, don't insult me," he says with a scoff. "Yes, her big brown eyes make me think of yours, but she's a sweetheart with an undercurrent of sass. She keeps me on my toes, love."

I laugh nervously. "And that's a good thing?"

"To be sure. I like a bit of mystery."

My nerves disappear as I burst out laughing. "Mystery? I'm the least mysterious person you'll ever meet. I work at a grocery store and study computer science, and I rarely go out or do anything spontaneous."

"No, lass," he says seriously. "You are the most mysterious creature I've ever come across. I never know what you're thinking, and it drives me mental. I can't tell if your smiles mean you're laughing at me or hiding some sort of secret. When you're looking at me, I can't tell if you like what you see or if you think I'm a big eejit. And I like having to work to get you to laugh."

Ay no. I'm in trouble with this one. He has to have a flaw somewhere. I'm about to tell him that he's definitely not a "big eejit" when my phone beeps through another call. It's Papá.

"Hey, I'm so sorry. My father is calling me. Can I take this and call you back?"

"No worries, Lovely. I know how important your family is to you. I need to at least try to do some homework anyway. Talk tomorrow?" he asks hopefully.

"Yeah, okay."

"Bye, love."

"Bye."

52

Chapter Eight

Teagan

"Good job, José! Excellent form, mate!" I cheer for the boy as he expertly blocks a ball from entering the net. The kid has some serious talent at such a young age.

After I ended my call with Layla, it took me a long time to focus on my homework. I hadn't intended to be so forward with our conversation, but there's something about her that makes me want to open up and show all of my cards. And that throaty laugh of hers is quickly becoming my favorite sound. It makes me want to work harder to earn her smiles.

I should have been doing a research paper, but instead, I spent my time looking up salsa dancing. My jaw dropped once I realized how sensual it was. I'd give up just about anything to watch Layla move like that. In private. No other wanker is going to look at her luscious body swaying and undulating so seductively. I'm thinking of learning how to do it myself just so I have the excuse of putting my hands on her while her hips sway.

Shaking those thoughts out of my head, I bring myself back to the present and see Gabriela sitting on the bleachers, pouting. She looks so sad that my heart just about breaks. Jogging over, I take a seat next to her.

"What's wrong, Gabriela?" I ask quietly. "Are you alright, lass?"

Sniffling, she peeks over at me before pointing to a boy around her age across the gym. "That boy over there told me girls can't play soccer as well as boys."

I frown, looking over at the boy in question. That won't do. "Now you listen to me, lass. He doesn't know what he's talking about. Girls are some of the fiercest soccer players around. Did you know that one of the best players in the world is not only a girl but she's Hispanic?"

Her head shoots up, face bright with excitement. "¡No mames! Who is she?"

The light in her eyes makes me smile.

"Her name is Marta Vieira da Silva. She's been named the FIFA World Player of the Year *five times.*"

Gabriela's eyes go wide. "¡¿Cinco?! Wow! Do you think I could be the best player in the world, Mr. Teagan?"

"I do! If you practice and work hard, you could be anything you want," I tell her sincerely.

She beams up at me before jumping up and wrapping her arms around my neck in a fierce hug. Chuckling, I give her a quick squeeze back.

"C'mon. Let's go work on your saves. We'll show those fellas how it's done, yeah?"

"¡Sí! ¡Vámonos!"

Gabriela proves to be quite the force to be reckoned with when challenged. She still roars like a lion when she pounces on a ball, but she doesn't hesitate to dive for it either. The look of determination in her eyes would stop anyone in their tracks. She means business.

In the last few minutes of class, I make it a point to discuss female soccer players. They don't get enough credit to begin with and definitely don't get paid enough as professionals. I'm going to start the next class by watching some footage from the Women's World Cup. That will surely put that little tosser in his place.

The rest of the week flies by in a blur, which is fine by me since I'll be seeing Layla tonight for the opening of Beauty and the Beast. I haven't seen her since that chance meeting on campus, and now I look for her every time I step out of Cameron Hall. I even go so far as detouring around the amphitheater on the off chance of seeing her. When I don't see her, I send her a text message asking about her day. She's usually quick to respond, which makes me grin like a fool every time.

Now I'm staring at my closet and trying to decide what to wear to the play. I don't usually fuss over clothes, but I'm clueless as to what kind of attire is appropriate for this type of event. Eamon just happens to walk by my door at that moment. He glances over, then stops in his tracks.

"What the feck are you doing, mate?" he asks, raising a brow.

"Ach. I'm trying to figure out what the hell I'm supposed to wear to this thing." I groan in frustration.

Chuckling, Eamon leans against the door frame and folds his arms across his chest. "Honestly, you could probably dress casually. It's not Broadway, so don't get fancy. "

"No," I say quickly. "I'm meeting Layla there."

Eamon's brows rise higher. "Yeah? That changes things. Have you asked her what she's wearing?"

"'Course not. What are you going to wear?"

"I'm…" He pauses. "Well fuck. I don't know. I hadn't even thought about it."

"See? This feels like an important event. It's an important night for your mot, and it's the first time Layla and I've gone to anything just the two of us."

"So it's a date?" he asks, smirking at me.

"No. Yes. I don't know. She asked if I was going, and I told her I was if she'd be there. So we agreed to meet up. I'm not picking her up. And I'm paying her back for the ticket. She wasn't going to let me, but I wasn't having that."

Eamon nods in agreement. "I'll ask Norah what the dress code is. Problem solved."

"Thanks, mate."

Layla

I'm a nervous wreck, and I have no idea what to wear. Normally I'd wear jeans and a nicer sweater, but this feels like a date, even if neither of us confirmed it as such. Thank god my best friend is a part of the production. If anyone will know what I should wear, it will be Norah.

Layla: *What's the dress code for tonight?*

Norah: *For the play? There's not really one. Some people dress up, some dress casual. I'll be in business casual since I'm on the crew. Why?*

Layla: *I might be meeting Teagan there...*

Norah: *WHAT?! A date?!*

Layla: *No. At least I don't think so? He insisted on buying Charlie's ticket off of me, and he's not picking me up.*

Norah: *Hmmm. Sounds kind of like a date to me. Wear that one black mini dress with the Queen Anne neckline. Play up the smoky eye. And your red peep toes!*

Layla: *You don't think that's too much?*

Norah: *Nope. You'll have him drooling. ;)*

Layla: *That's NOT what my goal is.*

Norah: *Added bonus. Do beach waves too.*

Huffing out a breath, I pull open my closet door, grabbing the dress in question. If I'm being honest, it's my favorite. The last time I wore it was to Charlie's wedding. If I really want to be truthful, I'd admit that I kind of love the idea of dressing up for Teagan. I've caught his hungry gaze running over my body more than once, and every time, I've been in jeans and a casual top.

A lot of women that are my size are self-conscious of their bodies, but Mami instilled in me from a young age that a woman's curves are one of her best assets that deserve to be accentuated just as much as her hair and eyes. Do these curves make shopping difficult at times? Absolutely, but I've learned what styles work on my hourglass figure and have stuck with it.

After curling my hair, I apply my makeup, carefully contouring and highlighting my features. Before beginning my eye makeup, I dust a shimmery bronzing powder over my cheekbones and decolletage. Following Norah's advice, I blend a few different shades to give my eyelids a smoky look, then add a sexy cat eye lining. I remember spending hours in front of a mirror perfecting this particular technique once I started high school. Finally, I add a couple of coats of extreme-length mascara and a deep red lipstick to match my heels. Stepping back, I admire my reflection with satisfaction. I look and feel confident and sexy. Snapping a selfie, I send it to Norah.

Layla: *Thoughts?*

Norah: *Holy shit, Lay. You're smoking. Can I date you?*

Layla: *Ha! I don't think Eamon wants to share you.*

Norah: *Good point. I'll just live vicariously through Teagan. Gotta get back to the dressing room. See you soon! xoxo*

Layla: *Break a leg! xoxo*

Taking a deep breath, I grab my cropped leather jacket and small clutch and head out the door.

* * *

Finding a parking spot proves to be a challenge. The play has been so hyped up that everyone wants to be at the first showing. Eventually, I give up and decide to park near Congdon Hall and walk. It isn't too long of a walk, and the weather is mild. Locking up, I pull out my phone to see a text from Teagan.

Teagan: *I just got here. I'm outside of Kenan Auditorium.*

Layla: *On my way. Had to park over by Congdon.*

Teagan: *I'm coming to you.*

Layla: *It's really okay. Be there soon.*

Teagan: *Nope. Not letting you walk in the dark alone.*

I roll my eyes out of habit, but inside, I feel all gooey like a toasted marshmallow.

After walking for a few more minutes, I see him. He's far enough away that I can't make out all of his features, but I know it's him just by his easy stride and the hands stuffed into his pockets. As he approaches, I almost trip. He's mouthwatering in a maroon sweater over a white collared shirt with charcoal gray slacks. While reminding myself to shut my gaping mouth, I notice his steps falter, his eyes going wide as they trail from my head to my feet and back up my body. Placing a hand over his heart, he lets out an almost pained sound.

"Christ Almighty," he breathes, stopping inches from me.

"Hola," I say softly, peeking up at him through my lashes.

Clearing his throat, he takes a step back and looks me over again. "Layla, you look...devastatingly beautiful."

"Thank you." I blush. "You're looking pretty good yourself."

I can't *not* compliment him. Even if he hadn't said a word to me, I still wouldn't have been able to refrain from telling him how handsome he is. If Niall Horan and Lucas Bravo had a love child, it would look just like Teagan. He has the boyish smile of Niall mixed with the sexy and pensive eyes of Lucas. His maroon sweater is stretched tight over his broad chest and shoulders. Does he actually have product in his hair? It looks like it has been artfully tousled and swept to the side. He even shaved. Oh, that jawline. *Damn.*

"I wasn't sure what the dress code was. I was afraid I might have overdressed, but now I feel like maybe I didn't dress up enough," he says, eyes continuing to roam.

"Uh, no. You look just right," I blurt out, which makes him grin, showing off that dimple. "Shall we, Lovely?" he asks, offering his arm to me.

Unable to stop myself, I run a hand down his bicep before looping it through and resting it in the crook of his arm. What I actually want to do is run my hands all over him.

"We shall. Hopefully, we'll find some good seats," I tell him as we begin walking towards the theater.

"I think Eamon said Norah reserved some for us."

That was news to me. "Oh yeah? She didn't mention it to me earlier."

He shrugs in response, and we walk silently the rest of the way, our eyes repeatedly darting towards each other. Each time I catch his gaze, he smiles, which makes me blush. Everything he does makes me blush. *Annoying.* When we reach the theater, I stop and pull the tickets out of my small handbag then turn and hand one to Teagan.

"Right. Here." He starts to pull his wallet from his pocket.

I reach out a hand to stop him. "We'll worry about it later."

"Is this your way of trying to get me to forget?" he asks with narrowed eyes.

I roll mine in return. "You're ridiculous. Let's just go find our seats first."

Teagan pulls the door open and ushers me through with a hand on the small of my back. I can feel the heat searing through my dress. How can such a small gesture be so telling? When we enter the lobby, we stop short. It's completely packed full of people. Half of them are just waiting to be seated, while the other half are visiting in large circles. I'm suddenly very glad I wore heels as they give me just enough height to see over all of the heads.

"Sheesh. I wasn't expecting this big of a crowd," I mumble to Teagan.

"C'mon. Let's try going around," he says as he slips his warm, rough hand into mine, holding it firmly and leading me to the outside edge of the room.

He doesn't release his grip once. Any time someone steps in front of us or blocks our path, he pauses and rubs soothing circles on the back of my hand with his thumb. Eventually, we find a side door and sneak into the auditorium. The room is half full with people milling about trying to find the best seats.

"Did Eamon say where our seats were?" I ask, craning my neck to find the man in question.

"No, he didn't. Not very helpful of him, was it?" Teagan teases before saying, "Ah! There he is."

Following his line of sight, I see Eamon standing to the left of the stage and about ten rows back, motioning us forward

"Hey," Teagan greets his friend. "Thanks for saving the seats."

"Yeah, mate, no worries," the tall dark-haired Irishman says. He looks at me and nods in greeting. "Layla. You look lovely."

Giving him a small smile, I murmur a quick thank you right as Teagan says, "Doesn't she just? I about fell to my knees at the sight of her. Took the breath right out of me."

My face heats, but I shake my head in amusement and Eamon chuckles before clapping his friend on the shoulder.

"Right, well your seats are in the middle there." He points. "I'm in the row ahead of you but down a bit. See you after the show?"

"Yeah, mate. 'Course."

Teagan turns to me and gestures for me to go ahead of him. It's a tight space, so I brush against him as I step by. God, he smells good. I'm suddenly very thankful I'm familiar with not only Beauty and the Beast but all of Norah's work because I don't think I'll be able to concentrate on anything other than Teagan tonight.

We find our seats with index cards taped to them that read, "Reserved for T. O'Brien and L. Diaz." Once we're settled, I realize just how great these seats are. We're far enough back that the actors' voices won't be booming at us but close enough to see details. I turn to remark on how good this spot is but stop when I find Teagan staring at me with an unfathomable look in his eyes. My breath hitches at the intensity of it.

"What?" I ask quietly, bringing a hand to my hair and looking down at my dress. "What's wrong?"

His mouth tips up at the corner. "Nothing. Absolutely nothing is wrong. I'm just mesmerized is all."

"Wow," I huff in an attempt to break the tension thickening around us. "I guess I need to make myself up more often, huh?"

A crease forms between his brows, and his lips turn down. "No, I wasn't saying you're not always beautiful— because, lass, you are stunning. I've just never seen you all decked out like this."

Snorting in amusement, I turn back to face the stage. I knew exactly what he was trying to say; I just wanted to tease him. Then I feel his hot breath on me as he whispers against the shell of my ear, "Those red lips are distracting, Layla. They have me thinking about *tamales.*"

A flash of heat shoots straight to my core, and I immediately press my thighs together. I slowly look over at him, not at all surprised to find his face so close to mine, but my pulse still quickens at the proximity. Unable to control myself, my gaze darts to his mouth and back to his eyes. My teeth latch on to my bottom lip, and Teagan's eyes zero in on the movement. The tension continues to press in as he angles his head closer, so close I can feel his breath fanning over my lips.

Then the lights in the auditorium dim momentarily, signaling the production will be starting in five minutes.

My eyes slam shut as I turn back to face the stage, and I hear Teagan curse under his breath. I'm immensely thankful for the program I managed to snag from the lobby on the way in. There's nothing subtle about the way I'm fanning my face with it, but I can't bring myself to care. I am on *fire.* Not from embarrassment, but from being so turned on it's unbearable. Twice now we've been on the verge of what I know will be an earth-shattering kiss only to be interrupted. I know for a fact I won't be able to control myself if we find ourselves in this situation a third time.

Chapter Nine

Teagan

The lights lower and the conversations around us silence in anticipation of the play starting, but all I can think about is grabbing Layla's hand and finding an empty room with a locking door. When I discovered that she had parked farther away from the building and would be walking alone, I automatically headed in her direction. I was nervous and excited to see her but not at all prepared to see her dressed like a wet dream, prowling towards me in fuck-me heels and with lips painted devil red. I actually tripped over my own feet. The closer she came, the harder it was for me to breathe. She's so beautiful that it's physically painful. When I said that I practically fell to my knees, I wasn't slagging her. I would have gladly crawled across the ground to worship at her feet.

As we entered the building, I was acutely aware of all the heads turning in her direction. I couldn't blame them, but a primal urge came over me to step in front of her and beat my chest, telling them all that she's *mine*. It was instinctual for me to grab her hand and lead her to the outskirts of the room in an attempt to hide her from wandering eyes. Eyes that kept drifting to the low- cut neckline of her dress.

I've more than noticed how her ample breasts fill it out and nearly groan out loud every time I let my own eyes roam, which I'm trying not to do. Really, I am. I respect her and will treat her accordingly, but *fuck me*, Layla Diaz is an absolute bombshell. Not to mention those lips. I want to mess up that red lipstick in all sorts of inappropriate ways.

The packed theater is the last place I want our first kiss to be— there *will* be a first kiss and soon if I have any say about it—but when she's sitting so close and smells that good, I can't think of a reason why this isn't as good of a place as any other. Then those fucking lights flashed and killed the moment.

I'm attempting to discreetly adjust my growing erection when I notice Layla fanning herself with a program she snatched from the lobby. Her face is flushed, a beautiful russet color traveling down her throat to her chest that's heaving slightly. *This is torture.*

Surprisingly, I'm actually able to focus on the play once it starts, which is a testament to the actors' skills and Norah's incredible costumes. The dresses she designed look like actual flowers, with Belle's resembling an upside- down yellow rose. Layla gasped audibly when it was revealed, pride in her eyes for her friend's work. I'm completely enamored by her. She catches me watching her, and those gorgeous brown eyes soften in a way I can't pinpoint, but I vow to do everything I can to make her mine.

At the end of the evening, we find Eamon in the lobby waiting for Norah, so we stay and visit a while. He's beaming with pride.

"Oh my god," Layla squeals. "That was incredible! Everything was absolutely perfect! And Norah's costumes! I can't get over Belle's dress!"

Eamon and I share an amused look. I don't think I've ever seen Layla so animated before, but I like It. Hell, I like everything about her.

"Yeah, she really did amazing," Eamon says, shoving his hands into his pockets. "It all really came together on stage, though."

"Hey!" Norah's voice sounds from behind us.

We all turn to greet her with hugs and congratulations, and Eamon pulls her into his arms to press a kiss to her temple.

"Well done, Acushla. That was incredible."

Norah beams up at him with nothing but love in her eyes. I sneak a glance at Layla, who's watching the couple with a small smile on her face. To anyone else, it would look like she's patiently waiting, but I don't miss how she takes in every touch between our friends. She looks…wistful.

"I have to get back. I just wanted to come out and say thanks for coming real quick," Norah says before looking back to Eamon. "See you tonight?"

"Definitely," Eamon answers.

The two share a heated look, and he watches her walk away.

"Well…" Layla clears her throat, but Eamon doesn't even flinch.

"Eamon, mate. You have a little bit of drool there…" I tease him and finally get a response.

"Fuck off, wanker," he says with a glare.

"I'm just messing with you. Good on you for being all about your girl. It's how it should be."

"Yeah, she's…" Eamon starts.

"Amazing," Layla finishes softly, giving him a knowing look.

He nods in agreement before adding, "Alright, I'm going to head out. You two good?"

"Grand," I reply cheerfully. "I'm going to walk Layla back to her car. I'm assuming you won't be back to the flat tonight?"

Eamon grins. "Nope. It's all yours, mate."

Layla looks away pointedly at the insinuation. I'd love nothing more than to invite her back to the flat, but I'm afraid I won't be able to keep my hands to myself. *Ach. Who am I kidding?* I know I won't be able to keep my hands off of her once I'm permitted the chance. With her consent, of course.

"Right. Ready, Lovely?" I ask, gesturing toward the doors.

"Yeah, I am. See you later, Eamon."

"Bye, Layla. Teag," he responds simply before heading back towards the auditorium.

The night has gotten colder since we were inside, and as much as I'd like to prolong this walk with Layla, I don't want her catching a chill.

"Do you work tomorrow?"

"Unfortunately," she grumbles. "I open, so as soon as I get home, I'm going straight to bed."

Damn. I can't keep her out much later, then. So much for making that kiss happen tonight. I don't want to rush it, but I also don't want her sleep-deprived before her busy day tomorrow.

"Are you stocked up on turkeys now?" I ask with a wink and am rewarded with the sound of her smoky laugh.

"Yes, finally. Which is good, considering Thanksgiving is in a couple of weeks. Do you and Eamon and Ro celebrate it?"

"Not in a traditional sense. Our first year in the States was spent eating pizza and drinking beer." I chuckle at the memory. "We've upped our game since then, though. Now we have stew *and* beer."

"That sounds good to me!" Layla says approvingly. "Norah and I usually go to Charlie's. My parents were trying to get me to come home for both Thanksgiving and Christmas this year, but I told them there was no way I was going to travel back to Texas twice in one month"

"So you'll be going home at Christmas, then?"

"That's the plan." She sighs. "I miss them and really can't wait to see everyone, but I'm also dreading it."

"Why's that?" I ask hesitantly. It's none of my business, but I hate the idea of her being unhappy.

Layla groans in frustration. "My Mami is *constantly* bringing up the fact that I'm unmarried and without children. She thinks that, because she already had two at my age, I'm wasting my life. She made sure to remind me that my brothers are both bringing their girlfriends to Christmas this year."

I raise my eyebrows in astonishment. "So let me see if I understand. Your Mam would rather you be a young, married mother than an independent woman choosing her own future? And somehow your brothers are better because they're bringing someone with them to dinner?"

Letting out a humorless laugh, she says, "Yep. That sums it up. It doesn't even matter that they bring a *different girl every year!* She just sees them as potential daughters-in-law who can provide her with *nietos*. I could probably bring a homeless man I found at the airport with me, and she'd be ecstatic."

We've reached her car and turn to face each other. I consider what she just told me, an idea forming. It may not be a very good idea, but I'm going to try anyway.

"Don't take a homeless man."

Layla rolls her eyes. "I'm not actually going to. I was just being dramatic."

"Take me," I say before she's even finished the last word.

Her eyes widen, and she gapes at me. "What?"

"Take me with you. It will give you some reprieve from the constant judgment, and I can make tamales with your Abuela." I wink again.

"That's ridiculous. Why would you do that?" she asks in disbelief.

Shrugging, I say, "Why not?"

"Because you...we're not...that's..." Layla stutters out.

I step closer, placing my hands on her shoulders and giving them a light squeeze. "Layla. It doesn't have to be complicated, lass. Don't overthink it. Just tell them you're bringing a friend if it makes you feel better. If anything, I can be there for moral support, yeah?"

She narrows her eyes at me. "You do realize that it's not just Mami and Papá and my siblings. It will be *everyone*. We're talking dozens of loud and nosy Mexican family members that have no respect for boundaries."

"Aye, I do. Sounds fun to me. Maybe your brothers and I can play a little footy and they can teach me some new tricks. Gabriela wants to become the next Marta Vieira da Silva. I could share what I learn."

Her gaze softens as her lips tip into a smile.

"Sleep on it and let me know tomorrow if you want me to come with you. Now get in your car and get warm. Go home and go to sleep, mo chroi."

Tilting her head to the side, her dark curls draping over her shoulder, she asks softly, "What does that mean?"

Flashing her my best smile, I say, "I'll tell you later. Text me when you make it home."

Layla

To say that I'm disappointed that Teagan didn't try to kiss me again is an understatement. I was considering taking matters into my own hands when he dropped that bomb on me. Take him home to Texas with me? Introduce him to my family? As what? Just a friend? *Yeah right.* Mami would be asking us why aren't we more than friends, making it incredibly awkward. Teagan would handle it with grace, no doubt, because that's the type of person he is. He'd probably take the teasing and give it right back.

This sounds like the start of those fake dating romance novels, which just so happens to be my favorite trope, but this is real life. Does the idea of having him by my side as a buffer sound appealing? Absolutely. My family would love him, but what happens after the holidays? What if all of this tension that's building between us is just physical? I haven't had sex in way too long, and Teagan is so hot. There's chemistry there, but what if we're not compatible otherwise?

I'm still pondering this as I let myself into my house, kick off my shoes, and get ready for bed. My phone buzzes right before I collapse onto my pillow. *Shit.* I forgot to text him when I got home.

Teagan: *Did you make it home okay?*

Layla: *Yes. Sorry. I got distracted.*

Teagan: *No worries, love. Glad you made it. Sleep well.*

Layla: *Goodnight, Teag.*

Despite my racing mind, I manage to fall asleep quickly. When the alarm goes off at the ungodly hour it was set for, I reluctantly roll out of bed. I was dreaming about making tamales while naked, and it doesn't take a genius to figure out what inspired that one. Chuckling to myself, I fix coffee and get ready for work, savoring this happy feeling. Once I clock in, it's going to be a long day.

Chapter Ten

Teagan

"You don't think they…" I grimace.

Eamon and I are sitting at our kitchen table, discussing the events of the previous night at Paddy's.

"Christ, he better not have pulled his normal shite," Eamon grouses. "Surely, he wouldn't shag and bail on *Alicia.* Not just because she's pure gold, but she'd murder him."

"I swear to god, if we have to find a new pub, I'll rip his bollox off and shove them so far up his arse, they'll hang out of his nose," I seethe. I'm usually a lover, not a fighter, but sometimes Ro makes me so raging mad with his antics. And I'm not about to give up O'Nelly's Pub.

Eamon barks out a loud laugh.

The wanker in question chooses that moment to barge through the door.

"What'd I miss, mates?"

"Just our plans to disfigure you if we have to find a new pub," I grumble.

"Why the feck would we have to find a new pub? What did you wankers get up to?" Ro sinks into one of the chairs and props his feet up on the table.

"Not us, you gobshite," Eamon says while pushing Ro's feet off the table. "Keep those boats of yours on the floor, will ya? Now tell us what you did to Alicia."

Ro lets out a loud groan. "It's not what you're thinking. In fact, it's quite the opposite."

Eamon and I share a look of disbelief before Rowan continues.

"Alright, so Alicia and I bumped into each other last week at a club. We'd both been drinking, obviously, and dancing. Next thing I know, we're in the jacks, snogging. It was getting heated, but I put on the brakes. Alicia's not just some random wagon, is she? Snogging is one thing, but shagging her is a different story altogether. If I'm going to shag her, it's not going to be while we're hammered in the jacks of some manky club. I have more respect for her than that. So, anyway, she was raging and ran out of there before I could even explain myself. It's been frigid ever since."

There's utter silence as we process what Ro just told us. When has he *ever* stopped a shag? And with Alicia of all people! He must actually *like* her.

"Stall the ball." I turn the ball cap on my head backward before leaning forward to rest my elbows on the table. "You're saying that Alicia wanted to hook up and *you* turned *her* down?"

"Not because I didn't want her! God knows how much I'd love to sink my..."

"Stop," Eamon interrupts. "No more, mate."

"Right. So anyway. That's the story. Every time I try to talk to her, she goes all ice queen on me." Ro shrugs.

"Well, Rowan, for once, I can actually say you did the right thing, but you're going to have to find a way to explain it to her," I tell him sternly.

"And how do you suppose I do that when she barely acknowledges me?" Rowan gives me a look like I'm dense.

Eamon hums and taps his chin. "Norah and I are hosting Thanksgiving at hers next week for all of our mates. She always invites Alicia. If I can make sure she's there, you can corner her at some point. We can orchestrate something."

"You and the fire sprite are getting serious, yeah?" Ro asks with a raised brow.

"Yeah." Eamon blows out a breath as he laces his fingers behind his head. "She's amazing."

Observing my friend and roommate, I notice the subtle changes on his face. Eamon was so guarded when he came to UNCW. Now his eyes are brighter and his normal scowl has been replaced with a softness that only one feeling in the world can bring.

"You love her, don't you, mate?" I ask quietly.

"Without a doubt." He answers without hesitation.

We sit around discussing what Ro should do or say to make things right with Alicia for a while. He's rarely serious about anything but seems to be genuinely bothered by what transpired between him and Alicia. She's fierce in every way, with long black hair and blunt bangs brushing her eyebrows and both arms covered in sleeves of tattoos. She usually wears all black, sometimes accented with deep purple or red. The girl is seriously intimidating and doesn't take shite from anyone. When a man hits on her at the pub, she's quick to put him in his place, and the guy doesn't bother her again. Except for Ro, who loves a challenge. He takes her insults and rebuffs to use as fuel for their next round.

"Have you considered just asking her out?" I suggest. "Clearly there's chemistry there. Maybe instead of immediately getting physical, take her to dinner?"

Rowan scrunches his nose like the air smells of rotten fish. "Teag, mate. I don't do dinner dates."

"Then how do you plan on moving forward with her?"

"I never said I wanted to date her." He scoffs.

"So," Eamon says slowly. "You want to fuck her, but you won't because you respect her. And you have no interest in attempting a relationship with her because...why?"

"Eamon, Eamon, Eamon," Ro says, addressing his friend like he's a small child. "I'm too young and hot to settle down. This body was made to entertain the *ladies*. Plural. I'm not a one-woman type of man."

Eamon rolls his eyes as he stands from his chair. "Whatever you say, Ro. I've gotta get to Paddy's. Slán," he says, bidding us goodbye in Irish.

I want nothing more than to hit Ro upside the head. *Fecking eejit.*

"Well probably better that you leave Alicia alone, then. She doesn't deserve to be another notch on your bedpost," I snap at him.

"That's my point exactly, O'Brien! She's a good girl who deserves to be with someone who can give her all of her heart's desires and stay the course. I'm not that man," Rowan says regretfully.

Ro hasn't shared much of his life in Ireland, but we know his family life has been rough. His mom walked out on them when he was a young wan, leaving him with an alcoholic father. He's implied that, in order to survive, he had to do some unsavory things but never expanded on it.

"But you could be. If you really wanted to be." I shrug.

Ro lets out a defeated sigh. "No, mate. I don't think I could be. I think I'd try and fail. So rather than becoming a huge disappointment, I'll just stick to what I do best."

"I think you cut yourself short, Ro. If you'd actually be serious for once, I think you'd surprise yourself."

He rolls his eyes dramatically.

"I'm serious. The fact that you were able to stop yourself from shagging Alicia, while drunk, speaks volumes. Even when you're banjaxed, you recognize she's different than your regular flings. Obviously, you don't lack complete common sense."

"Fuck off," Ro barks. "It took every ounce of willpower to take my hands and mouth off of her, Teags. I can't stop thinking about it. Half the time, I want to kick myself for stopping, and the other half, I actually feel like I did something honorable."

"You *did*, which is what I'm trying to tell you," I growl in frustration. "You *can* be what she deserves because you're already doing what needs to be done. Think it over, mate. Really think about what it would look like to give it a go with her. If the thought of waking up next to her, and only her, for the foreseeable future makes you cringe, then leave her be. But if that thought makes your heart stop, it might be worth giving up your wild ways."

Rowan sits there silently for a long while, just staring at the wall. I've never seen him so pensive before. Finally, he sucks in a deep breath and stands, stretching his arms above his head.

"Right. I'm off. Thanks, Teags. I know I give you a lot of shite, but you're a good bloke."

"Go on with you, now. Did Rowan Gallagher just pay me a compliment? I like this new you. Looking forward to when you pick up the next tab at Paddy's."

"Will I, yeah? You can go and bollox, how about that?" Ro says with a grin.

"There he is." I chuckle.

Layla

It's Thanksgiving Day, and I still haven't given Teagan an answer. I made a pros and cons list that didn't help at all. Deciding to call in reinforcements, I text Norah.

Layla: *Hey, any chance you need some help with meal prep and your guy isn't there yet?*

Norah: *I'm officially intrigued. Yes, come on over. Door's open.*

Layla: *Thanks xoxo.*

Not wasting any time with getting fixed up, I slip into my favorite sandals and head next door. I'll have time to get ready for the big meal later. Norah and Eamon orchestrated a *Friendsgiving* since so many of us don't have family close. Last I checked, the guest list included all three Irishmen, Alicia, Myra, Amelia, and myself. Since Charlie is the only one married, the couple spends the holiday with her husband's family. Norah is providing the main part of the meal, but everyone else is bringing some sort of side dish or dessert.

"Knock knock," I call out as I enter Norah's house.

She's sitting at the kitchen island with a coffee mug cupped in her hands, red hair in a messy bun on top of her head. There's a steaming mug of coffee waiting for me.

"*Mi amor*, you take such good care of me."

Norah sips her coffee before ordering me to sit and spill. "Alright, what is it that you don't want to say in front of Eamon?"

Sighing heavily, I say, "It has nothing to do with not trusting him. I just want to say that now. It's more of I don't think I could actually make the words come out if he was here."

"Understood. Now, spill."

"So, you know that Teagan and I saw the play together. What you don't know is that we almost kissed. In the auditorium. Five minutes before the play started."

Norah gasps, then starts bouncing in her seat. "Okay, *almost*. Then what?"

"Before you get too excited, we still have not kissed yet." I pause to laugh at my friend's pouting face. "However, after the play, he walked me to my car and we started talking about holidays with families. I told him how my family always hounds me about being single, never bringing anyone home with me for the holidays, my brothers bringing a new girl every year, yada yada. I made a joke about finding a homeless guy and paying him to come to dinner just so they'd leave me alone."

"And...?" Norah waves her hand, encouraging me to continue.

"Teagan told me to take him to family Christmas."

"He *what*?!" Norah claps her hands to her cheeks in shock. "Was he being serious?"

"Yes! Norie, I thought he was just messing with me, but he was dead serious. He said he could be my backup, my moral support against my family. When I asked him what he was getting out of it, he just said that he wanted to play soccer with my brothers and make tamales with my Abuela."

"Wait," Norah muses, not missing a damn thing. "Why did you blush when you mentioned making tamales?"

"Um. We might have had a conversation where making tamales became an innuendo?"

Norah bursts out laughing. "Okay, I need to know this story before we talk about anything else."

Groaning and blushing like crazy, I recount our first almost-kiss and the conversation following that. Norah is practically in tears by the end of it.

"Oh my god, Lay. I can't. That's so funny! I always knew Teagan was a fun guy, but I'm learning so much about him right now. Okay, now, back to him inviting himself to the Diaz Family Christmas. What did you tell him?"

Biting my bottom lip, I dig my pros and cons list out of the pocket of my hoodie. "I haven't answered him yet. I have no idea how to. On one hand, the moral support would be awesome. On the other hand, does this mean we're dating? Or just friends? Are we telling my parents we're dating if we're not actually dating? Also, *why* would he offer to do this? I'm so confused, Norah. I made a freaking list of why I should or shouldn't take him up on this, and it hasn't helped."

"This is a big deal, amiga! First, I don't think you and Teagan can be classified as *just* friends anymore. Not after almost kissing *twice*." Norah holds up two fingers, emphasizing her point. "There's some serious sexual tension between the two of you. Have you gone out since the play?"

"No," I groan. "Our schedules have been conflicting. We text every day. The last time I saw him in person was at your surprise party, and we didn't really get a chance to talk." I let my mind wander back to that moment.

* * *

The girls and I decided to throw Norah a surprise party in celebration of the play being such a huge success. Paddy, the owner of the pub, agreed to close it to the public so we could make it a private event. I'm sandwiched between Amelia and Charlie when Teagan saunters up to our table. He says hello before my friends start gawking at him and making the whole thing awkward as hell.

Realizing we aren't going to have any sort of privacy, he says, "I won't interfere with your fun. I just wanted to come over and say hi."

"I'm glad you did," I tell him, smiling softly.

He raps his knuckles on the tabletop before tossing me a wink and walking back to the bar. Once his back is turned, Amelia and Charlie start squealing and giggling.

"Please stop," I beg. "You made that so weird."

"Sorry, girl, but that man is hot. We're living vicariously through you right now."

"You just keep your hands and eyes to yourselves, and we won't have a problem, comprende?" I snap, earning a round of astonished gasps and giggles.

"Okay," Norah says, bringing me back to the present. "I think the first thing you two need to discuss is where this relationship is headed. That will make your decision easier, right?"

"That's true. See? This is why I came over here. I knew you'd be calm and level-headed while my brain went *loco*. Now I just have to find the nerve to bring it up." I sigh heavily at the thought.

Norah reaches out to squeeze my hand. "Don't worry. You have time. It's not something that has to be talked about today. Let's just enjoy the holiday, and if the conversation comes up naturally between the two of you, great! If not, table it for another day. He's a patient guy, and I don't think he's going anywhere."

"You're right. Thanks, chica. Now. What can I do to help?"

* * *

Teagan is sitting across from me, looking so ridiculously handsome it's distracting. He's in a hunter green sweater over a black collared shirt and a pair of light-wash jeans. The five o'clock shadow covering his sculpted jaw is somehow better than his clean shaven look. It's rugged and sexy. The group decided to keep the night informal, but everyone seems to have taken extra care in selecting their outfits. Ro's even wearing a tie!

I'd like to say I dressed for myself, but I chose my outfit with Teagan in mind: soft taupe dolman-sleeve sweater over black leggings with red accent jewelry and the red lipstick Teagan seems to love. I left my hair down, letting my natural waves come out to play. If anyone has noticed the way we keep eyeing each other, they haven't mentioned it.

We manage to find ourselves alone only once. I walk out of the bathroom to see Teagan leaning against the opposite wall, hands in his pockets, sleeves pushed up to his elbows. I stop and watch his eyes travel over me slowly.

"Hey, stranger."

He smiles warmly as he pushes off the wall and steps closer so we're toe-to-toe.

"Hello, Lovely. You look incredible," he murmurs.

"Thank you. So do you."

Leaning in, he moves his mouth to my ear, the faint scent of pine and something strictly male invading my senses, and whispers, "Did you wear those red lips for me, love?"

I swallow thickly. Not wanting a repeat of our almost kisses to be outside of a bathroom, I place a hand on his chest and push him gently back. Smiling broadly at him, I shrug before turning to walk away but pause to glance over my shoulder.

"Maybe, guapo."

Chapter Eleven

Layla

I'm at Paddy O'Nelly's with Norah, Eamon, and Charlie. While the girls and I chat, Teagan and Rowan saunter into the pub. My eyes roam over Teagan from the weathered royal blue ball cap on his head to the Converse on his feet, appreciating the way his green UNCW hoodie and dark-wash jeans cling to his muscular body. He makes casual look better than good. He greets the pub owner, Paddy, with a hug before swinging his gaze around the space. Once he spots me, he grins, putting those dimples on display, before making his way over to me.

"Evenin'. You're looking lovely, Layla," he says as he takes the seat next to me, throwing his arm over the back of my chair.

"Thanks," I mutter, my face heating.

As the night progresses, more drinks are consumed and our group chats, laughing for what seems like hours. Occasionally, I feel Teagan's fingers playing with my hair or grazing my shoulder. He never removes his arm from the back of my chair, and the more I imbibe, the closer I lean into him. We are like magnets, drawn together, unable and unwilling to resist the pull. His subtle touches sear me to my bones, stoking my fire from a simmer to a blaze. I am on the verge of suggesting we leave and go to my house when a commotion at the door has us all freezing mid-sentence. Mac, a fellow Seahawks teammate, stumbles in completely blitzed out of his mind, due to learning a few hours ago that Myra is pregnant with his baby, completely unplanned. While it is a complete shock to the rest of us, Norah and Eamon apparently already knew and, thankfully, are able to calm him down before sending him home safely.

"Mac as a father. Now that's something I can't believe," Rowan exclaims. "That wanker can't even take care of himself!"

Teagan barks out a laugh. "True enough. I hope Myra is prepared to raise the kid without him."

"You never know," I say, turning to him with a shrug, "maybe he'll wake up tomorrow a new man."

"Also true, love." Teagan winks and brushes my hair off of my shoulder. "I'll swing by and check in on him in the morning."

I smile at him, completely smitten with this act of kindness. "Text me after. I was thinking about going to Airlie Gardens. I might want some company."

Then, without giving him a chance to respond, I rise from my seat, hug Norah and Charlie goodbye, and leave.

* * *

I'm dancing around my living room, trying to expel the nervous energy coursing through me while I wait to hear from Teagan. He said he would check on Mac last night and I'm anxious not just for an update, but also to know if he plans on joining me. The sound of my phone chiming, has me tripping over myself as I rush to it.

Teagan: *Morning, love. Still want company today?*

Layla: *Good morning. I wouldn't turn it down if you're free.*

Teagan: *For you? I'm always available.*

Layla: *If only you could see how hard I'm rolling my eyes right now. Want me to pick you up? You're on the way to Airlie Gardens.*

Teagan: *You're not rolling your eyes. You're probably blushing. But yes, if it's not too much trouble.*

Layla: *I'm choosing to ignore that first part. I'll be there in twenty.*

Twenty minutes later, I'm pulling up to the apartment complex. It isn't fancy by any means, but it's nicer than what most college students live in. I spent the entire drive trying to regulate my breathing and calm my nerves. I park the car and sit there trying to decide if I should just text him to let him know I'm here or knock on the door. The decision is made for me when my phone buzzes in the console.

Teagan: *Want to come in? You don't have to wait in your car. I'm a little behind schedule. Door's open.*

I inhale deeply. Eamon had gone back to Norah's place with her after leaving Paddy's, so I'll be alone with Teagan in the apartment. No big deal, right?

Layla: *Okay. Be right up.*

Stepping out of the car, I tuck my hair behind my ears, suck in another deep breath, and climb the stairs to the second-story apartment. He said the door is open, but I'm hesitant to just barge right in, so I knock a couple of times before slowly opening the door. "Knock knock," I call out quietly, then freeze.

Teagan is leaning against the breakfast bar that separates the open floor plan with his phone to his ear, ball cap on backwards. And shirtless. He's holding the phone with one hand, while the other is resting on top of the hat, and the muscles in his arms flex in the most distracting way. I knew he had tattoos but never realized that the band around his bicep is actually an intricate rope of Celtic designs. The North Carolina sun has left his skin golden, and I let my gaze drift over his torso, appreciating every defined line on his chest and stomach. When my eyes drop lower, I realize the top button of his jeans is open, showcasing the V leading down below the waistband.

Holy shit.

"Ma, no, it's fine. Really." His deep, lilting accent floats through the room.

"I know you are, but it's grand. That's what public transportation and good friends are for."

He lifts his head, catching me staring, and winks at me. I can't tell if the flush of my skin is from being turned on or being caught ogling.

"Speaking of good friends, one just walked in. I'll call you later, yeah? Right. I love you too, Ma. Kiss Gran for me. Ta."

Teagan pushes off the bar and pads toward me on bare feet, a predatory grin spreading across his handsome face. He stops a few inches away and looks down at me. I'm average height for a woman, but he's certainly taller than the average man.

"Sorry about that. My Ma. She's been calling me almost weekly, which is unusual."

"It's fine," I squeak out, then clear my throat. "I think it's sweet. And relatable. I hear from mine just as much."

"Aye, then you understand why I'm running behind this morning. Mams and their incessant chatter." He laughs, but it's obvious how much he loves his mother, and I admire him all the more for it.

"Yes, definitely. Though mine takes at least ten minutes to just say goodbye. And that's just on the phone. In person, I have to start saying my goodbyes an hour before I'm supposed to leave."

He chuckles as he turns back towards the kitchen. "I'll finish getting ready. Make yourself at home. You want coffee or something?"

"I was going to treat you to coffee from my favorite spot, but I can pre-game it," I say, trailing behind him and trying my hardest to stop staring at his ass.

"I'm more of a tea guy, but if it's your favorite, I'd better try it."

I climb onto a stool at the breakfast bar and watch him saunter down the hallway before he steps into one of the rooms. I'm completely transfixed watching the muscles of his back shift. When he comes back out, he's pulling a navy blue Henley over his head, his pants are fastened, the hat is gone, and his shoes are on. As sad as I am to lose the view of his uncovered body, I can't deny that he looks just as delicious dressed.

"Well you're in luck. They have a pretty great tea selection," I inform him, propping my elbows on the bar.

"Yeah?" he asks, walking in my direction. "I'm not too picky, but you've piqued my interest. Back home it's just plain ol' black tea."

"Cream and sugar? Or do you take yours plain?"

He passes behind me, then leans in to whisper against the shell of my ear, "Just sugar. I like it dark and sweet."

A jolt of lust shoots straight to my core, making me squeeze my thighs together and squirm in my seat. Teagan and his food innuendos might just be the death of me.

"Alright," he says, interrupting my dirty thoughts, "I'm ready if you are."

He's standing on the opposite side of the bar, arms crossed over his chest, and grinning at me like a Cheshire Cat.

Jodón.

"Yeah, I'm ready."

Teagan jogs to the door and opens it, gesturing me through with an exaggerated bow. "After you, Lovely."

I roll my eyes at him but can't stop the smile that creeps over my face.

* * *

We stop at El Cafecito for the coffee and tea I promised. I found the small Mexican cafe after I joined the Hispanic Cultural Center at UNCW and they gave us a list of all the Hispanic-owned businesses and restaurants in the surrounding area. I've visited several, but El Cafecito is my favorite. They have the best *orejas,* and their coffee is spiced with the perfect amount of cinnamon.

When we enter the cafe, Esmerelda, the owner, is rolling out dough on a large workspace. She's probably in her mid-seventies but doesn't look it. Her daughter, Maria, is busy filling the pastry case along the adjacent wall. She looks up and smiles.

"Buenos días, Layla," she greets us. "¿Cómo estás?"

"Buenos días, Maria. Estoy bien, ¿y usted?"

"Bien! Who is your friend?" she asks, winking at me in a not-so-subtle way.

Naturally, I blush, while Teagan chuckles and extends a hand to her.

"Teagan O'Brien. Pleasure to meet you," he says amicably.

"Ooh! Hello, Teagan. ¿Eres irlandés?"

"Uh…" Teagan starts, looking to me for help.

God, he's adorable.

I smirk at him. "She asked if you're Irish." I glance back at Maria, the grin on my face widening. "Yes, Maria. Teagan is Irish. He's a student at UNCW as well."

Maria's grin widens as her gaze bounces between the two of us. "I didn't realize they were so handsome in Ireland."

Teagan beams at her. "They're not. It's just me."

Laughter spills from Maria's lips. "Oh, chica, he's smooth."

I scowl at both of them. *Of course, he'd have Maria wrapped around his finger too.*

"What can I get for you two? Are you staying or getting it to go?"

"To go, please. We're on our way to Airlie Gardens," I reply.

Maria nods her head knowingly. "Es un lugar hermoso."

Teagan looks to me again, and I say, "She said it's a beautiful place."

"Ah," he says, "I really need to learn Spanish."

We visit with Maria for a few minutes while she fills our order. I pay for our drinks, ignoring Teagan's protests, and then Maria hands us a bag of free pastries with a wink.

Chapter Twelve

Teagan

I really need to learn Spanish.

I should ask Rowan to teach me, but I don't trust the wanker to teach me the correct translations. I'd probably end up telling Layla she looks like a gargoyle rather than how beautiful she is. Ro would think that's the funniest gag ever.

After we leave the cafe, Layla drives us to Airlie Gardens, teasing me the entire time about my lack of Spanish language skills. I love every second of it. Her bashful side is endearing, but when her feisty side comes out to play, I can't get enough of it. My goal for the day is to see just how much fire she has.

We exit the car, and I cross my arms over my chest, glaring playfully at her. "Remind me to give you absolute hell for not being able to speak Irish when we go to Ireland."

"Who said I'm going to Ireland with you?" Layla quips, giving me a sardonic look over the top of her car.

"I did. Just now. You're not a very good listener."

We meet at the front bumper and walk side by side through the garden entrance. I've never been to Airlie Gardens, but I'm excited to explore with Layla today.

"I don't remember you asking if I *wanted* to go with you, O'Brien. What if I'd rather go with Ro?" She raises an eyebrow.

I know she's just slagging me, but the thought of her going to Ireland with anyone other than me has me feeling like a caveman. *Woman mine.*

"Pffft. The last person you'd want to go to Ireland with is Rowan Gallagher. He's from Galway."

"What's wrong with Galway?" Layla asks.

I shake my head dramatically. "Oh, it's beautiful, to be sure, but it's full of nothing but sexually devious culchies too busy smoking cannabis and drinking Buckfast. If you don't get out while you're young, you're there for the rest of your life." I shrug. "A mate told me, it's where ambition goes to die."

"Ouch, that was a little harsh, don't you think?"

"Nah, you should hear what they say about Kilkenny," I tell her. "Actually, now that I think about it, Rowan should be from Kilkenny with his red hair and affinity for alcohol."

Layla snorts in amusement. "Are you from Kilkenny?"

"Thomastown, which is in County Kilkenny. I grew up only twenty minutes from Eamon, actually. But we didn't meet until we got to the States. We probably drank in the same pubs and didn't even know it."

Layla starts digging in her purse as soon as we approach the ticket booth, and I'm not about to have that. Especially since she paid for my ticket to the play. I place a hand over hers to stop her.

"I've got it."

Her head snaps up, a look of indignation on her face. "No, you don't. I invited you, so it's my treat."

"Wrong. You used that excuse with the play. And you also bought our drinks. So, with all due respect, Lovely, it's my turn."

Layla looks at me with narrowed eyes and pursed lips. She isn't wearing that seductive red lipstick, which is a blessing in disguise. I wouldn't be able to concentrate on anything other than her mouth.

That mouth. The things I want to do with that mouth...

"It's not up for debate, Layla."

"Fine." She sighs heavily. "I concede. This time."

"That's a good lass." I didn't mean for my voice to go lower the way it just did.

After paying for the tickets, we set off along the path. The day is sunny, but there's a chill in the air, and I didn't bring a jacket. This is typical Irish weather, minus the rain. We walk quietly for a few minutes, soaking up the sights of the seasonal gardens and artwork scattered throughout the grounds. I can see why this is a popular place. It's gorgeous, even in late November.

"Do you come here a lot, then?" I ask as we near the infamous Airlie Oak—the massive tree covered with Spanish moss.

"I've been a couple of times. Never in the fall, though," Layla answers. "My favorite part is the Bottle Chapel, especially on sunny days like today. It's magical!"

Passing a rather large rose bush full of huge red blooms, Layla stops to gently cup one in her hand before leaning forward to smell it. The lyrics from an Irish love song pop into my head, and without second thought, I start singing softly.

Hmm, take me back again,

Take me back one more time,

Spanish rose.

Layla's eyes flick to mine, and her cheeks flood with the sweetest blush I've ever seen. I don't get embarrassed easily, but she sure does.

The way you pulled the gate

Behind you when you said, 'It ain't too late.

Come on, let's swing the town and
have a ball tonight.'

Giving her an impish grin, I continue, pressing a hand to my chest as I serenade her.

In slumber you did sleep.
The window I did creep
And touch your raven hair and sang
that song again to you.

"Oh my god, stop!" Layla begs, covering her face with her hands and peeking through her fingers at me.

"But I'm only halfway through the song! You're not saying I'm a poor singer are you, love?"

"No! Not at all! It's just... Ugh. I don't even know. Overwhelming?"

She sounds nervous, so I gently grip her elbow, bringing her to a stop in front of the Bottle Chapel. It really is stunning. A small structure sculpted entirely out of recycled glass bottles of every color cemented together. With the sunlight hitting it, the glass twinkles like a treasure trove of rare gems and jewels. Turning her toward me, I pull her hands from her face, keeping them both in my grasp.

"I'm sorry. I don't mean to embarrass you. Okay, that's a lie," I amend. "I love to see you blush."

Layla glares at me. "Taking pleasure in my suffering? That's rude."

I chuckle and release just one of her hands but keep a hold on the other, intertwining my fingers with hers.

"C'mon," I say, pulling her with me toward the chapel. "Show me this Bottle Chapel of yours. I want to see what all the fuss is about."

We amble along the spiral pathway until we're standing at the entrance. The open-air chapel sits in the middle of a raised platform with flowers planted along one side. That side is shaped like a large butterfly, with blue glass bottles outlining the shape of the upper wings, while green and clear bottles fill the interior. Each wing has a ring of amber bottles mimicking eyes. The lower wings are predominantly blue, with the occasional red glass scattered throughout. The opposite side is only a partial wall, but no less intricate in its design. The back wall is a set of bronze, branch-like fairy wings, stretched wide. The entrance is a solid wall with an arched doorway framed by two glass bottle trees and a blue glass bottle sky. It isn't large, by any means, but still remarkable.

"Wow," I say, releasing a slow whistle. "This really is spectacular."

Layla nods in agreement as she leads us through the doorway. In the center of the chapel sits a bronze sculpted tree with bronze birds littered among the branches. Along the back wall, below the wings, is a mosaic-topped bench.

"It was built in honor of Minnie Evans, an artist that used to man the ticket booth," Layla explains, looking up into the bronze branches. "Her artwork was inspired by dreams and visions. One of those visions came to her when she was forty-three years old and told her to 'paint or die'. So she painted."

I watch her carefully. She looks almost wistful as if she envies the life of the artist.

"Are you an artist, Layla?"

She scoffs. "No. Not at all. Why?"

With a shrug, I say, "Just curious. You seem invested, is all."

"I just love that she pursued what she loved. She had a vision and went after it. It didn't matter what anyone else had to say about it. She chased what brought her life."

This gives me pause. Someone, somewhere, told this gorgeous creature she had to do something other than what she loved. *What I wouldn't give to make her dreams come true.*

Hands still clasped, I take a step closer to her, bringing us face to face. "Tell me, Lovely. If you could do anything with your future, what would you do? If you had endless resources and people cheering you on, what would your vision be?"

Layla looks away from me. "It's a pipe dream, Teagan."

Raising my free hand, I gently grasp her chin between my finger and thumb, returning her eyes to mine.

"Hey, listen to me," I say seriously. "Your dreams matter. No matter how unattainable they may seem at the moment. If you truly want something, don't let anyone hold you back. Now," I pause, ensuring I have her undivided attention. "What's your dream, Layla?"

Her eyes pool with unshed tears and I could die right here. The last thing I want to do is make her cry. Layla inhales deeply, then releases her breath. It washes over my face and I do something foolish. Moving my fingers from her chin, I cup her cheek, leaning in to kiss her. It's a gentle press of my lips to hers. I don't demand more. This is not the time or place to ask for more than what I've taken. Just as I'm beginning to pull away, Layla abruptly clutches the front of my shirt and hauls my mouth back to hers. I grunt in surprise, but I don't waste a single second winding my fingers in her silky hair and grabbing her hip to pull her flush against me. Angling her head, I run my tongue along the seam of her lips and she parts them immediately. I coax her mouth open further, letting our tongues brush tentatively before I begin exploring her mouth fully. I've been aching for her mouth, and I'm not disappointed. Those lips are soft and pillowy, delicious and sweet.

She moans and arches into me, causing my cock to twitch behind my zipper and reminding me that we're in a public place. I slow the kiss gradually, eventually pulling away, and meeting her wide eyes. Her flawless skin has taken on a ruddy hue and those fecking lips are swollen in the sexiest way. We stare at each other until the sound of someone clearing their throat sounds from nearby. Whipping our heads toward the doorway, we find a middle-aged woman with a bleach-blonde inverted bob glaring at us.

"This is a family-friendly establishment. Not a brothel," she snaps at us.

Layla lets out a sharp bark of laughter, but I stare daggers at this imposing woman. *What the fuck? A brothel?*

"Excuse me?" I demand. "Did you just equate our kiss to an establishment where one might acquire a prostitute?"

The lady crosses her arms over her chest and sniffs in our direction. "People bring their *children* here."

Looking around dramatically, I take in the utter lack of children present before narrowing my eyes. "Aye, that they do, but they aren't here now.

And you stood there watching us, *for how long*? Seems like if you were that disgusted, you could have easily turned around and walked away."

Layla buries her face in my chest to hide her giggling. Instinctively, I wind my arms around her waist and hold her close.

"That is *not* the point. You should be ashamed of yourselves for behaving so indecently in a public place."

"Indecent? You think *that* was indecent? Clearly you've never been properly kissed," I fire off, then pause. "Oh. That explains it then."

"I beg your pardon?" she asks incredulously, her face turning beet red.

"Teagan…" Layla warns in an amused whisper.

I glance down only to be caught in those deep brown eyes. God, I want to kiss her again and never stop.

"Let's just keep walking," she says. "Don't fight with *The Karen*. It's not worth it."

Karen? Does she know this woman?

I nod once and turn back to *Karen*. "Well, as much fun as this has been, I think it's time for us to find somewhere more private to carry on our indecent behavior. Have a lovely day, Karen."

Layla bursts out laughing and quickly slaps a hand over her mouth before grabbing my arm to drag me away from the chapel, leaving *Karen* there gaping like a fish.

Chapter Thirteen

Layla

"I cannot believe you just called her Karen!" I can't contain my laughter as we approach the Pergola Garden.

We took off from the Bottle Chapel at a near run, hands grasped tight, not even bothering to stop at the Butterfly House. The more distance we put between ourselves and that hateful woman, the better. Had we been fully making out, I could have understood her outrage, but it was a short and barely heated kiss. Our hands weren't even roaming.

"Is that not her name?" Teagan asks with obvious confusion. "You called her Karen, so I just assumed you knew her."

This sends me into another fit of giggles, leaving me clutching my side and gasping for air.

"Teagan..." I choke out between laughs, "It's an expression. A *Karen* is a woman that constantly complains about everything or asks to *speak to the manager* over stupid, inconsequential shit! They find something to bitch about wherever they go."

He palms the back of his neck and blushes. It's almost as sexy as seeing him shirtless.

"So, her name isn't Karen?" he asks sheepishly.

I giggle and shake my head. "I mean, I don't know who she is, so I can't answer that, but based on her reaction, I'm guessing that's not really her name. But she's well aware of what it implies."

"Well fuck," he groans. "I feel like a right eejit now."

"Don't," I say with a laugh. "That lady was a bitch."

Teagan gasps in mock astonishment, "Layla Diaz! There are *children* present!"

When we reach the walkway to the pergola, our pace slows to a lazy stroll down the gravel path. Azaleas line either side before seamlessly blending in with the vining Carolina Jessamine and Star Jasmine that drapes over the top of the structure. A soft breeze ripples around us as we approach the multi-tiered fountain in the middle of a rounded platform with steps leading down to the lake.

"You mean the same children that we scandalized earlier?" I turn to bat my eyelashes at him.

"Yes," Teagan says, smiling warmly and pulling me into his arms, "exactly the same."

Placing my hands on his chest, I gaze into his bright green eyes, my pulse thrumming. His lips turn up in one corner before he leans his head closer.

Is he going to kiss me again? Please let him kiss me again.

"Layla," he starts.

"Yes?" I breathe.

"I need to apologize to you," he says remorsefully.

What? Oh no. He didn't really want to kiss me, did he?

My heart sinks into my stomach and the smile on my lips falls. "What are you apologizing for?"

Teagan brings a hand up to tuck my hair behind my ear. "I didn't ask your permission before kissing you. I've wanted to kiss you since the day I met you, but I shouldn't have taken it from you like that. I'm so sorry."

My eyes widen momentarily before I burst out laughing. I shouldn't laugh at him, but the fact that he thought I wouldn't give it to him willingly is comical. We've been dancing around this moment for weeks.

His brow furrows as he waits for me to get control of myself. Taking a deep breath, I try to suppress my giggles. Once I've composed myself, I run my hands up to his shoulders and then down his biceps, squeezing firmly.

Hijole, those muscles...

"Teagan O'Brien," I say seriously. "you are, without a doubt, the most thoughtful man I've ever met."

When his arms tighten around my waist, the butterflies in my stomach go soaring. "So why are you laughing at me, Lovely?"

"In what universe would I ever say no to you kissing me? " I ask quietly. "I'd have to be completely loco *not* to want you to kiss me."

That boyish grin takes over his face and all I want is to kiss him again and never stop.

"Honestly, this wasn't how I had planned it. I just hated to see you cry. I didn't even really think. I saw your tears and my knee-jerk reaction was to kiss you." he says softly.

Why is he so perfect?

I smile coyly at him. "So you *had* planned on kissing me at some point?"

Teagan cups the side of my face, lightly brushing his thumb over my cheekbone. "Oh, without a doubt. I told you. From the day we met, I took one look at this perfect mouth and was a goner."

His thumb moves lower, tracing over my bottom lip, eyes zeroing in on my mouth.

"I hope you're not waiting for my permission again," I whisper.

The last word has barely left my mouth before his lips are on mine. Using that damned thumb again, he pulls my bottom lip down, forcing my mouth open. There's nothing cautious about this kiss as his tongue plunges in, taking me captive. His other hand slips from the small of my back, creeping down until he's cupping my ass. I squeak in response but don't pull away.

If anything, I press myself closer, thankful that the pergola provides more privacy than the Bottle Chapel. My hands begin exploring, one slipping to the nape of his neck, where I run my fingers through his hair, and the other snaking down his chest to his hard stomach. Shuddering in response, he pulls his mouth from mine to deposit small, soft kisses along my jaw until he reaches my earlobe and nibbles on it. The moan I've been trying to keep at bay slips free.

"Lovely Layla," he whispers hoarsely, "if you keep putting your hands on me like that, we'll prove your friend, Karen, correct and behave indecently in a public place."

I whimper, convinced that at this moment, I wouldn't care if we were in the middle of a crowded room. My body blazes for him. I wasn't even this turned on when I had sex for the first time. The thought of sleeping with Teagan has me pressing my thighs together and gripping his hair tighter.

Teagan chuckles darkly against my neck. "Oh, the things I want to do to you, lass…"

"Oh god," I pant against his shoulder. "Should we go? We should go. Right?"

Pulling back, he smirks at me. "Nah, we haven't seen everything yet."

I gape at him. Is he kidding? The feel of his hard cock pressing against my stomach says otherwise.

"C'mon, love. What's next?" he asks, grabbing my hand to lead us back the way we came.

"You're evil," I grumble and pout dramatically. "Pure evil."

He barks out a laugh and slings an arm over my shoulders, pulling me close, and kissing the top of my head. "What's the saying? Good things come to those who wait?"

I scoff. "Eso es estúpido."

Teagan

It takes literally every ounce of self-control I have not to drag Layla to some sheltered spot and fuck her up against a tree or one of the pillars of the pergola. Her mouth is so soft and sinful, and those noises she makes! *Christ almighty.* The way her body molded to mine is full of all sorts of seductive promises. I'm not sure what came over me when I grabbed her arse, but I have no regrets. I want to sink my teeth into those luscious globes.

"I forgot to ask how Mac was this morning," Layla says, bringing me out of my dirty fantasies.

"Hmm? Oh! Right. Yeah, he had a bit of the fear in him alright, but seems to have realized he was being a bit of a prick last night. Said he was planning on going to Myra's later to properly apologize, like."

The tosser was downright surly when I checked in after my run this morning. His flat isn't far from the one I share with Eamon now, so I was able to keep my word to Layla.

"That's good. Hopefully, they can figure this out together as peacefully as possible."

"Aye."

We walk aimlessly down the path without saying a word for a few moments, just absorbing the scenery. Layla is still tucked under my arm and it just feels *right.* For the entirety of my relationship with Ashley, I thought she was *the one*, but it pales in comparison to the way I'm pulled to Layla. Obviously I think she's gorgeous, but it's so much more than being physically attracted to her. I want to know her secrets and deepest desires. I want to win all of her smiles and laughs. I want to put her on a pedestal so everyone can see how incredible she is.

"So are you ever going to give me an answer?" I ask teasingly.

She angles her head to look up at me questioningly. "To what?"

"Taking me home with you for the holidays."

"Oh." Her face falls and she bites her bottom lip.

Shit. Maybe now that we're...well, I don't know exactly what we are, but we're something...maybe meeting the family is too much too soon?

"Layla, it's okay. I understand if it's too uncomfortable for you," I say, trying to save the mood.

"No," she says. "It's not that. Well, okay maybe it is, but I won't be uncomfortable because of *you*. I wasn't kidding when I said my family can be a lot. I don't want them to overwhelm you, because they absolutely will ask you when we're getting married and having children."

The idea doesn't terrify me like she thinks it does. I've always wanted to get married and have a family. Not right this second, but someday.

"I'll just tell them we eloped because I knocked you up. It'll be grand."

Layla gasps so loudly that I'm afraid she's hurt herself. I whip my head in her direction to find her staring daggers at me, so I just grin back at her. Then she begins to let loose a string of Spanish that sounds like it's supposed to be intimidating, but the way her cheeks flush in anger just makes me want her all the more.

"Are you laughing at me?" she demands, eyes narrowing.

I school my features, biting back the laugh she's accusing me of. "Nah, definitely not laughing at you. I would never."

She rolls her eyes and darts out from under my arm, walking ahead a few steps. That won't do.

"Now hold on, lass," I say, catching up to her and wrapping my arms around her from behind, pulling her against my chest. She relaxes into my embrace, but I still plan on groveling. "I was just slagging you. Remember what I told you the night we met? About it being the Irish way and a form of affection between couples?"

"I know," she mutters, leaning her head back against my shoulder.

"But..." I hedge.

Turning in my arms, she places her palms flat on my chest then peers up at me. "You think they'd be shocked by that answer, but honestly, they'd be thrilled. Don't get me wrong, they'd be pissed about not being able to throw a lavish, Mexican wedding, but ultimately, they'd be ecstatic. And I hate that."

It's my turn to frown now. She doesn't want to get married and have a family?

95

"Explain this to me," I say.

"*Mierda*," she breathes. "All I've ever heard my entire life is that there's no greater achievement than getting married and having a brood of children. Yes, I do want to experience those things someday, but it feels like a cage, you know? Like no matter what I do, no matter what degree or job I have, no matter what passions I have, nothing will ever be as great as being a wife and mother, so why even bother? I'm young, Teagan. I want to live my life for me before I start living for others. I have two little sisters that I helped care for as babies, so I know how hard having kids can be. I'm not ready for that."

I blow out a breath as I process the truth she shared with me. It seems like it's been festering for a while, but she hasn't been able to let it out. And it's fucking heartbreaking. She should be able to pursue whatever she wants in life, without others telling her what's best for her. I get just as worked up over women's rights as I do corporate greed. There's no sense in any of it.

"Hey," I murmur, bringing my hands up to cup her face. "I don't fully understand what you're experiencing, but I do know what it's like to want a different life than what your family wants. My Da is constantly harping on me about not taking over the family farm. Don't get me wrong, if an emergency happened and I had to, I would, but that's not where I want my future. I want to make a difference in the lives of people, rather than sheep."

Layla snorts indelicately, but a smile starts to spread across her face.

"Atta girl," I say, kissing her forehead. "But seriously, it's not fair for your family to put those expectations on you. Their dreams aren't yours. And if you want, I'd be happy to stand by your side and tell them just how amazing and capable you are all on your own. Which you are."

"Thank you," she tells me, stretching onto her toes to place a chaste kiss on my lips. "Anything for you, Lovely."

Chapter Fourteen

Layla

"Oh my god, Norah. That's so scary."

On our way towards the exit of Airlie Gardens, my phone chimes at the same time as Teagan's. We glance at each other before opening the message. It's a group message to the two of us from Norah and Eamon, telling us that Eamon's sister was found unresponsive and is currently in a coma. They are leaving for Ireland tonight. I immediately call Norah.

"What do you need me to do?" I ask worriedly.

"Just keep an eye on the house, I guess?" She suggests, her voice quiet. "I don't have anything pressing going on over the break." She sounds so tired.

"You got it, chica. Anything you think of that you need me to do while you're gone, just let me know. And keep us updated."

"Thanks, Layla," she says over a yawn. "You're the best."

When I hang up, Teagan is looking at his phone with a furrowed brow.

"This is awful," I say, thinking he's having a similar conversation with Eamon.

"Oh, absolutely, but Eam sent me a separate text." He angles his phone towards me.

Eamon: *Hey mate, Norah and I booked a place up in Avon for a short holiday, but with us going back home for Caity, we can't keep our reservation. I'm putting it in your name. Take Layla.*

I stand there dumbfounded. Is he suggesting we take a vacation together? Just the two of us? "Um..." I begin.

"You're going home to see your family, so I know you can't go."

It takes me less than a second to make a decision.

"I'll cancel." I blurt out.

"What?"

"Seeing my family. I'll tell them I'll visit during Spring Break. I need to be close by to watch Norah's house anyway." I shrug.

Teagan's green eyes light up. "Yeah? You want to go?"

"Yes. Let's go."

This is not only what I want, but what I need. I need to do something that's just for me, that makes me happy. And spending time with Teagan at some beach house away from normal day-to-day living is perfect. Nerves flutter through me at what this trip implies, but it feels right.

"Alright. The reservation is for tomorrow through the rest of the week. Will that work for you?" he asks.

"I was going to be heading back to Texas anyway. I'll have Mami change the flight for a later date."

* * *

"Lo siento, Mami. I know, I know. But this is important. I need to stay here for Norah. She doesn't know how long they'll be gone."

"Layla, this is so unlike you. Are you sure there's not something going on?" My mother asks suspiciously.

"No, Mami. I'm not canceling, I'm just rescheduling. I could try for a weekend visit if you absolutely cannot wait until Spring Break. Or, like I've said a million times, you are always welcome here!"

I know that will fall on deaf ears, but really, why is she allowed to be upset about me rescheduling when my family never comes here?

"Ugh, mija, we've talked about this," my mother says in frustration which has me rolling my eyes so hard they might get stuck that way.

"I know, just offering." I sigh heavily. "Anyway, let me see what Norah says once she arrives in Ireland, and then we can go from there, okay? I promise I'm going to come home to see you soon."

"I'm holding you to that, chica. I'll get your plane ticket taken care of."

"Gracias, Mami. Kiss Papá for me?"

"Sí, sí. Hablamos pronto, cariño."

"Talk soon. Love you." I tell her, feeling only slightly guilty for not telling her the whole truth.

After leaving Airlie Gardens, I took Teagan back to his apartment but didn't go inside this time for fear of jumping his bones. The goodbye kiss he gave me was long, deep, and sinful. Leaving me breathless, he promised he'd pick me up in the morning and drive us to Avon for our getaway.

Now I'm stuck staring at the pile of clothes on my bed, trying to decide what to pack. It's cooler on the East Coast this time of year, so I'm not expecting us to be beach bums, but I'll still bring a swimsuit. I'm well aware of my figure, having come to terms with the fact that I will always be considered plus size. It took me a long time to learn to love myself and my body, and while I'll never get to live out my ultimate sexual fantasy of being picked up and slammed against a wall, I love the way I look—in *and* out of my clothes. So I pack the white bikini with high-waisted, lattice-side bottoms.

I start a load of laundry before making my way to the shower. It's safe to assume that Teagan and I will be *up close and personal,* so shaving and exfoliating is a must. My heart races every time I think about the possibility of sleeping with him. The last time I had sex was three years ago, and other than my vibrator, I'm out of practice. But the drive is in no way missing. Kissing Teagan has proven that.

* * *

¡Carajo!.

I overslept and forgot to put my clothes in the dryer last night, so the underwear I was going to wear won't be dry in time. Teagan will be here in about thirty minutes and I'm not fully packed. Looking into my underwear drawer, the only clean panties and bra I have are a red, lacy set I bought on a whim. Whatever. It will have to do.

There's a knock on my door just as I'm zipping my bag. Taking a deep breath, I glance in the mirror hanging in the hallway and give myself a reassuring smile. I'm an independent woman capable of making decisions, of taking control of my life. With that, I open the door confidently.

"Morning, Lovely," Teagan says in a low voice, eyes roaming from my head all the way down to my feet.

"Buenos dias," I murmur as I check him out in return. Why is a tight, black t-shirt so hot? And that ball cap?

"Like what you see?" His lips pull up into a knowing smile and I don't even want to deny it.

"I do," I tell him. "You look good in a hat."

"Fan of the cap, are ya?" When he lifts a hand to pull on the bill of the hat, his shirt raises, showing off a sliver of skin. "I'll wear one every day if you want me to."

"I might let you."

He chuckles before asking, "Ready?"

"Yeah." With a nod, I say, "Let's do this."

Teagan

It's late afternoon by the time we reach the rental. The drive took about five hours, but passed by in a blur thanks to easy conversation with Layla. We talked about nearly everything, except that we are spending nearly a week alone together—and the elephant in the room that is our physical attraction to each other. I want her. Christ, do I want her, but the last thing I want is for her to feel like the whole reason we're taking this trip is so I can fuck her. She's calling the shots. If she wants to spend the entire time binging her favorite TV show, that's fine with me. I'm delighted just to be able to have a conversation without Rowan interrupting.

Following the prompts from the SatNav, we find the rental with relative ease. The property sits right on the beach, with a small wooden walkway that leads from the porch to the water. I park the car in the drive and we exit, stretching our limbs from the long drive.

"This is adorable," Layla says, eyes roaming over the sage green exterior.

"Aye, looks really nice. Well found, Eamon."

She turns her eyes towards me and smiles sweetly. "I hate that they weren't able to come here. Norah would have loved this."

I nod in agreement, though I don't think I know Norah well enough to make that assumption.

"Shall we?" I gesture towards the door.

"Sure. I think I'm going to walk the beach as soon as we unload though. Would you like to join?"

"'Course I would," I tell her as I unlock and open the door.

The space is clean and cozy. A big, over-stuffed couch and chair with soft-looking pillows and blankets fill most of the living area. There's a small fireplace in one corner, and an entire wall of windows facing the ocean. Connected to the living area is an eat-in kitchen and a small, round table with two chairs. On the other side is a short hallway with three doors. The first turns out to be a linen closet, and the second is the bathroom, which leaves the last door—the bedroom. One bedroom with one bed. I'm just about to call out for Layla when she comes to stand next to me.

"Oh."

"I'll take the couch," I say quickly, not wanting to put any pressure on her.

"Teagan, neither of us is sleeping on the couch," she tells me firmly, crossing her arms over her chest. I definitely do *not* notice the way her breasts are pushed together like that.

"But…" I start, then she places a finger on my lips to silence me. Chills race down my spine at the contact.

"Come on, let's go take that walk," she murmurs.

* * *

It's December, but the temps are in the high sixties, so we remove our shoes when we reach the end of the boardwalk. The air is warm, but the water is frigid. When the waves wash over our feet, Layla squeals and jumps a little, grabbing onto my arm to keep from falling. She's fucking adorable.

"Ach, come on. It isn't that cold." I tease her, relishing her touch on my skin. "The Irish go skinny-dipping in water like this!"

"Then you're all loco!" she says, shaking her head in disbelief.

"Shall we take a swim?" I suggest, wagging my eyebrows at her.

"Abso-fucking-lutely not! I'm from South Texas, remember? A day in the eighties is considered temperate!"

Chuckling, I say, "That's a scorcher where I'm from. And we've no cooling units there."

She stops in her tracks, looking at me like I'm crazy. "What? You're not serious."

"Aye, I am. The average high temp in the summer is what we're walking in right now. No need to own one when we can just open the windows."

"I can't even imagine a world without air conditioning," she mumbles.

Linking our hands, I give her a tug. "C'mon then, Lovely. Let's stroll a little more."

We walk for about ten more minutes before turning back towards the rental. I drape an arm around Layla's shoulders, pulling her close to my side. No words are spoken, but I can physically feel the electricity charging between us. All it will take is one small spark. When we reach the place where we left our shoes, we slip them on silently before ambling back up the boardwalk. Opening the door, I gesture for her to go first, but I don't move out of the way. Her shoulder brushes against my chest as she passes, and she pauses to glance up at me, eyes dipping to my mouth for a brief second. She licks her lips, then bites down on that bottom one. The tension thickens around us. I want nothing more than to lean down, claiming that lip between my own teeth.

"Teagan..." she whispers in a pleading voice, big brown eyes full of invitation.

Then my fecking phone rings. We both inhale deeply, creating some space between us.

Clearing her throat, she says, "Go ahead and take that. I'm going to take a shower."

Holy god. My brain is flooded with the image of Layla naked under the spray of the shower, rivulets of soapy lather and water cascading over those luscious curves. And I'm fucking jealous. When the bathroom door clicks, it brings me out of my stupor, and I answer the call without looking at the caller ID.

"What?" I growl.

"Whoa, mate. Everything alright?" Eamon asks, worry lacing his words.

"Shite. Sorry. Yeah, everything's grand. How are you? How's Caity?"

"Hanging in there," he breathes out. "No change in Caity's condition. We just got back to Mam's. Norah is resting, so I thought I'd check in to see if everything is okay with the rental."

"Right, yeah," I grunt, turning my hat backwards on my head. "We got here not long ago. Just getting back in from a stroll on the beach. The place is great. Thanks again for letting us take your reservation, mate."

"Aye, it's no problem. Glad you and Layla could go. How's that situation, anyway?" Eamon asks. I can hear the amusement in his voice.

Cheeky wanker.

"Oy. That's none of your fecking business, Kennedy. Mind your own mot!"

He laughs. "Sure, yeah."

"Actually," I sigh heavily. "There's nothing to report, but damn if I don't want it to. I'm letting her call the shots though. I don't want her to think all I want is a quick fuck from her."

"Remember what Norah said. Layla hasn't really dated anyone, so this is all new to her. She's probably waiting for you to make the first move."

Fuck me. He's right.

We talk a few more minutes, but I'm anxious to end the call. It's time I claim my lass. The bathroom door opens, and Layla steps out in a puff of steam, her skin flushed, and wearing a tank top and these skimpy silk shorts. She must see the hunger written all over my face because she stops, her eyes going wide. Fuck it.

I prowl towards her.

Chapter Fifteen

Layla

Teagan stalks in my direction, his eyes burning with determination. I wanted him to kiss me when we walked in the door, but it felt like he was hesitating. Now, he slips his fingers into my hair, angling my face up toward his.

"Layla, I'm going to kiss you now."

I can't breathe and my heart is pounding out of my chest. Unable to form words, I just nod. That's all the confirmation he needs before his mouth crashes into mine in a kiss so heated, I can feel it all the way down to my toes. When I part my lips slightly, he claims my mouth fully. Slowly, he slides a hand from my hair, down to my throat, where he squeezes gently. Whimpering, I press myself into him, trying to erase any and all space between us. Teagan groans at the contact, the sound is so erotic I think I might orgasm where I stand.

He steps forward, beginning to slowly walk us backward, one hand still on my throat, while the other winds around the small of my back. Not paying a bit of attention to where we're going, we collide with a wall. I let out an *umph* which makes Teagan release my throat and pull way, his eyes clouded with a mix of concern and lust.

"Are you okay? Shite, I'm so sorry. I should have been looking..."

"I'm fine," I breathe, pressing my mouth to his. "Don't stop."

"Fuck," he groans, possessing my mouth once more.

I link my fingers through his belt loops, pulling him closer. When his hips meet mine, I can feel how hard he is and I moan, knowing it's for me. Tearing my mouth from his, I start placing wet kisses along his jaw until I reach his ear, where I pull the lobe between my teeth and nibble. The way he's panting and grinding against me is the most empowering moment of my life.

"Teagan," I whisper in his ear, "I want you."

"Aye, I'm yours," he groans against my neck before sucking the sensitive flesh and biting down.

"*¡Ay si!*" I yelp, returning my mouth to his.

Releasing his belt loops, I slide my hands under his shirt, grazing the dips and planes of his abdomen with my fingernails. I've fantasized about touching these abs since the first time I saw him shirtless at soccer practice. Teagan's hands tighten on my waist before traversing over my ribs and up the sides of my breasts. It feels like a wake of burning flames everywhere he touches me.

"Bedroom," I pant. "Now."

Grunting in agreement, he dips down to clutch the back of my thighs and hoists me up.

"Teagan, what are you doing? I'm going to break you," I shriek as my legs lock around his waist, my arms looping around his neck.

"Wrong," he growls, pressing kisses to the swell of my breasts that are peeking over the top of my tank top.

"I'm too heavy," I complain until I feel his tongue run from my cleavage to my jaw.

"You're fucking perfect, Layla," he mutters into my skin. "I plan on worshiping every inch of this perfect body."

Those words turn my core molten. If I don't have him inside of me soon, I'm going to die. Completely cease to exist. The need I have for him is so strong, I feel like I'm drowning. As if reading my thoughts, he turns us into the bedroom, and we fall onto the bed, our mouths fusing together in a brief, sloppy kiss. Teagan pulls away, sitting back on his knees. His hungry eyes roam all over my body, stopping to zero in on my heaving breasts, before meeting my gaze.

"What?" I pant out.

A feral grin slowly spreads over his face. "I can't decide where I want to start. I could kiss that luscious mouth of yours for the rest of my life, but I want to taste *all of you.*"

Holy fuck.

I shiver in anticipation. "I don't care where you start, I just need your hands and mouth on me."

Teagan's eyes flare wide. "Protection?"

"I'm on the pill," I rush out. "And I'm clean."

"Me too," he confirms, running his hands up my thighs to my hips, where he holds me tightly. Leaning forward, he takes the bottom of my tank top between his teeth to guide it up my body. When it's around my throat, he buries his face between my breasts, inhaling deeply. My fingers shove the hat from his head and tangle in his hair, giving a sharp tug. I feel his laugh rumble against my skin before he sits up again.

"Jaysus, Layla. Look at you," he mutters in awe.

I blush, biting my bottom lip. The way he's looking at me is almost reverent. I'm suddenly very thankful that the red lace bra was the only clean one I could find this morning. The hunger in Teagan's gaze is enough to make me want to burn all the others in my hamper. He grazes a knuckle over the peak of one breast before hooking his finger over the lace and pulling it down slowly. The cool air is in harsh contrast to my heated skin.

"Fuck me..." Teagan groans, lowering his head to suck a nipple into his mouth.

My back arches off the bed as I cry out. The last sexual experience I had was nowhere near this intense, even when I climaxed. I'm pretty sure he can make me come just by sucking my nipples. God, if this is what happens when his mouth is on my breasts, what about when he moves lower?

Teagan

I take my time paying homage to each of Layla's perfect breasts. As much as I love her in red, this sexy-as-sin bra needs to go. Slipping a hand behind her back, I unhook it and slowly pull it from her body. Then the air leaves my lungs in a low *whoosh.* Her breasts are glorious—full and heavy with perfectly peaked nipples that I can't help but brush the pad of my thumbs over before sucking them into my mouth. I love every lush curve of her body. When she protested me picking her up, I vowed to make it my life's mission to make sure she never feels anything but worshiped like the goddess she is. It's not completely selfless though. Touching, kissing, and pleasuring her is something I'll never tire of.

While laving at her nipples, I can feel my cock growing harder by the second. The noises she's making, and the way she's pulling my hair, have me so turned on, I'm afraid I won't make it longer than a few seconds once I'm inside of her. Groaning, I tell myself to stop thinking about it or I won't even make it that far. I can tell she's getting impatient by the way her body bucks against me, but fuck if I haven't waited for what feels like ages to get this beautiful woman under me. I want to spend hours with her.

Somewhat regretfully, I move from her breasts, starting to rain kisses down her torso. When I reach her navel, I swirl my tongue around it, chuckling as she shivers. Her hands are pushing at my head, urging me lower. Lifting my eyes to hers, I hold her gaze as I tuck my fingers into the sides of the small shorts she's wearing, pulling them over her curvaceous hips and down her shapely legs. Red catches my eye, and I discover that her underwear matches her bra—red, lacy boy shorts hug her hips. I raise a fist to my mouth, biting my knuckle.

"Were you planning on me undressing you today or is this just a happy little accident?" I ask, voice low and rough.

Layla props herself up on her elbows, smiling shyly at me. "It's the happiest accident of my life."

With a wolfish grin, I say, "It's the happiest accident of *my* life, Lovely."

"I'm glad you approve," she says shortly, "but can we get rid of them now?"

A bark of laughter escapes me.

"So impatient," I mutter, lowering my head to lick her roughly over the lace.

"*¡Dios mío!*" Layla cries out, falling back onto the bed.

Fucking hell.

This woman will be my undoing. Tired of waiting to taste her, I yank her knickers down her hips, tucking them into my back pocket. I own them now. When Layla starts to press her legs together, I grip her thighs, spreading them wide, before taking a brief second to admire her pussy. I groan at how wet she is already. All I do is groan when her body is involved.

"Lovely Layla, you have no idea what you do to me," I mutter before dipping my mouth back to the apex of her thighs.

I don't waste time teasing her. Repeating what I did while she was covered, I press my flattened tongue over her seam, licking all the way up to her clit. I take my time, adding pressure when I reach the swollen bud. She gasps loudly, bucking her hips in response. I do it again and again, soaking up her moans and reveling in the constant string of Spanish flowing from her mouth. Her thighs clamp over my ears and I feel them quiver. She's getting close. Latching my mouth to her clit, I pull it between my lips, sucking hard. She yells out her release, undulating against my mouth until her orgasm fades.

When her legs go slack onto the bed, I finally raise my head. She's panting heavily, eyes hooded when they meet mine. I lick my lips, watching those big, brown eyes widen as I crawl back up her body, planting kisses along the way. When I reach her mouth, I gently kiss the corners of her lips before devouring her again.

Layla's hands snake down my sides, causing me to shiver, and yanks at the bottom of her shirt, pulling it up to my shoulders. Breaking the kiss, I rock back on my knees and reach a hand behind my neck, grabbing the shirt by the collar before tearing it over my head. Sitting up, her eyes and fingers rake over my chest, to the waistband of my jeans. She pops the button and my cock twitches in response.

Meeting my gaze, she purrs, "Take these off, Teagan."

Her wish is my command. If she were to demand that I bark like a fucking dog, I'd do it gladly. Especially while she's sitting there, gloriously naked, her skin flushed from the orgasm I just gave her. Christ, I love her body.

Rising from the bed, I take a step back to remove my jeans and briefs. I watch Layla's heated gaze travel from my face, over my chest and stomach, then coming to a stop at my raging erection. Her eyes widen, and that luscious mouth falls open slightly.

"Hijole..." she whispers.

Chuckling, I climb back on the bed, hovering over Layla, who is still propped up, leaning back on her hands. I dip my head to kiss her softly, gently pushing her back on the bed. She shudders and a hint of hesitation flashes in her eyes.

"Is this still okay, love?" I ask. "Do you want to stop?"

"No," she breathes, shaking her head, "Just...go slow. It's been a while."

"How long?"

"Um...since the beginning of freshman year," she answers, biting her bottom lip.

Three years?

How has she not had sex in three years? How does she not have a line of men waiting at her door, *begging* for just a scrap of her attention? The fact that I'm her first after so long is a heady sensation.

"Okay," I whisper, brushing a kiss to her jaw. "We'll go slow. I want to savor you anyway."

"God, the things you say, and do, with that mouth," Layla moans, gliding her hands up my biceps, and into my hair.

"We're just getting started, love," I mutter, letting my body settle on hers so that we're *finally* skin-to-skin.

Kissing her again, I force her mouth open with my tongue and wind it around hers. We lose ourselves in the rhythm of the kiss, our bodies naturally moving in tandem. Layla's legs fall open wider as I nestle myself between her thighs. I run a hand down her throat, over her chest and stomach, before palming my cock, guiding it towards her entrance. Rocking my hips forward, I slowly push in an inch or two at a time, letting her adjust to me. It's a slow form of torture. She feels so good clenching around me, that I can't contain the groan forming in my throat. Once I'm fully seated inside her, she gasps softly against my mouth. I freeze instantly.

"Are you okay? Did I hurt you?"

"No. God, no. Please don't stop." she begs, rolling her hips and flexing her inner walls around me.

"Fuck..." I grind out, burying my head in her neck and breathing heavily. "If you do that again, I'll come, Layla. Your first time in three years will not be with a two-pump chump."

She laughs out, causing those muscles to squeeze again. I groan loudly, then bite her shoulder in retaliation, before pulling out of her slightly.

"Teagan," Layla whines, "please."

Propping myself up on a forearm, I cup her face with my hand, staring into her eyes as I thrust deeply. She mutters a string of Spanish that I can't understand, but take as encouragement. On the next thrust, her eyes shut and she grips my arse, pressing me closer. The act is so carnal, I abandon the idea of controlled movements. I start fucking her, harder and deeper. Her cries of pleasure push me closer and closer to the edge, but I refuse to come before I get her off again. Reaching between us, I press the pad of my thumb to her clit, moving in tight circles.

"*Ohmygod*. Yes, keep doing that," Layla pants. "I'm going to come again."

"Fuck yes, you are," I growl, unable to take my eyes off her face. The way her mouth falls open, combined with the noises coming from her, is enough to make me explode. "I want you to come all over my cock, Lovely."

Layla throws her head back against the bed, screaming out her release. When she clenches around me again, I come so hard, I see stars. I moan her name, over and over, as I spill inside her. I collapse on top of her as she wraps her arms around me, pressing my head to her chest. Layla just holds me there and her heart is racing as fast as mine. That was hands down, the most intense sex of my life. My shy Layla isn't quite as timid in the bedroom.

Chapter Sixteen

Layla

I wake up feeling deliciously sore between my legs, more than eager to get my hands—and mouth—back on Teagan. Last night was perfection. He's such a Golden Retriever out in public, but behind closed doors? He's a wolf. The way he uses his body to make mine sing is such a new experience. I never expected to feel so feral with Teagan, especially since my former lovers left me lacking. I just thought that was the standard. Now that I've had a taste of what good—no, *great*—sex can be, I'll never settle for anything less. And even though I was completely sated when we fell asleep, now that I'm awake? I want him. *Bad.*

He's asleep on his back, and that *morning wood* just makes it so much easier to slip down the bed before taking him into my mouth. The moment I close my lips around his cock, he stirs, mumbling incoherently. Those mumbles soon turn into groans before morphing into expletives as his hands tangle in my hair. With one hand gently squeezing his balls, I slide the other up to his chest, raking my nails back down before fisting the base of his cock. His fingers tighten in my hair almost painfully, but it only turns me on more. Knowing that I'm the reason for his loss of control makes me feel so powerful and sexy.

"Fuck," he groans, his voice rough with sleep. "Yes. Yes. Oh Christ, Layla. I'm going to come."

"Mmm," I hum, running the tip of my tongue under the head.

With a strangled moan, Teagan's release shoots into my mouth. I swallow it all before climbing back up his body, kissing and licking every inch of skin in my path. Moving his hands from my hair to my face, he pulls me up until our mouths connect and our tongues begin a frantic dance. As much as I love sucking him off, kissing him is addicting. If kissing were an Olympic sport, Teagan O'Brien would win the gold every time.

Breaking the kiss, he drags his lips over my jaw - not kissing, but actually dragging them.

"Sit on my face," he commands against my throat.

"What?" I ask incredulously. "I'm not sitting on your face."

"Yes, you fucking are," he growls, then bites down on that erogenous zone where my shoulder meets my neck. "Now, be a good lass and get up here."

A rush of heat surges between my legs, but I pull back. "It's one thing for you to pick me up and toss me around, but I'm pretty certain that I will suffocate you."

"I can't think of a better way to go than drowning in your pussy," he tells me. "But, that's not going to happen. Whatever misconceived notion you have about your body is complete bollocks. Do you understand? Every single part of your body is perfect and tempting."

I have no words, just overwhelming emotions. It took a lot of work to get to the point where I love my body, but hearing Teagan's praise makes me feel like a goddess.

He must see the surrender in my eyes, because he cups the back of my neck roughly and says, "Now. Get on your knees, drop that sweet pussy on my mouth, and hang on."

¡Ay güey!

Cautiously, I rearrange my legs so that my knees are framing his face and I'm hovering over him. When I don't immediately lower myself, he grabs my ass and raises his head to my center. He moves so quick, I barely have time to grab the headboard before he's licking a broad path over my seam. I cry out, slamming a palm against the wall as he spears his tongue into me over and over. *"¡Ay que rico* Teagan!" I moan, but then yell out when he sucks my clit into his mouth, rapidly flicking the tip of his tongue over it. I lose all control chasing my orgasm and start riding his face, grinding while twisting a hand into his hair tightly to keep him where I want him.

He makes a low noise in his throat then squeezes my ass cheeks hard as he pulls me tighter against his mouth. The tension builds and builds to the point where I start to see stars. My cries of pleasure get louder the closer I get until suddenly, I'm screaming as I explode all over Teagan's mouth in the most intense orgasm I've ever experienced. Wave after wave of pure ecstasy courses through my body, leaving me breathless. I'm gasping for air as he slows his rhythm, bringing me back to earth. Finally, he relents, turning his head to place a soft kiss on my inner thigh before grinning up at me, the evidence of my release glistening around his mouth.

"Good morning, Lovely," he says gently. The way he looks at me is all-consuming; like I'm the first bit of sunlight he's seen after an eternity in darkness.

"Buenos días," I murmur as I run my fingers through his hair.

He pushes gently, letting me know he wants me to move back. Sliding off of him, I snuggle into his waiting arms, laying my head on his chest and draping a leg over his. He runs his fingers up and down my arm as we lie there silently. It's not awkward, but I'm not sure what to say. Do I thank him? Ask him how he slept? Suggest breakfast? This is the first time I've actually spent the night with a guy.

"What's going on in that pretty head of yours, Layla?" Teagan mumbles into my hair.

"Who says I'm thinking about anything?" I challenge.

"Ach, I can practically hear the wheels turning. And you're so tense. I thought I had you nice and relaxed."

Snorting a laugh, I lift my head, resting my chin on his chest. "I'm sorry. I'm just overthinking this."

His brows furrow with concern. Brushing a thumb over my cheekbone, he asks, "Overthinking what exactly?"

"Um. I've never spent the night after…"

A wide grin spreads across his face. "Aren't I the lucky one?"

"Don't let it go to your head, guapo," I tease.

"Too late. You're obsessed with me. Just admit it."

I roll my eyes and act like I'm going to get up, but he bands his arms around me, rolling me to my back. Teagan's strong body settles over me.

"Layla, listen to me," Teagan orders, his eyes darting back and forth between mine. "This doesn't need to be complicated. I don't have expectations. I just want to be with you—in whatever capacity you'll let me. We can make up our own rules and tell everyone else to fuck off, yeah?"

Nodding, I cup his cheek, drawing his lips to mine in a tender kiss. It's meant to be just a quick kiss, but as his tongue caresses mine, we get lost in each other. This time, he's gentle. Every slow thrust is intentional, each push filled with purpose. His green eyes burn into mine so intensely it's impossible to look away. There's not a wild rush to reach release; we're just enjoying each other and making a statement that we're not ready to put into words yet. This isn't fucking, it's love making. I never understood how people could fall so quickly, but I think I'm beginning to understand how Norah felt when she first started seeing Eamon.

Teagan

There's a shift happening, and it's both electrifying and terrifying. Layla and I have explosive chemistry. Our bodies burn for each other, but the tether between us—the one I feel as I thrust languidly into her, staring into those dark chocolate eyes, feels like it's changing from a paltry rope into a steel cable. It would take a force of nature to break it.

When I feel her body begin to quake with impending release, I keep the pace slow but deep. Her arms wind around my neck, pulling me flush against her and she holds me there. I bury my face into her neck, breathing her in. I want us to come together. It feels important that we do. Her panting quickens, and as my name topples from her lips, I know I'm a goner. We fall and there's no going back.

* * *

After forcing ourselves out of bed, we shower together, but I don't fuck her again. As much as I want to, I need her to know that this is so much more than me wanting her body—which is so fucking gorgeous. With those wide hips, round arse, and full breasts, I'm practically drooling every time I see her. But Layla is so down-to-earth and genuine, it's impossible not to want to be around her. She's funny, intelligent, and compassionate. The fact that she gave Mac the benefit of the doubt about becoming a dad speaks volumes to her character.

Once we've finished showering, I wrap a towel around my waist, heading for the bedroom where we rummage through our luggage for clothes.

"Shall we get breakfast?" I ask.

Layla drops her towel, glancing up at me while she steps into another pair of those fucking lacy underwear. She smirks. "Food is fuel. I think we've burned quite a bit of energy, don't you?"

"Aye," I say with a wink, enjoying the way blush fans her cheeks. "I could probably go another round, but I like the idea of being ready for a marathon."

I take deep satisfaction in the way her eyes go wide and her sweet mouth drops open.

"You're trouble, *Papi*," she purrs.

I know enough Spanish to know what *Papi* means and it does something to me. I stalk towards her, backing her against the wall and pressing my naked chest to hers. Placing my hands on her hips, I skim my nose along her jaw and down her neck. Her breath hitches as her fingers creep to the towel tucked around my hips.

"Say it again."

"Papí," she whispers.

I kiss the corner of her mouth before pulling back to say, "Hello there, Cailín."

"What does that mean?" Layla asks breathlessly.

"Little girl," I answer, pushing my hips into hers so she can feel how hard I am for her. How hard I *always* am for her.

"Teagan," she groans, rolling her hips in response. "We're never going to leave this house, are we?"

Chuckling, I kiss her quickly before reluctantly taking a step back. "Come on then, Lovely. Let's get dressed."

She sticks that bottom lip out in a pout and my first thought is how much I'd like to bite it. I've always had a pretty healthy sexual appetite, but this Spanish rose of mine has me fecking ravenous.

Chapter Seventeen

Layla

"Left foot forward."

We eventually left the house and found a small cafe nearby. We drank coffee, ate breakfast tacos, and then spent a good amount of time playing our version of Twenty Questions. During our conversation, Teagan asked me about Salsa dancing and then demanded that I teach him when we got back to the house. Now we have the living room furniture pushed out of the way, and we're standing side by side as I teach him the basic steps.

"Right. Got it, yeah. Step forward with the left, rock back on the right," he repeats.

"Don't forget to move your hips."

"Show me how again."

Turning towards him, I say disbelievingly, "I've shown you about ten times now!"

"Aye, I know. I just like watching you do it." He grins at me like a Cheshire Cat.

Tanta problema.

Leveling him with a glare, I say, "You can't Salsa without moving your hips. That's half the fun of the dance."

"I think we move our hips together rather well, if I do say so myself."

Heat surges in my core thinking of how true his statement is, but I keep a straight face, letting him believe I'm not amused.

"Fine," I say with a shrug, stepping away from him. "We don't have to learn."

"Hold on there," he says, grabbing my hand and spinning me back towards him. I slam into his chest and he immediately slides his other hand to the small of my back, spreading his fingers to press me closer. Then he steps forward with his left foot, forcing my right foot back. His hips sway, then roll against me. Instinctively my body moves in tandem with his, as if we've been dancing together for years.

Teagan holds my gaze as he murmurs, "Was that right?"

A small smile plays along my lips and I nod. "Yeah, that was perfect."

He leans in to capture my mouth with his in a softly passionate kiss that we could easily get lost in. Tumbling right back into bed would be so easy, but I'm determined to do more during this getaway than fuck Teagan all day every day.

Forcing myself to break the kiss, I clear my throat and say, "Let's move to the next steps."

I'm pleasantly surprised to find that not only is he a fast learner, but he has pretty good rhythm for a white guy. When I say as much, he barks out a loud laugh.

"You'd be surprised by how much dancing and football have in common when it comes to coordination and footwork. In fact, a lot of times during practice, Ro will have us do some viral dance he found on social media. Eamon is the only one who can't seem to follow along."

This little fact has me giggling so much, I have to sit on the couch. Teagan plops down next to me, raising an eyebrow in confusion.

"Did you know he and Norah were taking Salsa lessons at the rec center?" I ask between outbursts.

His eyes widen in surprise. "No fucking way."

"I'm so serious," I wheeze out. "Norah said he's a *terrible* dancer! But so is she, so they really are perfect for each other!"

Now Teagan is laughing right along with me, which only makes us both laugh harder. It takes a few minutes for us to get control of ourselves, but eventually, the giggles taper into the occasional chuckle.

"Thank God he's good on the pitch at least," Teagan says. "You'd think with as talented as he is with a ball, he'd be able to do basic dance routines."

"He doesn't strike me as someone who enjoys dancing anyway," I reply.

"Nah, he'd rather play the music than move to it."

"Speaking of," I start. "How long has the Irish trio been playing together?"

"Football?" He looks completely baffled.

"No, music! I've seen you play at Paddy's."

The three of them are frequently requested to play at O'Nelly's Irish Pub. Teagan usually plays the harmonica or banjo, Eamon is on guitar and lead vocals, while Ro plays violin.

"Oh right. We didn't start playing music together until sophomore year. Our first year in the States was spent in survival mode—learning a new culture, bonding with the other Seahawks, stuff like that, yeah?"

"Did you play as a kid?" I ask.

Teagan leans back on the couch as he throws an arm around my shoulders, tugging me close beside him.

"A bit. My Mum put me in lessons when I was a wee wan. I enjoyed it, but I didn't really have an interest in playing in front of anyone until Paddy's. Even now, my skills don't go past basic pub songs."

It's fascinating to hear about Teagan's upbringing. It was so different from mine. My family is affectionate to a fault and wants to be completely involved in everything, while it sounds like Teagan's parents were very hands-off and less nurturing. I'm amazed that he's as sweet and tender-hearted as he is when his siblings sound just as aloof as his mom and dad.

We stay snuggled on the couch for a little bit longer before I ask if he wants to join me in the hot tub.

Teagan jumps up so quickly that I practically topple over to where he was sitting. Holding a hand out to me, he says, "Aye. Do I ever."

Teagan

"Want to get in the hot tub?" Layla asks out of nowhere.

I'm immediately hit with the image of her in a bathing suit, and my mouth goes dry. I've seen her naked. My lips have kissed every inch of her, but I'm still chomping at the bit to see her in a strappy garment—one that only covers a fraction of her skin. Leaping from the couch, I extend my hand.

"Aye. Do I ever."

Layla laughs, her eyes sparkling. She places her hand in mine and I pull her into my arms, kissing her forehead before leading her back to the bedroom. After digging in her suitcase, she pulls out something white and shuts herself in the bathroom. I quickly shuck my clothes, pull on my black swim trunks, then sit on the edge of the bed. When I hear the door open, I look up and feel all the air leave my lungs.

Goddamn.

Layla stands there in a white, triangular bikini top and high-waisted bottoms with strings on the sides making a lattice pattern. She's put her hair into a messy knot on top of her head. It's hot as fuck, but I prefer her hair down for the sole purpose of wrapping it around my hand to guide her where I want her.

Letting out a low whistle, I rise from the bed and prowl towards her. When we're only inches apart, I brush the knuckle of my index finger over the swell of her breast, watching as goose flesh spreads over her skin.

"This," I say, lifting my eyes to hers, "looks amazing on you."

"Thank you," she mutters, looking away in what appears to be embarrassment.

I can't have that, so I grip her chin firmly between my thumb and forefinger, guiding her face back.

"Mo chroí, I mean it. And every other time I've told you how beautiful you are. You. Are. Perfect."

Her cheeks darken and those rich brown eyes are full of doubt. If I could have any super power, it would be for Layla Diaz to see herself through my eyes. I don't know what it's like to be a woman, let alone a woman with a full figure in a world where being beautiful is defined by how thin you are.

"What does your ex look like?" Layla asks suddenly.

"My ex?" I'm completely flummoxed.

"Yeah," she says. "What does she look like? Is she tall or short? Blonde hair or dark hair? That kind of stuff."

"I mean, yeah, she's tall and blonde, but what does that have…"

"Is she skinny or curvy?

"Layla…" I'm beginning to see where this is going, and I don't like it one bit.

"Please just answer the question," she begs, her voice beginning to tremble.

Sighing deeply, I say, "I will tell you whatever you want to know, but I want you to listen to me. There is no comparison."

"You're stalling…"

"Jaysus, you're persistent," I tease her. "Fine. Ashley is tall, blonde, and thin. But she's also a cheating bitch, one that didn't have the decency to talk to me when she started to feel our relationship going south."

Layla opens her mouth to say something, but I push my index finger against her pillowy lips. "Just leave it, Lovely."

She squeezes her eyes shut tight. "Teagan, I don't think you understand. Regardless of what you say, or how you feel, that doesn't stop the little voice in my brain that tells me I'll never live up to your standards. I am the complete opposite of your ex, who apparently is the type you're into since you dated for so long." She sighs, shoulders drooping in defeat. "I'll never be tall, skinny, *or* blonde. And while you make me feel sexy and desired when we're together, I can't help but feel that if you had to choose a girl out of a lineup based on looks alone? You wouldn't choose me."

My heart plummets. It isn't because she's right, but because she truly believes that. I wish I could go back to when I first met Ashley and lose her number. Had I known that Layla Diaz was in my future, I would have waited for her.

Tipping her head up, I hold her gaze. "The day we met, I watched Eamon run across the field to Norah. But from the moment I saw you standing there, I never looked away. I couldn't. You were—and still are—without a doubt, the most beautiful woman I've ever seen. So no, Lovely, I didn't choose you out of a lineup, but I did choose you out of a stadium full of hundreds. And I'd choose *you*, again and again."

Layla's eyes turn glassy, but her lips morph from a small smile to a full-face grin that is so radiant it nearly blinds me. But if that smile is the last thing I see before losing my eyesight, it will be worth it.

Chapter Eighteen

Layla

Is this what newlyweds feel like on their honeymoon? We've been in Avon for three nights now, but each one just keeps getting better and better. We don't have a set agenda, so there's no rush to be anywhere. Our evenings are spent eating dinner either at the house or out somewhere quiet with mood lighting, followed by fucking until our bodies give out, limbs tangled and sweaty. In the mornings, we wake up slowly; kissing, touching, and making love. The need for food is the only reason we make it out of bed. Once we're up, we explore the quaint shops or go shelling along the beach. When our mouths aren't busy tasting each other, we take advantage of the uninterrupted time to get to know one another better. We talk about family traditions, favorite music, bucket lists, and anything else that comes to mind. I've learned that sheep farming isn't just walking around a bunch of white fluff balls carrying a stick and whistling at a dog. While they are a responsibility, they're also easier to manage than most other farm animals. This doesn't leave me with a sudden desire to start raising sheep, but I now have more respect for the farmers.

Earlier this evening, we took a blanket from the house and settled on the beach with an array of snacks. The temps started to drop, so I stole Teagan's hoodie and pulled it on over my tank top. He didn't object, only giving me a heated look that had my toes curling. After eating, we put everything away and he began firing off question after question about my life in Texas and the first years at UNCW, claiming he's making up for lost time.

"Tell me about your boyfriends during high school and at UNCW," he demands.

Groaning, I flop backward on the blanket and stare at the clouds sailing overhead. "There's not a lot to tell."

"I still want to know," he says laying down beside me, lacing his hands behind his head.

"I didn't really date in high school. I'd have dates for events like prom and homecoming, but nothing more than that."

"Who was your first?" he asks quietly.

"My first, what? Date?"

"No...," he draws the word out. "The first one you gave your body to."

Oh.

"Um...his name was Brian." I glance over at him to see the muscle in his jaw feather. "We graduated together."

"How old were you?" His voice is laced with something I can't identify. Not exactly anger, but he isn't thrilled. I turn to my side, propping my head on my fist.

"Eighteen. About a week after graduation. We were at a party."

Teagan rolls to face me, mirroring my position. The sun is beginning to descend but shines bright enough to make his eyes sparkle like emeralds.

"I hope he was good to you."

He's dead serious, but I burst out laughing.

"What?" he asks incredulously.

126

"Teagan, it was the first time for *both of us*." I raise my eyebrows. "It was awful."

"Oh, yeah. I imagine that was awkward," he mutters. "Now I want details."

"No way!" I exclaim, reaching out a hand to playfully shove him.

"C'mon," he begs, grabbing my hand and intertwining our fingers. "I want to know everything he did wrong so that I can show you how it should have been done."

Snorting in amusement, I remind him that he's already shown me how good he is. Repeatedly.

"Ach, no. Your first time, and every time after, should be nothing short of incredible."

"You really want to know about my first time having sex? With someone that wasn't you? Are you a sadist?"

He can't be serious.

"Aye, I mean, no!" he blurts when he sees my eyes widen. "I'm not a sadist, but I do want to know about your first time."

Sighing, I relent. "Fine. Like I said, we were at a party at a mutual friend's house. I went outside to get some air and saw Brian sitting in a deck chair. I sat down in the chair next to him. We ended up talking for a couple of hours. We decided to go in, but when I stood up, my foot caught on something and I sort of… fell on him. We both froze, but then he kissed me and it turned heated. Next thing I know, he's leading me through a side door and sneaking us into an empty bedroom."

"Then what?" Teagan asks when I don't say anymore.

"What do you mean 'then what'?" I quip, confused. "We made papier-mâché eggs. What do you think we did?"

"Oy, don't get smart! Obviously, you had sex, but what did he do first?"

I stare at him, dumbfounded. "You weren't kidding about wanting to know everything he did."

"Nope. Where did he touch you first, Lovely?" His voice is low, slithering over my skin in a sensual caress.

I clear my throat. "He, um, immediately grabbed my breasts."

Teagan's eyes narrow. "Did he kiss you first at least? Or did he lead you into the room and just grab you?"

For some reason, describing my first time having sex to Teagan is a turn-on. I can feel heat pooling between my legs. Breathlessly, I say, "When we got in the room, he kissed me, grabbing me at the same time, then we kind of fell on the bed and he reached under my shirt, grabbing me again." I pause, inhaling deeply. "It didn't feel good, but I just went with it."

Releasing my hand, Teagan leans in, pushing me onto my back. A warm hand creeps under my sweatshirt until it reaches my breast. He squeezes gently, brushing a thumb over my nipple. I suck in a sharp breath, immensely grateful that I didn't put on a bra.

"What next, Layla?" He whispers, eyes locked on mine.

"He…uh…he kissed and sucked on my neck while pushing my shorts down…*oh God*," I gasp when he lowers his mouth to my throat, trailing his other hand to the band of my shorts before yanking them down. The cool ocean air has goosebumps spreading over my body. I don't even care that we're out in the open.

"Keep going," he growls in between kisses and nips, his hand just resting on my hip bone.

"Um. He…"

"What did he do after he took your shorts off?" Teagan trails a finger over the top band of my panties, making me shiver.

"He cupped my pussy over my underwear, rubbing his heel into my clit," I moan as he acts out my words on my body. I grip his arms like I did Brian's.

"Did he make you moan like this, Lovely? Were you this wet for him?"

"No!" I rasp.

Teagan chuckles darkly, still kissing my throat. "What did he do with his mouth while he rubbed you?"

I arch my back, pressing my aching breasts into his chest. I wish his shirt was off. "Fuck, I don't remember, Teag…"

"I'll improvise then."

Rucking my shirt up to my chin, he languidly licks one nipple while rolling the other between his thumb and forefinger. My hips buck, and he grinds his heel into my clit harder, making me groan loudly. "Keep talking, Cailín," he orders, his brogue thickening on that Irish term of endearment.

I want to listen to him say all the dirty things in Gaelic.

"He rubbed me for a few seconds then got up to take his pants off." It's exceedingly difficult to form coherent thoughts, let alone speak, while Teagan is running his teeth over my nipple. "We didn't even get fully undressed. Our shirts stayed on the entire time."

"Fucking eejit," he murmurs before licking the valley between my breasts. "Did he make you take your own knickers off or did he have the honor?"

"I took them off. *O caray...*"

I didn't know the underside of my boobs were a hot spot for me until just now.

"That's a shame," he grumbles, suddenly pulling away to stand, discarding his sweats and briefs.

I jolt upwards. "What are you doing? We're outside!" Okay, maybe I do care that we're out in the open.

"Relax, mo chroí. There's no one out here *and* it's dark enough that we won't draw attention."

He's right. It's nearly dark out. Only a few deep pink and purple streaks are still visible in the sky. "Now take off your knickers."

Carajo.

Glancing around to make sure there really are no people nearby, I shimmy out of my panties, pulling my knees to my chest before tossing the garment at his face. He grins gleefully, dropping to his knees. "Go on. What did this wanker do after he made you undress yourself? Did he taste you?"

"No," I say quietly. "You're the only one."

Teagan rocks back on his heels in shock. "Stall the ball. You're telling me that I'm the only one to ever taste that sweet cunt?" I nod, my face heating in embarrassment. "Fucking hell," he mumbles. "We'll come back to that later. Right now I want to finish what we've started. What happened next?"

"He crawled on top and kissed me for a few seconds, before nudging my pussy with his cock," I say, laying back on the blanket and letting my legs fall open. Teagan's eyes go feral as he licks his lips, clearly wanting to devour me.

129

"Did he go slow?" Teagan asks with concern.

"He did," I say with a nod. "I'll give him credit for that at least. He was considerate and only went in a little at a time until he reached my hymen. Then, once I gave the okay, he pushed through."

"Did it hurt?"

"Of course it did. But he stopped and waited for me to adjust before continuing."

Teagan leans over me, dipping down to kiss me. His tongue winds around my own, before he reaches down to fist his cock. We both watch as he slowly sinks inside of me. I'm significantly more lubricated now than I was back then, so there's no resistance. Once he's halfway in me, he stops, bringing his eyes to mine in silent question. I dip my chin in a nod and he thrusts deeply. I don't wince in pain like the first time, but I do cry out his name.

"He fucked me slow at first," I moan. "Trying to figure out the right rhythm. Once our bodies synced up, he sped up."

Teagan follows suit, pulling out slightly before sinking back in. Our bodies are already so attuned to each other, we don't need to find our rhythm. It's automatic.

"Fuck," he grunts, dropping his head to the crook of my neck. His breath is hot against my skin. "You feel so good. I can only imagine what you felt like then. If he managed to last long enough to get you off first, then he has my respect."

Giggling, I run my fingers through his hair. "He definitely did not last long enough, but he did make sure I came shortly after."

"This is where our reenactment ends." He raises himself, bracketing my head between his arms. "I can't, in good conscience, come before you do."

He keeps his word, fucking me deep, grinding against my clit every time he bottoms out. I come faster than I ever have. Whether it's from all of the foreplay and build-up, or the way he hits all the right spots, I don't know. It doesn't take him long to reach his release either, and when he comes, a growl sounds from his throat before he collapses on top of me.

It's fully dark now, the only sounds to be heard are the waves crashing on the shore mixed with our labored breathing. Teagan gently brushes my hair back before kissing me softly.

"That," he whispers, "is how your first time should have felt."

Chapter Nineteen

Teagan

"He did what?"

Layla's voice hisses from the other room. When I woke up to an empty bed, I was disappointed. I love waking up next to Layla.

"I can't believe he did that." A pause. "No, I haven't heard from Teagan."

Fully awake and intrigued, I toss the covers back and amble into the living room where Layla is curled up in the corner of the couch. Her dark chocolate eyes meet mine, and I immediately rush to her side when I see them lined with tears. Winding my arm around her shoulders, I tug her close and give her a questioning look.

"Hang on just a sec, Charlie." She pulls the phone from her ear, putting it on mute. "Have you heard from Eamon?"

A foreboding sensation sinks into my stomach. "No, at least not that I know of. Let me check my phone. What's going on?"

"Eamon broke up with Norah in Ireland," she mutters, those tears now spilling over.

"He what?!" I practically shout. "What the fuck? No, that can't be right."

Layla shrugs. "Charlie got a text from Norah just a little bit ago, saying that Eamon dumped her and she's headed back to Dublin to catch a flight home. She didn't give any other details."

Rising to my feet, I stalk to where my phone is plugged in and yank it off the cord to call my roommate

"Norah! Norah, where are you?" Eamon answers immediately, completely frantic.

"It's Teagan, mate. What the fuck is going on? Layla said that you broke up with Norah and she's on her way back to the States. Please tell me this is some sort of sick joke."

He groans. "It's a long story."

"You fecking eejit," I snarl, shocked that it's true. "What on earth possessed you to make such a dick move? I thought you were in love with her?"

Now I'm right pissed. Eamon doesn't make brash decisions like this, so something must have happened.

"I was. *I am*," he says. "It's complicated, Teag. My Mam and sister need me here. Caity is doing poorly, and Mam shouldn't have to do this alone. I need to be here for my family."

What?

"I get that, but how does ending things with Norah factor into this? Surely she'd give up everything to be there with you. Everyone can see she's head over heels for you."

"I can't do that to her." He sounds so sure of himself. "She has a life in Wilmington. I won't ask her to give it all up just so I can selfishly keep her by my side. I love her too much to tie her down."

Laughing humorlessly, I ask, "You're a thick gobshite, aren't you, Kennedy? Did you even think to ask her what she wanted? Because it sounds like you made the decision for her."

"But," he tries to interrupt.

"But nothing. This isn't the Middle Ages, mate. Women don't need men making the decisions for 'em."

"Fuck off," he growls. "That's not what I was doing. I was trying to save her from a miserable life. She might be willing now, but what happens when the years drag on, and she starts resenting me? Better to end it now after a few months than years."

For fucks sake.

"You don't believe that," I call him on his bullshite.

He spews some other excuses, then has the audacity to sound annoyed with Norah for leaving him high and dry. My eyes roll so far back into my head, I'm afraid they might stay that way.

Layla pads into the bedroom and I stretch my arm out to her. She comes to stand between my legs, but I pull her down to sit on my lap, then scoff at my mate on the line. "You think she really wanted to spend all that time in a car with you after you basically sent her packing? And then to say goodbye at the airport?"

When Eamon asks if he's bolloxed things, I don't hold back, telling him that he really has. Pulling Layla a little tighter to me, I ask him, "So, what are you going to do about it?"

"I don't know, Teag. I really hurt her."

"Aye," I agree. "Does your Mum want you to stay in Ireland to help her take care of Caity?"

"I don't know," he mumbles.

"Hold on." I sit up straighter, pressing a kiss to Layla's shoulder as I do. "You told Norah to leave so you could take care of yer Mum and sister, but didn't even have that discussion with yer Mum?"

My accent thickens with each word as I process the mess my mate has gotten himself into.

"It's a given though, isn't it?" Eamon asks. "My Da's not here to do it, I am."

"Christ's sake, man. Go talk to your Mum, then figure out how to make things right with your lass."

He sighs heavily. "Right. Yeah, I will."

"Talk soon, mate." It's not a question of will or won't. I'll be badgering him until the eejit fixes this.

"Yeah. Bye."

I drop my phone on the bed beside me and press my forehead against Layla's chest. She stayed quiet while I reamed Eamon, letting me know she was there by wrapping an arm around my neck. She smells so fecking good and looking down, I want nothing more than to bury my face in her tits...or between her gorgeous thick thighs. My cock twitches against her leg and she huffs a little laugh.

"Sorry." I look up at her apologetically. "Not the time, right?"

"Probably not right now," she says, placing a quick kiss on my mouth. "What did Eamon say?"

"Basically he made decisions not just for Norah, but his Mum and sister too. He didn't discuss it with anyone, just decided he's going to stay on in Ireland to take care of his family. There's a lot of guilt eating at him for not being there, especially since his Da is no longer alive."

Layla winces. "It sounds like his mind isn't in the right place. The stress from his sister, mixed with being back home after so long, has to be weighing heavy. That doesn't excuse what he did to Norah though." She shakes her head slightly. "Not at all."

"No, she's a good lass. She's good *for* him."

"And *he's* good for *her*," Layla adds.

We sit there quietly, both of us lost in our thoughts for a minute before she says, "I think we need to head back to Wilmington. I'm going to go to the airport with Charlie to pick up Norah."

Nodding, I heave a sigh. As much as I'd love to stay here, and horde Layla to myself, she's right. Her friend will need her more than I do right now.

"Aye, Lovely. I'll start packing."

There's a beat of silence before Layla says that we shouldn't tell anyone about us.

My head jerks in her direction, causing me to drop the armful of clothes I just collected onto the bed. My first reaction is to become indignant. "Sorry, lass, but are you ashamed of me?"

135

"No, of course not! Why would you think that?"

"Why else wouldn't you want people to know that we're together?"

Layla closes her eyes, inhaling deeply like I'm some petulant child, as she mutters something in Spanish under her breath.

"Well?" I'm anxious now.

"Teagan," she sighs, stepping up to me, looping her arms around my neck. My hands instinctively go to her hips. "Let's imagine that you just had your heart broken and one of your friends comes bouncing in, all smiles and boasting about a new relationship. Tell me, how would you feel?"

"Oh. Right." She's got a good point. Wasn't I jealous of Eamon and Norah not that long ago? "I don't love keeping us a secret, Layla. So Eam better pull his head out of his arse and fix this."

"Not arguing with you there. Let's just wait and see what state they're in, and go from there."

Nodding, I lean in to kiss her. When she presses herself into me, slipping her tongue into my mouth, I know we aren't packing up just quite yet. We're both feeling the impending separation and, even though we know it's not permanent, there's no telling when we'll have a moment alone again. It's not like she can come over to my flat since I live with Eamon; since she lives next door to Norah, there's no hiding when I'm over there.

Layla's fingers knot into my hair as a whine escapes her. The sound detonates something in me, and the next thing I know, I'm spinning her so that her back is to my chest. I band an arm under her breasts, sliding a hand around her throat to angle her face as I murmur against her neck. "If this is the last time we have for a while, I'm damn well making sure it's memorable."

She gasps but her body rolls against mine, and I know she wants this as bad as I do. The hand under her breasts snakes across her belly, under the band of the little shorts she's wearing, and slips into her knickers. When my fingers creep into her folds, she's soaked. I groan and circle her clit with the pad of my middle finger, before yanking it out, ripping her shorts off and falling to my knees behind her. I palm the globes of her luscious arse with both hands, leaning in to bite one of the cheeks, making Layla squeak in surprise. Standing, I press my hand to the small of her back, pushing her forward until her hands hit the mattress.

"Get on the bed and stay on all fours," I command, my voice rough with desire.

She obeys instantly. Seeing her on her hands and knees has me on the brink of combustion. My hands roam up her back, shoving that tank top up and over her head. When it falls down her arms, I lean over, pressing her down until those heavy tits are flat against the bed. Gripping her wrists in one hand, I extend her arms, wrapping the tank top around them.

"Leave them there."

Layla nods vigorously in response.

"That's a good lass," I croon, trailing kisses down her spine. I bite the other arse cheek when I reach it. Her lust-filled groan makes my cock jerk. Tired of not being inside her, I line myself up with her entrance and slowly sink into her, hands latching around her waist. Once I'm fully seated, I don't move.

"*Coge me*," she exhales. Those inner walls flex around me, tempting me to lose control.

Releasing her side, I scoop up her long hair and twist it around my hand. Gently pulling, I watch in fascination as her back arches. Holding her in this position, she starts to squirm.

"Am I hurting you, Lovely?"

"No. I need you to fuck me, Teagan. Please."

A feral groan leaps from my throat and I pull out to the tip before slamming back into her, grinding my hips against her arse before retreating to do it all over again. With every punch of my hips, she cries out in pleasure and begs for more.

"Aye, that's it, Lovely. Let me hear you," I grunt.

"¡Si, Papí!"

Fuck, do I love it when she calls me that.

"You're doing so good, Cailín."

"Más duro," Layla pleads. "Harder, Teagan!"

Her wish is my command. I release her hair to latch onto those wide hips so I can fuck her the way she needs me to. The sound of our bodies slapping together is pushing me closer, but my lass will always come first if I have anything to say about it.

"Come for me, Layla," I command through gritted teeth. "Now."

She screams when she shatters, and it's a symphony to my ears, demanding that I go with her. So I do, with her name on my lips.

Chapter Twenty

Two Months Later

Layla

"We've been seeing each other for a couple of months now."

It's been two months since Eamon and Norah split, but it was barely weeks before they were back together. Eamon realized the error of his ways and flew back to North Carolina with a contrite heart *and* a ring in his pocket. They both learned the importance of trust and communication. And now they're engaged!

Which is how Norah found out about Teagan and me. Shortly after arriving back in the States, she caught me texting him. I couldn't lie to her, so I came clean. She was happy for me, but I could see the pain in her eyes, and I didn't want to make it worse by flaunting our new relationship.

We didn't make it public knowledge until after Eamon returned and they worked out their issues. Well, mostly public knowledge.

"What do you mean you've been together for a couple of months, mija?" My mother is incensed that I'm just now telling her, but I have my reasons. "Why am I just now hearing about this? Where did you meet? Have you slept together yet?"

"Mami! I am not answering that last one."

That's the first reason why I haven't told her until now.

"I'm not asking for details, but I want to make sure you're being safe! Unless you're calling to tell me you're giving me a grand baby…"

"Enserio, Mami. No, I'm not having a baby." I glance up at Teagan to see him wide-eyed from his side of the couch where he's been rubbing my feet. That look of panic quickly turns heated when his gaze skims my body, lingering on my midsection. I jab him in the side with my foot, which earns me a grin.

"Okay, so tell me more about this Teagan." She demands.

"What do you want to know?" I pull the phone from my ear and set it to *speaker* so that Teag has to endure this with me.

"Everything, mija! Is he cute? Does he have a job? Where's he from? What's his family like?"

The grin on his face grows with every question she asks, and I just know that he's dying to hear my answers. I have the immense pleasure of watching that grin turn into a glare when I switch to speaking Spanish with my mother.

"Yes, Mami. Teagan is very handsome. He works with kids at the YMCA, is the goalie for the Seahawks soccer team, and…he's Irish."

She misses the cue, continuing in English, "He's Irish? Is he a redhead? Will I have redheaded grand babies?"

I groan loudly while Teagan tries to disguise his laugh as a cough.

"Do you have me on speaker, Layla? Hello? Teagan? Let me talk to him!"

"Hello, Mrs. Diaz. It's nice to unofficially meet you." Teagan winks at me before taking the phone from my hand.

"Likewise. Are you the reason my Layla didn't come home for the holidays?"

"Um…" Now it's my time to laugh as he flounders for an answer.

"I'll take that as a yes, then. So you're going to come with her to Texas on Spring Break, yes?"

I freeze as he looks at me questioningly, before responding. "Aye, if that's what Layla wants, I'd love to meet you all."

The corner of my mouth tips up as I nod. I'm worried about him being overwhelmed by my family, but can't deny that having him with me will make the stay more bearable.

"Good answer," she tells him. "I'll book the flights."

"No, Mami," I rush out. "You don't have to do that. I can transfer my ticket from Christmas, and I'll get Teagan's."

"Ach. I don't think so, lass. I'll be getting my own."

"Hush." I wave a hand at him to be quiet, but he grabs it, nipping my fingertips with his teeth.

"Both of you hush," my Mamá's commanding voice sounds through the speaker. "I already have the website up. Now, how about flying out that Friday night, and then flying back the following Friday?"

"Mami, we aren't staying the entire week. How about three nights?"

"Three? No way, mija. That's hardly enough time to catch up!"

Groaning, I look to Teagan for help but all I get from him is silent laughter. He's definitely enjoying this, but eventually takes pity on me and holds up five fingers.

"What?" I hiss. "Five nights? You want to stay for *five nights*?"

He shrugs then mouths, "Sure. It'll be fun."

I roll my eyes at him. *Hombre loco.*

"Mrs. Diaz? How about five nights? Will that be enough?"

"Ah, he's the reasonable one of the relationship. Yes, you can fly out Monday morning and back on Saturday. Sound good? Yes, okay. See you soon! Love you, mija!"

And then she hangs up before I can even utter a word. Turning to glare at my Irishman, I ask, "What have you done?"

Teagan laughs heartily, eyes shining with delight. "Ah, c'mon, Lovely. It won't be that bad."

Scoffing, I swing my legs from his lap and walk towards the kitchen. "You don't know what you're getting into, guapo. Do you not remember me telling you about my family? Not just how many members it has, but how *involved* they make themselves?"

I'm pulling a glass from the cabinet when I hear him padding across the floor in my direction.

"Aye, I remember." Strong arms wrap around me from behind and his chin rests on my shoulder. "And I'm not scared, Cailín. You shouldn't be either. I've got you. Anytime you start to be overwhelmed, or start to feel like your family is taking shots at you, I'll be there to intercept them."

Leaning into his embrace, I feel some of my anxiety subside. "You're not nervous at all?"

"No, why would I be?"

I spin in his arms to loop mine around his neck. His hands settle on my hips, squeezing gently.

"Isn't meeting the girlfriend's family a big deal for guys?"

Shrugging, he leans in to place a chaste kiss on my lips. "Honestly, I can't answer that. I never met Ashley's. It never even came up. And back home, I already knew everyone, so I didn't have to be introduced."

A small part of me loves that he'll be experiencing this with my parents. Even if the idea of my family swarming him and making all sorts of comments terrifies me. I shouldn't be surprised though. Teagan is outgoing, always finding a way to have conversations with those around him. He's 'Mr. Social Butterfly' while I'm 'Ms. Anti Social'.

"Promise you won't give up on me once you see how crazy they are?" I ask teasingly.

"Promise. It would take a hell of a lot more than that to scare me off of you now."

He winks and kisses me again. I so badly want to let this kiss morph into something hot and heavy, but we both have to go to work and be responsible adults. I didn't love working at a grocery store to begin with. But after being with Teagan? All of my shifts have felt so lackluster. I go through the motions, putting forth the least amount of effort possible without losing my job.

My mind has been drifting lately to the future. I'm pursuing a computer science degree, but what will I do with that? Nothing in the field is remotely interesting to me and being stuck at a computer all day feels like torture. The point of having a job is to earn money, but would it be so bad to not make as much money while doing something I enjoy? I know my parents and grandparents had to work their asses off to provide the life they gave us—and I'm forever grateful, but does that mean I have to follow in their footsteps? They had families to care for at my age, so their options were limited, but I'm not a parent and I'm taking measures to keep it that way for a while.

* * *

"Mr. O'Brien! Ms. Diaz! It's a pleasure to be seein' ya this fine evening."

Paddy O'Nelly is behind the bar, drying glasses with a white bar towel when Teagan and I walk into the pub. He smiles warmly at us, eyes darting to where our hands are joined. He knows we've been dating, but still acts like it's new information whenever he sees us together.

"Hiya, Pat. How's she cuttin'?" Teagan greets him, releasing my hand long enough to shake Pat's.

"Ah, grand. Are ye here to celebrate the two love birds as well?" Paddy nods toward our usual table where Norah and Eamon are cozied up, chatting with Rowan.

"Aye. Glad Kennedy pulled his head out of his arse, yeah?"

"Teagan," I chide, lightly smacking his arm, "be nice."

Paddy chuckles as Teag turns wide, innocent eyes on me. "What? It's nothing he hasn't said himself!"

I roll my eyes at him. "I'm going to sit."

Teagan draws me close, his arm tight around my waist as he kisses my cheek. "Go on, love. I'll get us drinks."

"Good to see you, Pat," I beam at the pub owner before heading in the direction of our friends. As soon as my back is to them, a hand pats my ass. Wheeling around, I find Teagan with a huge grin on his face. He winks when I scowl at him.

"You're lucky I like you, guapo."

This makes both men chuckle, so I spin on my heel, aiming for Norah.

"She's got spunk, she does," Paddy says not so quietly. "Keep her around, O'Brien."

"Aye. That's the plan."

A rush of delight floods me at the thought of Teagan making plans to keep me. This isn't just a fling, but it's entirely too soon to label it as love. Isn't it? Norah knew with Eamon, and look where they are now. Is that my future with Teagan? Am I ready for that level of commitment? I'd like to think I am, but *marriage*?

"Layla!" Norah's voice breaks through the cycle of thoughts in my head.

"Hey, chica!" I stoop to hug her before giving the other two Irishmen a little wave.

"I'm so glad you came out. I know you're usually tapped out after work."

She's not wrong. On the nights that I close, I'm too tired and cranky to venture out into the crowds, completely content just to stay home and unwind. But since dating Teagan, he's been slowly pulling me out of my shell. He has this innate ability to tell when I need a distraction from myself...and when I need to decompress alone. Well, not completely alone. There hasn't been a time when I haven't wanted him with me.

"True, but I wouldn't miss celebrating with you two!"

"Too right, lass." Rowan raises his glass in my direction. "Better them than me!"

Eamon tosses a coaster at the redhead. "Wanker. Yer just jealous."

Ro makes a disbelieving noise. "Of being weighed down with a ball and chain? No offense, Norah love."

Following her fiance's lead, she tosses her coaster at him too, which has us all laughing. I love seeing how Norah has come out of her shell since being with Eamon. The fear in her eyes has been replaced by confidence and trust. It looks good on her.

"Who's up for a little competition?" Rowan asks, rapping his knuckles on the table as I slide into the booth beside Norah and Eamon. I don't know him that well, but the guy has seemed a little off lately. We all know he has a thing for Alicia, so it's not surprising to catch his eyes following her around the pub, but his usually jovial persona seems forced tonight.

"Depends on what you have in mind," Teagan says as he places a beer in front of me, sliding onto the bench beside me.

"Ah, nothing big. Just a little drinking contest. For old times' sake." Ro winks at Norah, who just rolls her eyes. "I'm thinking *'Never Have I Ever.'*"

To everyone's surprise, Norah agrees. "Yes, let's do it! This seems safer than a one-on-one challenge."

"Acushla," Eamon warns. "With Rowan coming up with the questions, do you really think this is a good idea? Knowing him, he'll ask something like, 'Never have I ever taken a piss standing up.'"

"Oi!" Rowan yells. "Fuck off. I'll make it even-steven. I swear on the Blessed Virgin."

"I'm game," I chime in with a shrug. "I don't have to work until tomorrow afternoon and it's been a while since I've done anything like this."

Teagan turns his head in my direction, face speculative as he searches my eyes for any hint that I'm bullshitting him. "You sure about this, Lovely?"

Lifting the glass to my mouth, I hold his eyes as I down the entire beer. Once I've swallowed, I hand the empty glass to him. "I'm going to need another drink."

Chapter Twenty-One

Teagan

"Fucking hell, Norah. Of course I've never done that! You're as bad as Gallagher!"

Eamon's girl has been giving me a run for my money with this *"Never Have I Ever"* game. Somehow, we're the only two still going. Layla held on as long as she could, but after four drinks she was done. It was cute how she thought she could outdrink me though. Her friend, however, must have some sort of superpower that absorbs alcohol.

"Answer it, Teagan!" Norah demands. "Never have I ever gotten my skirt tucked into my underwear after using the bathroom."

The fire sprite raises a brow, wiggling the pint in her hand. I roll my eyes and chug the last of my beer.

"Happy now?" I ask, glaring at her. She laughs before chugging her own drink. "What the hell? You've never done that either? I was ready to bow out and declare you the winner!"

"Alright, O'Brien," she slurs, pointing a finger at me. "I challenge you to a tequila shot contest."

"Ach, tequila?" I grouse. "I fucking hate tequila."

"Well, if you don't take the challenge, you automatically lose."

There's a nagging voice in the back of my head telling me that we've started a new game, but I'm drunk enough to not care. I'm only hearing that I'll lose and, even though I just told her I was ready to call it quits, the competitive side of me has decided we're good for one more.

"What happens if I lose, Grady?" I smirk at her.

Norah grins maliciously at me. "If you lose—or don't accept the challenge—you, Eamon, *and* Ro have to be my models for the costume fittings for the drag show."

I hear Eamon curse under his breath. "Don't do it, mate."

"What kind of costumes?" Ro asks curiously.

My stomach sinks when Norah starts giggling and sings out, "Wellllll…It *is* a drag show. And I a*m* the costume designer, so you do the math."

She's mental. "No fucking way, Grady!" I yell.

"You must really think I'll beat you then."

Glaring at her, and trying to focus, I nod. "Alright. If you outdrink me, then we'll agree to play dress-up. But," I point at her, "If I outdrink *you*, then you and Layla have to come up with *and perform* a cheer at our next match. In front of the whole crowd."

The color drains from Norah's face and my lovely Layla is looking at her friend with such hatred it's almost scary. She then turns those eyes my way, and I feel my balls shrivel a bit.

"Absolutely no fucking way, Teagan."

I grin and drape an arm over her shoulders, pulling her into me so I can kiss her cheek before looking smugly at Norah.

"What's the matter, Norah? You look a little scared. Afraid I'll beat you?"

"Norah, don't you dare agree to this," Layla seethes next to me.

The red-haired lass and I have a tense glare-off before she nods. "Alright.

Deal."

"What?" Layla shrieks. "Shit. You better win or we're not friends anymore."

Laughing, Norah clumsily makes her way to the bar where Alicia is pouring drinks. I move closer to Layla, attempting to kiss her neck, but she shoves me away.

"Uh uh," she says, shaking her head. "You better hope she wins or this relationship is going to take a turn for the worse."

"Ah, c'mon, Lovely. Will it really be so bad to cheer for me at a game? You're a dancer, so you'll be grand."

"Teagan, I swear to god. Look at this face," she points to it, not realizing that I'm always looking at her. "Do I look like I'm joking about this?"

No, she doesn't, but my drunk arse is too busy thinking about her in a cheer leading costume. "But think of how good you'll look in that little skirt," I purr, gripping her thigh before sliding my hand up her inner thigh.

"Don't." She clamps her legs together and grabs my wrist, pulling it away. I watch her exit the booth and stomp to the bar.

I chuckle, thinking that maybe I should be worried, but she's sexy even when she's angry. I have a feeling the make-up sex will be worth it. On that thought, I stumble up to our group where Norah is informing Alicia of our plan.

"Alright, Teags. Our fate is in your hands. Don't fuck this up." Ro is rubbing my shoulders like I'm Conor McGregor about to begin a fight.

Norah lets out a bark of laughter. "Oh, Ro. I have a denim thong with your name on it."

We all laugh, but none more than Alicia. She's holding her sides as she giggles away. Rowan, abandoning my shoulders, stalks toward her, growling, "That will be enough out of you, lass. I bet you'd enjoy seeing me in that, wouldn't you?"

Alicia snorts indelicately. "I'd pluck my eyes out with these bar tongs if I saw your ass in a denim thong." She waves the tongs in the air.

I can tell that Ro is about to get fired up, so I decide to get a move on. "Let's do this, Grady. I hope you and Layla enjoy coming up with your cheer."

148

The cheeky sprite actually salutes me before saying, "Bring it, Irish."
Oh, I'll bring it.

* * *

The only thing I brought was my body to the floor. I'm curled up, arms folded over my head, as the lasses sing some drunken version of "We Are The Champions". I feel a pat on my head and lift my eyes to find a gloating Norah.

"Don't worry, O'Brien. I'll make sure your costume is a flattering color." A small smirk dances on her lips. "With a matching boa."

"Fuck me," I moan. "How are you even standing? This whole pub is spinning right now."

She giggles. "It's okay, Teag. There's no shame in being a lightweight. Some of us can just hold our liquor better than others."

Before I can form a retort, Eamon has his arms wrapped around her from behind, pulling her away. He better keep an eye on that one. She's trouble.

"Oh, baby boy. You're looking rough." Layla squats down next to me, brushing my hair back in what would be a touching gesture if not for the fecking smirk on her lovely face. Or faces, rather. There are three of her right now.

"Kill me now. Just put me out of my misery," I mumble.

A husky laugh leaves her before she turns her head—heads—over her shoulder. "Rowan, come help me get this *borracho* up and into the Uber." She's so loud and my head spins.

I'm not sure if I'm walking, floating, or being dragged to the car because I can't feel my legs. My stomach is roiling and I know, beyond a shadow of a doubt, that when I wake up tomorrow, my head will be in ribbons. My head lops to the left where Ro is grumbling about kicking a ball directly into my bollocks at the next practice. I grimace and roll my head to the right. Layla' eyes meet mine and she smirks at me again.

"You're so beautiful," I slur. My eyelids are getting heavy now.

She huffs a laugh. "Thank you."

"How'd I get so lucky?"

"Good question," Ro mutters on my other side and Layla snorts.

"Layla," I mumble. "I love you."

She jerks her head to look at me, those brown eyes blown wide, her perfect lips falling open on a soft "oh".

Then the world goes black.

* * *

I was right. My head is in absolute ribbons. It feels like someone is taking a garden dibber to the back of my skull while riding upside down in a waltzer. The last thing I remember is Rowan and Layla hoisting me up off of O'Nelly's floor.

"Fucking Christ," I groan into the pillow.

Based on the scent embedded in the pillowcase, I assume that I'm at Layla's house. She always smells so good—a mixture of soft florals and citrus.

"Buenos dias, guapo."

Slightly turning my head, I crack my eyelids open to find her lying in bed next to me. Her raven hair is pulled into a high ponytail, sleep lines nestled along her cheek. There's something in her eyes that I can't identify. She almost looks nervous.

"Morning, Lovely. What time is it?"

"Just after ten." Her voice is much softer now. "How are you feeling?" .

"As shook as a hand at mass."

Layla giggles. "What does that even mean?"

"It's an Irish saying for very hungover." Slowly, I roll from my stomach to my side and face her. "We've a good amount of terms and lines related to drinking. Shocking, I know."

Her lips tip up in a smile, but she doesn't say anything. Lifting a hand, I trace my fingertips over her cheek.

"What is it, Cailín?"

She inhales deeply, like she's steeling herself for a difficult conversation.

150

CHAPTER TWENTY-ONE

"How much of last night do you remember?"

My brow furrows in confusion. I remember making an arse of myself, but I don't recall anything too concerning—other than losing that fecking bet to Norah.

"I lost a bet to Norah, but I'd think you'd be pretty happy about that," I confess.

Her face transforms into a full-blown smile for a second. "Oh, I am. Absolutely. This morning would be going completely different had you won."

I cringe. "Aye, I imagine. You're welcome then."

Layla rolls her eyes but then her smile falls. "Do you remember leaving the pub?"

"Not at all. I vaguely remember floating from the floor to the door, but nothing after that. Why? What's going on, Layla?"

She squeezes her eyes closed. "It's nothing."

"Hey." I grip her chin. "Look at me."

I wait for her to open her eyes and when she does, they're glistening with moisture.

"You said something," she whispers. "But if you don't remember, I'm guessing it was just from being drunk, so it doesn't count."

"What did I say?"

She shakes her head. "It doesn't matter. Just forget I said anything."

Layla starts to slide out of the bed, but I wrap an arm around her, tugging her into me. "Layla, please. Talk to me. If I said something terrible, I need to know so I can make it right."

She hesitates. As her lips part to speak, the doorbell rings. The shrill sound lances through my head, making me cringe. Layla takes advantage of my misery to jump out of bed and dash out of the room, leaving me floundering at what I could have possibly said to make her act so strange.

Chapter Twenty-Two

Layla

Literally saved by the bell.

I can't decide if I'm happy or upset that Teagan has no recollection of telling me he loves me. I'm not even sure if I should tell him what he said. Shouldn't the first time those words are uttered be memorable for all parties? Will he feel obligated to keep saying it if he didn't actually mean to tell me?

Do I love him?

Maybe...yes...I don't know.

I always hoped that when I found the right person, professing our love would come organically. There would be a defining moment or event that lead us to confessing our mutual feelings for one another. It would be romantic and emotional. Followed by passionate love-making.

God, I sound pathetic. That's books and movies, not the real world. The real world is your boyfriend of only a handful of months getting drunk off his ass, slurring that he loves you as his buddy helps you haul him into an Uber.

I could tell him what he said and have a super awkward conversation that would lead to him telling me he loves me because he feels obligated to or telling me that he doesn't love me. Both options are shit.

For now, I put those thoughts away, padding down the hallway to the front door. When I pull it open, I'm stunned to find my oldest brother, Marcos, standing there with a duffel bag at his feet and a grin on his face.

"¡Qué tal, Layla! ¿Qué pasa?"

"¡Marcos! ¿Qué estás haciendo aquí?"

I don't give him the chance to answer before flinging myself at him and wrapping my arms around his neck.

My brother is the spitting image of my father. Tall, muscular, dark brown eyes, and a mop of black curls on his head. His complexion is darker, not surprising considering he plays soccer professionally for Juárez. I haven't seen him in over a year and am surprised at how much I've missed him. My eyes sting with tears as I pull back to look at him. He seems to be in good health, but he looks tired, and the mischievous sparkle I'm used to seeing in his eyes isn't there.

"Güey, what's wrong?"

I watch as Marcos plasters on a fake grin. "What? Can't a guy visit his sister?"

"Don't be stupid," I admonish him. "Of course you can. It's just that a guy would usually inform his sister ahead of time so she could be prepared."

"I'm easy. Why would you need to be prepared?"

"Who was at the door, Lovely?" Teagan's voice travels from the bedroom. Marcos and I both jerk our heads in that direction as my gorgeous boyfriend drifts down the hall, wearing nothing but a pair of black boxer briefs.

God, he looks good enough to eat, even hungover. He's rubbing his hand over his hair when he stops short, eyes going wide before narrowing at my brother, whose arms are still around me.

"Hullo there. Who the feck are you?"

Marcos, sensing an opportunity to fuck with me, pulls me closer, placing a smacking kiss on my cheek. "Clearly you didn't tell him about me. What am I going to do with you, *preciosa*?"

"Cerdo. I hate you," I seethe, untangling myself to step toward Teag. He winds a possessive arm around my waist as I lay a hand on his chest. "This is my oldest brother, Marcos. He's an idiot."

Teagan lets loose a relieved breath and then extends his hand. "Sorry, mate. I'm Teagan O'Brien, the boyfriend."

Marcos grips the outstretched hand, muscles flexing as he squeezes harder than necessary. "Marcos Diaz. Nice to meet you. Especially since she failed to tell me she had a boyfriend."

I roll my eyes. "I'm surprised Mami didn't tell you."

"Oh, she did. But *you* didn't."

"Really, Marcos?" I give him a scathing look. "How many of your girlfriends have you called to tell me about, hmmm? Pretty sure I meet a new one every Christmas."

"None of mine have ever been serious enough to move in with me though," he says, looking pointedly at Teagan.

"No, mate, we're not…" he tries to interject.

"No. No, no, no, no, no, no," I spit out rapidly, shoving my finger into Marcos' chest. "You do not get to show up on my doorstep, unannounced mind you, and start throwing around judgments and demanding answers."

Before my brother can argue, I turn back to Teagan. "And you're not helping matters by standing here in just your underwear. Go put on some clothes while I deal with this."

"Go easy on him, Lovely. He's just looking out for you." Teagan winks at me before sauntering back to the bedroom, closing the door behind him.

"So, an Irish guy?"

Rounding on Marcos, I jab my finger at him again. "Shut up, *cabrón*. You don't get to ask any questions right now. Go sit down. I'll make coffee then you can tell me why you're really here."

* * *

154

"So let me get this straight," I say, scowling into my café de olla. "Because you've been drafted by the Charlotte Football Club and are now moving, she's unwilling to attempt a long-distance relationship. Even though she says she loves you?"

After Teagan put on some clothes, I poured us all a cup of coffee before settling in to hear Marcos' story. Teagan nestled into the corner of the couch, wrapping an arm around my shoulders when I joined him, while my brother stretched out in the armchair across from us. His legs are spread wide, head resting against the back of the chair.

"That sums it up," he sighs. "I don't know what to do. I've been playing for Juárez my entire career and the goal has always been to move up. CFC is sixth in the League. It would be huge for me."

"Fair play, mate!" Teagan exclaims, raising his mug in salute. "That's incredible!"

"Seriously, Marcos, that's amazing. You should be so proud. And if she really loved you, she would be too."

My brother has never been interested in someone enough to have this kind of reaction. He normally drops them once they start to get too clingy. The fact that he actually still wants this woman, even after her refusal to attempt to make a relationship work, speaks volumes.

Marcos sits up, resting his elbows on his knees and letting his hands hang before them. His eyes dart between me and Teagan. "What if you two were in this situation? What would you do?"

This gives me pause. What *would* I do? I try to put myself in my brother's girlfriend's shoes. Imagining Teagan telling me that he's leaving and I won't see him every day makes my heart hurt, but knowing that he's finally achieved his dream would give me so much joy. Honestly, I'd probably find a way to go with him. I can get a job anywhere with my degree. But what happens if we break up and then I'm stuck in a city where I don't know anyone?

Oh.

"Tonto," I say gently. "She's scared. I'd put money on the fact that what she really wants is to follow you wherever you're going, but she is terrified that the relationship will end. She'll be left alone in a place she's not familiar with if that happens."

"Why would the relationship end? I love her and want to be with her for the long haul," he says defensively.

I quirk a brow at him. "The *long haul* for you is maybe six months. You don't exactly have the best track record for long-term relationships. She's cutting ties now, before things get too involved, so it's less painful. She's not going to make a huge move unless she is absolutely certain that you're her endgame."

My brother glares at me, so I glare right back. He may be older, but that doesn't mean he's the wisest.

"So you're saying I should marry her?"

"Jesus, Marcos. No, I'm not telling you to marry her, but the only way she's going to even consider staying together is if she feels secure enough with you."

Teagan clears his throat. "Do you think she'd consider a long-distance trial period of sorts? Maybe give it a go and reevaluate every so often?"

Marcos tilts his head to the side, considering this option. "That's not a bad idea."

Nodding, I expand on Teagan's idea. "You're going to have to put in a lot of work for her though. Stay in contact with her as much as possible, provide proof that you aren't fucking around on her. Make trips back to see her every chance you get...or fly her out to you."

"That seems excessive," he grumbles, refusing to meet my eyes.

"Hey," I hold my hands up and shrug. "You're the one that wants to figure out how to make it work with this chica, so that means you've gotta do the work. If you love her, it should be worth it."

"When the hell did you turn into a relationship guru, Layla?"

"When you decided to drop in uninvited, *burro*. Which," I state, pointing at him, "there's no way you came all the way here just so you could get life advice from your sister."

Laughing, he interlaces his fingers. "No, I'm actually meeting a new teammate and roomie. He lives here, but we got matched up to share a space when we're not on the road. Someone named Rowan Gallagher. You know him?"

Teagan chuckles under his breath. "Yeah, mate. I know him."

Chapter Twenty-Three

Teagan

Marcos looks at me questioningly, clearly hearing the amusement in my voice. "What am I missing?"

Layla puffs her cheeks before releasing her breath. "Rowan is... something."

I give Marcos a brief history of how I know Ro, including how we play together, which leads to a full-blown conversation about playing footie. Layla eventually gets bored and leaves the room under the guise of taking a shower. I'm only slightly resentful of the fact that I don't get to join her, but I'm enjoying getting to know her oldest brother. He's a good chap. We're close in age and have been playing football most of our lives, though he's been playing competitively longer than I have. Getting promoted to CFC is a huge accomplishment for both him and Ro.

"So," Marcos says, clasping his hands together. "As Layla's big brother, I'm obligated to make sure you know that if you hurt her, I'll be forced to kick your ass. I really don't want to do that because you seem like a decent guy and someone I'd get along with."

He laughs, but I can see how serious he is, which I respect. I have a sister and while we aren't exactly close, I get where Marcos is coming from.

Looking him in the eyes that are so similar to Layla's, I level with him. "I can assure you that I have zero intentions of ever hurting Layla." The sincerity of my words is evident. "She's important to me and the only thing I want is to make her happy."

He peers at me for a moment before nodding. "I can tell. She's glowing, amigo. And it's definitely not because her brother is visiting."

We both laugh, but inside I'm absolutely busting with pride. I know that Layla and I are good together, but when her family can see it too? Yeah, that makes a man feel good. The big test will be when we meet the rest of her family during spring break.

"Thanks, man. I appreciate you saying that. I hope your parents feel the same. I'm looking forward to meeting them in a few weeks."

A mischievous grin spreads across his face. "Layla did warn you about our family, didn't she? Mami is a force to be reckoned with."

I grin back at him. "Aye, she did. Must be where she gets it, yeah? She doesn't have a problem putting me in my place."

He nods knowingly. "Our twin sisters are just the same. Papá, Raf, and I all know exactly where we stand. Word of advice? When it's that *time of the month,* just agree with whatever they say."

"Marcos Diaz!"

We both jolt in surprise and turn towards Layla, who is standing behind the sofa with her hands on her hips. I didn't even hear her sneak up on us. If looks could kill though, Marcos would be dead meat. He only laughs, standing and walking over to her with outstretched arms.

"Awe, c'mon chaparrita. You know it's true!" He attempts to wrap her in a hug, but she steps back.

"Oh no, you don't," she hisses at him. "I know what you're doing. Trying to get Teagan to agree with you so he gets in trouble."

"Actually, I like Teagan and hope you don't do anything to scare him away. It was a genuine warning so he'll know what to expect. You, Mami, and the girls are scary."

She slaps him upside the head, muttering a string of what I assume are Spanish curses. Watching the two of them is immensely entertaining. My sister doesn't joke around with me like this, no matter how much I've tried.

Layla notices me enjoying their tiff and narrows her eyes at me. "Something funny, guapo?"

I stand and round the couch, gently grabbing her arm and pulling her into me. I kiss her temple, my lips brushing against her soft hair. "Nah, just love watching the two of yous go at it."

Her eyes dart to mine, brows furrowing. I can tell she wants to say something, but she presses her lips together before turning her attention to her brother.

"Are you planning on staying here, Marcos?" she asks.

"That's why I brought my bags with me, but I'm not sure if I want to share space with lovers. You might keep me up at night."

Layla blushes so violently I can feel the heat radiating from her. Before she has a chance to fly off the handle at him, I intervene.

"Hey, I'll stay at my place, so don't worry about that." Layla makes a noise of protest, but I hold up a hand. "It's okay, Lovely. It's just for a little while, yeah? I need to do some stuff at the flat anyway."

She sticks her bottom lip out in a pout, and only because her brother is standing less than two feet from us do I refrain from sucking it between my teeth.

* * *

"How do you think Marcos will like Ro?"

Layla and I are in the kitchen washing dishes shortly after her brother leaves to meet with Rowan. I offered to take him, but he insisted he go on his own so that he could get a feel for Ro without his mates around.

160

"Honestly," she says, drying her hands on the towel next to the sink. "He'll probably love him. They have a lot in common. Football, lots of girlfriends… okay, well that's all I can think of off the top of my head."

Chuckling, I place the clean and now dried mugs in the cabinet. It's a mundane task, but the sense of rightness I have sharing space with Layla is at the forefront of my mind.

"You think he's serious about this mot of his?"

A delicate snort leaves her before she turns, resting against the edge of the counter. She crosses her arms over her chest, pushing those luscious tits up. I'm going to miss burying my face in those every morning and night while I'm back at my flat.

"It's hard to say with Marcos. He's only ever been this serious about playing pro, so it's throwing me off. I'd be interested in meeting her just to see what the fuss is about. He's brought so many girlfriends home over the years and always behaves in a certain way. We'd be able to tell a lot by the way he acts."

"Aye, that makes sense. Not that I ever brought a string of lasses home to meet the family, but the ones you feel more serious about bring out a different side of a man."

Layla doesn't respond, so I glance over to find her narrowing her eyes at me and her jaw clenching. Abandoning the dishes, I stalk towards her and wrap my arms around her waist and snake my hands down to cup that lovely arse of hers. Those brown eyes flare with desire.

"Ach, you're not jealous, are ya, Lovely?"

"No," she lies.

Chuckling darkly, I yank her hips into mine so she can feel what she does to me. She whimpers at the contact. "Have you not realized that I know you?" I bring my lips to her ear. "That I know your body? I can tell when you're happy, sad, angry, *jealous…turned on.*"

She shivers, a small gasp leaving her before she whispers, "Can you read my mind too?"

Skimming the tip of my nose from her ear to her shoulder, I say, "Not yet."

"Good," she breathes, sinking to her knees before me.

161

"Cailín," I growl out. My heart is thundering and my cock twitches in anticipation.

Layla places her hands flat on my thighs. "Tell me what I'm thinking, Teagan."

Her voice is soft but there's a fire in her dark brown eyes. I'm ready and willing to let her consume me. It's not often she gets the jump on me like this. Not that I don't love when she sucks me off, but I'm usually chomping at the bit to get my mouth on or my cock in her pussy. All I want is to please her and make her come, over and over. I can't get enough of her.

"Show me."

Her gaze doesn't leave mine as she tugs my gym shorts down to my knees, taking my briefs with them. My cock springs free and her eyes drop to it greedily. Her soft hands glide leisurely up my legs to my stomach where her fingers trace the lines of muscle before she rakes her nails back down. Goose flesh erupts all over my skin.

"Layla…"

Her eyes flick to mine before those perfect fucking lips close around the tip. My hips buck reflexively, forcing my cock further into her mouth. She hums and runs the tip of her tongue along the sensitive underside of the head, making me simultaneously groan and twist the fingers of both hands into her hair. Layla doesn't move, just keeps me in her mouth, tracing me with her tongue. Breaking out into a cold sweat, I'm about to start begging when she finally sucks me to the back of her throat.

"Fuck!" I cry out at the sudden sensation then follow up with a string of random words of affirmation as she works me over. "Cailín…baby…fuck… yes…".

Just as I start to come, she pulls to the tip and stops. Completely flustered, I gape at her. She winks at me, scraping her bottom teeth lightly over that spot, and my vision tunnels as I spill my release into her mouth. My fingers loosen from her hair and skim down her cheek until I reach her chin. I grip it firmly, making sure she's paying attention.

"Swallow it, lass."

She obeys so beautifully. Gently, I extend my arm, pushing her off of my cock. Her lips are so red and swollen, that it's distracting.

"Come here," I quietly order, offering her a hand.

She takes it and I help her to her feet. After righting my shorts, I fold my arms around her. She smirks at me, so I capture those lips with my own and kiss her deep and slow. When we come up for air, I murmur against her mouth, "Let me make one thing *very* clear, Lovely."

Layla hums and leans back, probably thinking I'm about to take her to bed, which I am, but right now she needs to hear what I'm about to say.

"There is not a single woman on this earth that you need to worry about. Do you hear me?"

Her eyes soften and she nods. "I hear you."

"Do you believe me when I tell you that my eyes, mouth, hands, and heart are only yours?"

She goes rigid in my arms, eyes flaring in alarm. Not the reaction I was expecting.

"Hold on, what's that look for?"

"Teagan, don't say things unless you really mean them."

I'm properly confused now. When have I ever not been completely open with her?

"Layla, what are you talking about? I'm always honest with you."

She looks away, biting her bottom lip. "That thing you said last night? While you were drunk?"

Shite. Now I'm really worried. "Aye. What did I say?"

She inhales deeply, still not meeting my gaze. "I feel really stupid for even bringing this up. Because I want what you said to be real, but only if you absolutely mean it. I don't want you to say it because you feel obligated."

Something clicks in my brain, a flash of a memory. My drunken arse looking at her as she and Ro drag me to a car and knowing at that moment that she's my everything and there's no turning back.

"I said I love you."

Her head snaps back in my direction, eyes wide. "You remember?"

A corner of my mouth tips up in a small smile. "Aye. Once you started talking, it clicked."

"Oh." She worries that bottom lip with her teeth again. "Did you…"

She stops herself and looks away again. Gently cupping her cheek, I bring her eyes back to me and hold her gaze. "Aye. I meant it then and I mean it now. And I'll mean it every day until the day I die. I love you, mo chroí."

"You never did tell me what that means," she says with a sniffle.

"My heart. It means you're my heart."

Tears well and spill onto her cheeks, but her face lights up in a radiant smile. "I love you too."

Then she's raising herself on her toes to kiss me. It's consuming, like kissing Layla always is, but this time it holds so much more weight. We've been heading in this direction since the beginning. I think we both knew going into this that it wasn't just a casual fling.

Breaking the kiss, I brush strands of hair from her face and tell her earnestly, "I'm sorry that the first time I told you was while I was in rag order. If I could take it back and do it over, I would in a heartbeat."

A breathy laugh bursts from that perfect mouth. "It's okay. You more than made up for it."

"Ach, I owe you for something else too." I tell her, a wicked grin forming.

Her head tilts to the side, eyes questioning. "What's that, guapo?"

"A mind-blowing orgasm." Then I scoop her into my arms, eliciting a shriek and peals of laughter, and carry her to bed.

Chapter Twenty-Four

Layla

"How are you not nervous? It's *my* family and I'm freaking out."

We just landed in Brownsville for our Spring Break visit and we're waiting to deboard the plane. I'm ready to bounce out of my skin. Yes, I'm excited to see my family, and I want them to meet Teagan, but I'm also worried they'll be too much for him. Even though he's proven over and over again that he can handle anything and anyone, no matter the level of their energy. He welcomes the challenge of meeting new people and figuring out what makes them tick. He's genuinely interested in the people he strikes up conversations with, giving them his full attention. That's probably why the kids he works with love him so much.

Love.

He loves me. I love him.

Trading those words that day was better than what I had ever pictured. I was so worried that I wouldn't feel the butterflies and overwhelming surge of emotions since he'd said it while drunk the first time, but they were there in force. I had no idea that actually saying *I love you* would elevate our relationship. We were already in such a great place. Our honeymoon phase, so to speak.

I thought we couldn't keep our hands off of each other before, but that doesn't hold a candle to how we are now. Somehow we manage to keep our PDA to a minimum when we're with our friends, or in public, but once we're alone, all bets are off. We've fucked or made love on every surface in my house. The stamina of my Irishman is otherworldly. When our bodies are spent, we still find ways to be touching in some capacity.

"Why?" Teagan asks from the seat beside me, bringing me back to the present.

"Because!" I exclaim, pulling my hair over my shoulder and anxiously twirling a strand around my finger. "You're finally going to see what I mean about them being over the top and I don't want it to scare you away."

"Layla," he says, pulling my hands from my hair. "There's not a damn thing that's going to scare me away from you. We've talked about this."

Releasing a heavy sigh, I drop my forehead to his shoulder. "I know. I'm just so anxious."

His lips press into my hair. "You worried they won't like me, Cailín?"

A chuckle escapes me at the ridiculous idea. "No. They're going to love you. I think maybe I'm not prepared for all the comments they'll aim at me. The teasing will be relentless."

"Ah, love," he croons. "Don't you know I'm a goalie? I'll block every shot that comes your way."

He means what he's saying, but I know he's also trying to lighten my mood. What he doesn't realize is that those words are exactly what I needed to hear. After years of my family thinking they know what's best for me, I've never had a single person come to my defense. No one to jump in front of me and take the hits. But here's Teagan, ready and willing to do just that.

Lifting my head, I place a kiss to his jaw. "Thanks, babe. I love you."

166

He grins, that boyish smile lighting up his entire face, then leans in to whisper against my ear, "I love you, Cailín. And I quite like the sound of you calling me *babe*. Almost as much as I like it when you call me Papí."

This makes me shiver and regret that we weren't able to become a part of the Mile High Club.

"We're not going to be able to share a bed, you know?"

He jerks his head back, eyes wide. "Why the feck not? I thought your Mam was all about a healthy sex life, and that, lass, is something we absolutely have."

He wags his eyebrows, making me laugh.

"Yeah, yeah, but talking about it and being in the same house with it is a different story. Not to mention that my Abuela is very traditional and would make me go to confession. Actually, she'll probably have me do that anyway."

Teagan groans as he runs a hand over his face. "So you're telling me that I won't get to sleep with you the entire time we're there? That's five days, Layla. I'm not sure if I can make it that long."

"Ah, Papí," I purr, placing my hand on his thigh and slowly sliding it up the inside of his leg. "Just because we won't be *sleeping* together doesn't mean we won't be fucking."

* * *

"Mija!" Mami squeals with delight the moment she sees me walk through the airport doors.

I tried to tell her we'd rent a car and meet them at the house, but she wouldn't hear of it, insisting she had to come to pick us up. I was looking forward to driving Teagan around Brownsville though, prolonging our arrival at my childhood home.

"¡Hola Mami!" I greet her with a lingering hug.

As crazy as she makes me, there's something about being hugged by your mother - especially after going without seeing her for so long. She holds me tightly, brushing a hand over my hair before pulling back and holding my shoulders.

"Oh, hijita, it's so good to see you! You look so good!" She glances over my shoulder, presumably at Teagan, then back at me, wagging her eyebrows. "He's good for you, no?"

I hide my face in my hands, but I can hear Teagan chuckling as he comes up behind me, placing his hand on my lower back as he extends the other to my mother.

"Mrs. Diaz, it's lovely to meet you finally."

"Oh, and he's so polite too! No need for formalities, Teagan. You can call me Raquel. Thank you for bringing my daughter home for a while. It's been so long since we've seen her."

Rolling my eyes, I open my mouth to give her the same talk I give her every other time she brings this up, but Teagan slides closer, angling himself toward me, and says, "Ach, to be sure, but thank god travel works both ways, yeah? You lot are closer distance-wise than my family is. My parents would only love to be as close as you all are to Layla. They'd probably be visiting a few times a year."

I watch Mami's brow furrow as she processes this information, and then her gaze flicks to me. "I thought North Carolina was bad. I can't imagine being across the ocean from you, mija."

Teagan catches my eye and winks, saying without words that he's just blocked the first shot. The relief from not having to argue with my mother is palpable - a weight lifted from my shoulders. I grin back at him and mouth my thanks.

* * *

After retrieving our bags from the conveyor belt, we quickly loaded everything into the white Honda Pilot my father surprised Mami with on their anniversary. She'd been driving around the same old minivan since Rafael was born. She never complained, but when Papá revealed the new SUV to her, she jumped up and down, shrieking with delight and crying the happiest of tears. She now refers to it as her baby and is very, *very* strict about eating or drinking anything in it.

When Teagan opened the door for me to climb into the front passenger seat, Mami *ooh'd* and *ahhh'd* over how chivalrous he was. She didn't see the way he slapped my ass before I sat down though...or the way I palmed his dick through his jeans while she rounded the front of the car.

The drive to my family home from the airport is short, which means we're pulling into the driveway of the brown and tan brick house within no time. I think I'll always feel a sense of comfort here, even with my parents' antics and wild siblings. I know that, at any time, I can walk through that front door without invitation and know it's home.

Their first house was a tiny two-bedroom structure that they rented from Papá's uncle. It was cheap and they were young, so they didn't care. Once they found out Marcos was on the way, they knew they'd need something bigger eventually, as they wanted multiple children, so they skimped and saved, working two jobs a piece, to save up for the down payment.

Nearly every day, Mami would drive through a specific neighborhood, looking at all of the houses, knowing this was where they'd raise their family. The day they reached their goal, fortune was on their side as a house she had her eye on had gone up for sale. Not only was it the exact size they wanted, but it was priced just below what they were looking for. It needed a little TLC, but neither of my parents were afraid of a little hard work, so they fixed what needed to be fixed, remodeled what needed to be remodeled, and made it into the place we call home.

Mami puts the car in park, shuts off the engine, and turns to me. "I am under no illusion that the two of you don't share a bed, but you know how your Abuelos feel about sex before marriage. To keep them from sending us all to purgatory, I've put you in your old room mija, and Teagan is in Marcos'. I don't care what you do after lights out, just don't get caught."

Teagan chuckles in the backseat, but I'm about to burn to ash in embarrassment. Why I'm surprised that my mother would say such a thing, I'll never know. This is par for the course as far as she's concerned.

"Now, your Papá and Abuelo won't be home for another hour or so, but Jaz and Cori are inside with Abuela. They're getting set up to make tamales tomorrow."

I glance back at Teagan, who grins and winks at me, making my face heat again.

It's going to be five very long days.

Chapter Twenty-Five

Teagan

Layla wasn't kidding when she said her family is huge. After being introduced to her twin sisters, I was greeted warmly by her grandmother, who pinched my cheek and called me *guapo*. She's tiny in stature but makes up for it with her quick wit. Her eyes are constantly taking in her surroundings, tucking away information that she probably plans to use later as fuel to roast her family members.

Her brother, Rafael, was next to arrive. He looks more like Layla and their mother, with a rounded face and straight black hair. He's shorter than I am, but formidable. The bloke clearly spends time at the gym. He doesn't say much, but when he does, it's concise and thoughtful. Prying any information from him is nearly impossible. In the two hours I've been here, all I've learned is that he's twenty-four, plays center midfield for Austin FC, and still lives at home when he's not on the road.

There's a lull in the conversation for the first time since arriving. Layla and I are perched on the forest-green loveseat in front of the bay of windows facing the front yard. My arm is draped across the back of it, while she's nestled into my side. Across from us on the matching sofa sit her mother, grandmother, and Rafael. The twins, Cori and Jaz, are scrunched together in a brown leather recliner, busy on their phones.

"So tell me, Teagan," Raquel says, breaking the silence. "How do you like working with kids?"

Layla tenses beside me, so I pull her closer, giving her shoulder a gentle squeeze. "Aye, I love it. They're a great group. We recently finished up a segment on basketball, but are getting ready to get back into football, which is a relief. Basketball isn't my thing. I'm rubbish at it."

This earns an easy chuckle from the family and Layla starts to relax. It's only temporary though because the next question has her clenching her fists and looking down at her lap.

"Do you want a family someday?"

Cutting right to the chase then.

"Sure," I say honestly. I won't add fuel to the fire but I'll be as truthful as possible. "If and when the time is right. I'm in no rush though. There's a lot of life to live before bringing wains into the world, yeah? I'm only a young boyo, after all."

"How old are you?" One of the twins - I haven't figured out who's who yet- asks, glancing up from the screen in her hands.

"Just twenty-seven, lass."

"¡Ay! ¡Veintisiete!" Raquel exclaims. "Layla and her brothers were barely out of the toddler stage when I was that age! Surely you want niños before you're thirty?"

"Mami…" Layla warns.

I mentally brace myself for the retort I can see coming.

"What, mija? You're nearly twenty-four. If the two of you are planning on babies, you better get started soon."

"Actually," I interject, "I read an article recently from a medical journal

172

stating that they no longer consider age thirty to be the threshold for fertility issues anymore. In fact, a large majority of women are waiting until their thirties so they can establish themselves in their careers, providing a more financially stable environment for their wains. I think this is amazing. Good for the women taking charge of their lives and bodies." I lift my hand, hoping to emphasize what I say next. "Now, I realize I'm privileged as a white male, but I just don't understand the mindset of women being only for breeding. You lot aren't livestock, am I right?"

It's so quiet you could hear a pin drop. Most would be uncomfortable in this situation, but I've never had a problem speaking my mind. Respectfully, of course.

"Well, when you put it that way..." Raquel says thoughtfully.

"*Nieta.*"

Layla whips her head up finding her grandmother looking directly at her sternly.

"When I was your age, I didn't have the options you do. I love your Abuelo, and wouldn't trade our family for anything, but had I been given the freedom, I would have gone to college before having my babies."

"Mamá!" Raquel gasps at her mother's confession, eyes wide in astonishment, but the older lady only shrugs and pats her daughter's leg placatingly.

Rafael is smirking and the twins are staring open-mouthed at their grandmother. Glancing at Layla, I can tell she's holding back tears. The tip of her nose has taken on a ruddy hue like when she blushes, and there's moisture pooling along her lower lids. I'm racking my brain trying to find a way out of this because I know the last thing she wants to do is cry in front of her family, but I'm saved by the sound of the front door swinging open and feet strolling in the entryway.

"Is my Layla here?" A booming voice sounds and seconds later a tall man rounds the corner of the dividing wall, arms spread wide, with a huge grin spread over his face. His eyes immediately lock on Layla. "There's my princesita!"

Layla gets to her feet immediately and goes to her father, letting him fold her into his arms in a bear hug. The resemblance between him and her brother, Marcos, is uncanny. They both have the same angular face with a straight nose, pronounced brows, and black, curly hair.

"Hola Papá," she murmurs, squeezing him back.

He looks over her head at me, a welcoming smile stretching over his face. "This must be Teagan."

Layla pulls away, peeking at me over her shoulder with a wink. "Oh him? No, that's Rowan."

"The hell I am." I glower at her, hoping she reads the promise of retribution in my eyes.

Giggling, she returns her attention to her dad, grinning broadly. "Sí, Papá. This is Teagan O'Brien, my boyfriend."

Standing, I cross the space in a couple of strides, extending my hand toward the main man in Layla's life. "Nice to meet you, sir."

"Roberto, please," he says, clasping his hand with mine, no sign of animosity or dominance in his grip. "It's nice to meet you too, Teagan. Looks like you've been taking good care of my baby girl."

"Aye, that's the goal." He doesn't need to know *all* of the ways I take care of his daughter.

An older gentleman shuffles out from behind Roberto, white bushy brows raised in surprise as he looks me over. Clearly I'm not what he was expecting his granddaughter to bring home.

"Hello, sir. Pleasure to meet you." I hold my hand out for him to shake, but instead of the customary greeting, he traps my hand between both of his. I can feel the calluses he earned from years of hard labor as he built a life for his family. The wrinkles from age and sun mingle with scars he's acquired from what I can only hope is from working and not violence incurred during their immigration.

Layla gave me a brief rundown of her family history before arriving in her hometown. Having been born and raised in Mexico, they didn't venture to the States until they were well into adulthood. During that time, it was exceptionally daunting to make the trek across the border as many Americans accused them of stealing their jobs and taking advantage of the welfare system. Never mind the fact that the jobs they were accepting were the ones Americans didn't want because of low wages and social status. While I am an immigrant of sorts, I'm not a minority, so my transition was smooth sailing, whereas theirs was considerably more challenging. More often than not, Mexican migrants were victims of muggings because attackers knew that undocumented individuals would refrain from reporting the violence because of their unauthorized status.

As Layla's grandfather holds my hand in his, he examines it. Looking for what, I don't know, but he must have found something satisfactory because he scans my face, holding my gaze for a moment before nodding. He turns to Layla and says something in Spanish causing her eyes to widen and lips curl into a sweet smile. When she glances back at me, I give her an inquisitive look, but she just shakes her head.

* * *

"We're going to the rodeo tonight. I hope you brought your boots, Teagan."

Marcos showed up not long after Layla's father and grandfather and greeted me like an old friend, pulling me in for a one-armed hug and a whispered, "you ready to run for the hills yet?" I shook my head, laughing, because while the Diaz family is loud and lively, they're also kind and involved. None of the conversations have felt forced or awkward, aside from Layla's mom telling us to have babies, and even that was tolerable for me. Layla wasn't amused. She's apologized repeatedly for her mom's behavior.

"Erm...I didn't bring any boots with me. Just my runners. Those will work, yeah?"

Marcos wedges himself on the sofa between his mother and grandmother, earning him a playful slap on the arms from each of them.

"Sure," he says with a shrug. "You ever been to a rodeo, Teag? There's a reason we wear cowboy boots, and it's not just to look good."

For the first time since arriving, I'm actually feeling slightly nervous. Growing up on a sheep farm has given me enough experience to know to watch your step around the livestock, but I'm gathering that a rodeo in Texas isn't even remotely close to raising sheep in Ireland.

"So, what you're saying is that I need to go shopping?"

Chapter Twenty-Six

Layla

I've been sitting in our backyard with my sisters waiting for Teagan to finish getting ready for the last half-hour. It's unusual for him to take this long. He was a good sport about Marcos' teasing, but I could tell he was feeling apprehensive. I tried to get us out of going, but my parents managed to convince us to accompany them to the rodeo tonight. As a teen, I always enjoyed going, but taking my Irishman to a Texas rodeo seems so out of place. He's a farm boy, not a cowboy.

"What's taking him so long?" I mutter to myself, but the twins hear me and start giggling. I glare suspiciously at them. "What?"

"Nothing," they sing in unison.

"¡Mentirosas! You forget that I know your tells. Fess up."

Before they can respond, the screen door squeaks open and we all turn in our patio chairs, a collective gasp spilling from our mouths.

Ó—ra—le.

Teagan in a cowboy hat is something I didn't know I needed until right this minute. When he told me he was going to talk my brothers into lending them one of theirs, I thought he was joking. The white hat sits securely on his head, strands of his brown hair curling beneath the rim. He didn't just stop at the hat though. Clad in black jeans that hug him perfectly, a huge, silver belt buckle, and a trim-fit, short-sleeved denim shirt that is unbuttoned enough to show off the smattering of hair on his chest. And boots! He's wearing cowboy boots! He looks hot as fuck and I'm really regretting that we agreed to go with my family tonight. If I could work out a way for us to stay—or to arrive later—without raising suspicion, I'd do it.

Pinching the brim of the hat, he winks before nodding his head. "Ma'am."

En la madre. I'm speechless.

The silence stretches and he starts to fidget nervously, a flush creeping up his neck. "Um...is it too much?"

"No," I say in a rush, standing to move toward him. "It's just a...uh...shock to the system."

His smile falls and it breaks my heart.

"No!" I cup his cheeks in my hands. "You look amazing, Teagan."

"Yeah?"

A grin slowly spreads across his handsome face, so I step closer and murmur just for his ears, "*Sí, Papí.* Makes me wish we were alone."

Blazing green eyes meet mine and I forget where we are until someone clears their throat behind him.

"Layla." My brother, Marcos, steps next to Teagan, throwing an arm around his shoulders. "I'd tell you two to get a room, but the last thing I want to think about is my little sister and her guero bumping uglies."

"For fucks sake, Marc!" I shove his face with my hand, feeling Teagan slide his around my waist. "Bumping uglies? Really?"

My brother laughs and pokes my side, making me squeal.

"Would you rather I say, 'My sister and her boyfriend fucking like rabbits.'?"

"Ugh. ¡Eres un cochino! I'd rather you just keep your mouth shut, cabrón."

Teagan is watching in amusement as my brother and I exchange insults like we did as kids. Only now, we can actually say the bad words we once had to whisper when our parents were nearby.

Chuckling, Teagan steps around me, encircling my waist with both arms from behind. "Alright, Cailín. Let's get out of here before you and Marcos start a war."

Marcos grins at us mischievously and says, "That's right, Teag. Keep your woman in check."

"Oh, you did not!" I yell, lunging for him, but Teagan's arms tighten around me and my stupid brother darts back inside, laughing like a hyena.

Teagan

I've never been to a rodeo, but the energy in the air is intoxicating. The cheering crowd and the screams of people on the carnival rides mixed with fresh turned dirt from thundering hooves, and the various food vendors scattered around us is a hit to all of my senses.

I love it.

The fact that I'm here with Layla and her family, who have welcomed me into the fray with open arms, makes it that much sweeter. When her brothers started slagging me about my lack of rodeo attire, I asked them to get me set up, without telling Layla. They were only delighted to be keeping a secret from her. Somehow her little sisters got involved and now I'm, as they say, *vaquerito guapo*.

Layla's reaction was confirmation of that. After keeping her from murdering her brother, she decided she wasn't dressed right and needed to change. I thought she looked fucking gorgeous in her tank top and tight jeans, but when she came back outside in a dusty pink dress, I was instantly regretting the Wranglers I put on. I drank her in, my gaze traveling over her, from those dark, loose tresses to the brown cowgirl boots with flowers embroidered on them, spending an extended amount of time appreciating the low neckline, off-the-shoulder capped sleeves, and slightly flared skirt resting mid-thigh. When she sauntered my way, I had to remind myself that her teenage sisters were only feet from us. Had we been alone, the list of things I wanted to do to her...

"What do you want to do first?"

My eyes snap to Layla, bringing me back to the present. She's looking at me expectantly and it takes me a minute to realize she's not talking about my dirty list.

"Um...you pick. What's the typical order of business here?"

She smiles softly and laces her fingers with mine. "Come on, let's start with something to eat."

I let Layla lead me through the different vendors, immersing myself in her world. As anxious as she gets around her family, she seems in her element here. Bantering with her siblings, waving and smiling to people she's known for years. When she turns to look over her shoulder, it's like watching a slow-motion scene in a movie. A tendril of raven hair drifts over her face and she beams radiantly at me, a dimple popping in her left cheek. The urge to draw her to me and kiss the life out of her is so strong, I can barely stand it.

We decide on a street taco stand, then grab a funnel cake from the vendor next to it. The fried food options are endless and I know I'll be paying for it at practice next week. Finding an empty picnic table, we sit on the bench, straddling it to face each other. Layla lifts a piece of the fried batter and powdered sugar drifts down to dust the swell of her breasts. She must catch me staring because I hear her, very pointedly, clear her throat. My eyes dart up and I know I'm busted by the raised eyebrow and smug smile she's giving me. Holding my gaze, she takes a finger and swipes it through the white powder before bringing it to her mouth. She sucks the sugar off, releasing it with a pop. I swallow thickly, willing my cock to calm the feck down, when she makes a second sweep and holds her finger out in offering. Without breaking eye contact, I lean in, slowly closing my lips and twirling my tongue around it before gently biting her. Those coffee eyes flare as she lifts her other hand and snatches the hat from my head, placing it on her own.

Chuckling, I tilt my head to the side, making a show of inspecting her, before giving a resolute nod. "Aye, that looks better on you anyway."

Layla bats her lashes then bends her head forward to whisper seductively, "Remind me to tell you the rule of the cowboy hat later."

"Yes, ma'am," I agree wholeheartedly.

The rest of the evening is spent watching small children chase piglets around with flyswatters, barrel racing, bull riding, and carnival rides. I can honestly say that it's the most fun I've had in ages. I'm completely taken aback when Layla's mum links her arm through mine and leads me toward a small stage where a band is playing and people are dancing.

"Do you know how to line dance, Teagan?"

"Aye," I say with a laugh. "But I don't think your line dancing and mine are quite the same."

"¡Bueno, pues You're going to learn."

Raquel drags me out to the dance floor and begins showing me the steps to the dance. After salsa lessons with Layla, I catch on quickly. We dance through a few songs before my lass takes her mother's place. There's just something about watching her body move, the way the round curve of her arse sways with the music. When the music switches to a slower song, she starts to make her way off the floor, but I catch her, twirling her back into my arms. She starts to protest but gives up the fight when I take her hand with one of mine and slide the other to the small of her back.

"I'm not done dancing with you yet, Lovely."

Tipping her head back so she can see me over the brim of the hat, she smirks. "What if I'm done dancing with you?"

Her words are innocent, but for a shadow of a moment, I'm pitched back to when Ashley dumped me. I wasn't ready to end things, but she was. She'd already ended our relationship when she cheated, I was just too blind to see the signs. "Hey," she says softly, her palm cupping my jaw. "You okay?"

I blink, coming back to the present, and give her a reassuring smile. "Aye, sorry. Just had a moment."

Her brows furrow and she brushes the pad of her thumb over my cheekbone. "Want to talk about it?"

"I'm okay, promise. Just…" I start but shake my head. There's no point in even bringing this up because Layla isn't Ashley. "Nah, never mind."

"Teagan." She presses her body closer to mine, eyes pleading. "I need you to talk to me or I'm going to assume the worst."

Softening my features, I hold her tighter, and fess up. "The way you said that, about being done dancing with me? It just triggered a memory from when Ashley dumped me. I don't miss her in the slightest, but it had me briefly wondering if there would be a time when you were done with me too."

"Baby," she whispers. "I'm not…"

"No, I know. You're not her." As awkward as I feel, I make it a point to look her in the eyes when I say, "Just, do me a favor and let me know if your feelings start to change, yeah? Even just a little? I'd rather know so I can try to fix the issue, rather than have you come to me months later saying you're completely done."

Layla holds my gaze for a long moment while we dance, then nods. "I promise. But Teag, you have to do the same. I want this to work just as much as you do, so let's make it our goal to always be open and honest with each other, okay?"

The way she's looking at me, so earnestly, makes my eyes prick with emotion. Our chemistry is off the charts, it's true. I could spend every hour of every day buried between her legs, or with my mouth on her body, but it's more than a desire for physical release. The love I have for her runs so deep that words aren't enough. Only actions can properly convey the magnitude of my feelings. I told her I loved her, and I meant it, but I can see it all so clearly now. Before, it was like a cloudy day but I could see fine. Then the clouds parted, allowing the sun to break through, exposing everything hidden in the shadows. Layla is that beacon and I'll intercept anything that attempts to dim her light.

We've paused, standing still in the middle of the makeshift dance floor. Removing my hand from her back, I take the hat from her head, just so I can press a soft kiss to her mouth.

"Aye. You have my word."

Chapter Twenty-Seven

Teagan

By the time we get back to Layla's family home, it's after midnight. Rafael and Marcos decided to stay out and head to a local bar for a nightcap, while the rest of us returned to the house. Layla's parents bade us goodnight and the twins locked themselves in their room, leaving Layla and me to either go to our separate rooms or...not.

We choose the latter.

Leaving our boots by the door, Layla leads me into her room, quietly shutting the door and locking it behind us. I sit on the edge of her bed and let my eyes roam from the top of the cowboy hat to her now bare feet.

"C'mere, lass."

In a few steps, she's standing at my knees. Widening my legs, I bury a fist into the fabric of her skirt and pull her closer. Slowly Layla straddles me, her legs sinking into the bed. My palms immediately go to her thighs, coasting up under her dress. She leans in, giving me a chaste kiss before settling over my lap.

"Are you going to tell me the rule for the cowboy hat now?"

"Whoever wears the hat," She pauses to place a hand on top of the hat. "Rides the cowboy." She rolls her luscious body, grinding over my belt buckle.

"Fuck," I growl out, my head falling back. "Don't you ever take that hat off."

Rocking her hips again, a whimper escapes her mouth. I press a kiss to the exposed skin of her chest, thanking my lucky stars that she chose a low-cut dress.

"Ride me, sweetheart," I mutter against her soft skin.

With one hand holding the hat in place, she braces the other on my shoulder and grinds over the buckle. The thought of her getting herself off on it has me so hard it's painful, but I'll be damned if I stop her. So I grip her hips with both hands, raising my own to give her better access. Her eyes snap closed and she throws her head back, working herself faster.

"That's a good lass," I murmur against her neck. "Keep going."

"Teagan," she gasps. "I'm close."

"Aye. Come for me, Cailín. Make a mess on this buckle."

Her chest is heaving, those gorgeous tits bobbing in my face. Her nipples are peaking through the fabric of her dress, and since my hands are busy, I bite one through the fabric. Layla shatters, crying out softly so as not to wake her family.

"That's it, Lovely," I grunt against her breast. "Give me another."

"I can't. I can't," she pants, head still thrown back, hair flowing past my knees.

"Yes, you can." I pull her flush against me, snaking my hand around the curve of her arse until I find her soaking wet pussy. I thrust two fingers inside her roughly, finger fucking her like I wish I was doing with my cock. My hips snap up to meet her, over and over reflexively. Christ, I want to be inside her.

184

"Oh god! Teagan!"

"That's it, baby," I praise her. "I want to feel this pretty pussy come all over my fingers. Come on, give it up, Layla."

"Fuck!" she gasps as that second wave crests.

"Such a good fucking lass," I grunt, grinding harder.

Moaning, she slumps against me, her forehead pressed against mine. I don't give her a chance to catch her breath before I'm standing to turn, placing her gently on the bed, her hair fanning out around her. I kiss her long and deep before getting to my feet. She watches me as I start unbuttoning my shirt, tucking that bottom lip between her teeth while I shuck the fabric off. My fingers reach for the belt, the buckle wet from Layla's arousal. Pulling it from the loops, I bring the metal to my mouth and lick it slowly.

"Teagan," she breathes, her eyes filled with wanton desire. "I need you."

I drop the belt to the floor and remove my pants and briefs. Taking my cock in my hand, I stroke it lazily.

Layla whines and moves her hands to cup her breasts. "God, I love watching you do that."

My eyebrows lift in surprise. "Yeah? Does it get you wet, Layla? Watching me fuck my hand, knowing that this," I start pumping faster, "is because of you?"

She nods, biting that lip again.

"Show me," I order. "Take off everything and let me see you."

Layla sits up, pulling the dress over her head. She quickly removes the thin bra and shimmies out of her knickers before stretching herself back on the bed. I feel ravenous watching her snake her fingertips up her stomach to circle her nipples. She pinches them roughly before roaming back down. I stand there, mesmerized, as she spreads her legs wide, revealing her glistening sex. A delicate finger feathers over her clit before sinking into where I want to be.

Groaning, I slow my pumping hand and tell her, "You need to tell me right now where you want me to come, Layla, because I won't last much longer watching you do that. I can fill you up or I can paint your body with it."

"In me," she blurts out quickly. "I need you in me, *Papi*."

"Thank fuck."

That's all the direction I need before I'm climbing on the bed and slamming my cock into her heat. I fuse my mouth to hers to swallow the noises I know she makes when I fuck her roughly. I should probably keep it nice and easy so we don't risk waking her family, but there's something enticing about testing the limits with her. She'd be embarrassed if her family heard us, but the idea of the world knowing that *I'm* the one making her scream? It makes me *feral*.

Abruptly I pull out of her.

"What are you..." she starts, but I grab her and flip her over.

"Hands and knees, Cailín."

She obeys instantly and I fill her again, pumping a few times before snaking my hand around her and pulling her up so that her back is flush with my chest. I cup her tits with both hands, squeezing them firmly and plucking her nipples.

"Ay Dioscito santo" Layla gasps, the chant falling from her lips as I slam into her. *"Que rico"*

Banding an arm under her breasts, I bring the other up and wrap my hand around her throat, tipping her head back. I don't restrict her airways, but I hold her firmly while I continue fucking her.

"Are you going to come for me again, Layla?" I growl into her ear and she nods.

"Yes, oh God, yes."

My hand darts from her rib cage, reaching her clit and pinching it. Her body goes rigid as her third release rockets through her. The way her pussy clamps around my cock at this angle sets off my own orgasm and I bury my face into her neck to muffle the strangled noise coming from my own throat. I come so hard, my vision tunnels.

Collapsing to the bed, I roll us so we're face to face, and drape my arm over Layla's waist to drag her closer. With a sated smile, she kisses me tenderly. We don't speak, just settle into the bliss of the most explosive sex we've had yet. Every time we're together is passionate and mind-blowing, but this time felt like *more*. Maybe it was the realization that I don't just *love* Layla, but I'm inescapably *in love* with her. She's my endgame, the one I want to spend every waking and sleeping moment with for the rest of my life. I want to be the one that encourages and empowers her to do what makes her happy and be what she wants to be, rather than living by what others expect of her. One day—when and if it's what she wants—I hope to marry her and have a family. But if she never wants to take those steps, I'd be perfectly content just to be in her presence.

Layla's breathing deepens as she drifts off to sleep, her long lashes brushing the tops of her cheekbones. The air conditioner kicks on causing goose flesh to pebble her skin, so I pull the blanket over us. I should sneak out and back to my room now, but I don't want to let her go just yet.

"I love you, *mo chroi*," I whisper into her hair.

Chapter Twenty-Eight

Layla

"The coast is clear," I whisper when I duck my head back into my room.

Teagan fell asleep in my bed, and considering Abuela tends to be here early on tamale days, I have to make sure she's not lurking in the hallway when he sneaks out. When I turn around, he's pulling his jeans over his hips and I get momentarily mesmerized by the way his muscles flex and bunch. He catches me staring and smirks.

"Unless you want your Abuela to hear me fuck you against the door, you better stop looking at me like that, Lovely."

"Your filthy mouth..." Shaking my head, I stoop to pick up his shirt and toss it in his face.

"Ach, you love my filthy mouth and you know it."

He's right. I do.

"Get out of here. I don't want to incur her wrath or be sent to Confession."

He reaches for the doorknob, still shirtless, while planting a quick kiss on my lips. Just as he pulls it open, I stretch an arm across.

"Put your shirt on! What if someone else sees you leaving my room half-clothed?"

"You just said the coast is clear." He reminds me. "It'll be fine. I'm just stepping across the hall."

"Teagan," I hiss as he yanks the door open. Standing there, with her arms crossed over her chest, stands my Abuela, eyebrow raised.

Shit.

"Abuela! Hi! Teagan was just…" My face flames in mortification.

"¡Basta! I can see what he was *just doing* and you should be ashamed of yourselves!"

"Ah, Mrs…" Teagan starts, hurriedly yanking his shirt on.

She cuts him a scathing look that stops him in his tracks. When Abuela gives that look, everyone stops.

"Clearly, your mother didn't teach you correctly. If you're going to sneak a boy out of your room, you always check twice before shoving him out the door! I expected better."

Wait…

"I'm sorry, what?" I ask dumbfounded. Mami has always ingrained it in me that Abuela is the one to watch out for.

"You better be glad it was me, and not your Abuelo, that found you! He would be carting you off to the church faster than you can blink." She eyes Teagan appreciatively, a small smile stretching across her face, before looking back at me. "Otherwise, good for you, cariño. Muy guapo."

With that, she scurries down the hallway toward the kitchen, leaving Teagan and I gaping at each other in disbelief.

"So…" he says slowly. "Does this mean I can share a bed with you for the rest of the trip?"

Snorting, I push him into the hallway and close the door in his face. God, I love him. And against my better judgment, I've loved having him here in Texas with my family. It hasn't been quite as horrible as I originally thought.

He fits so perfectly, weaving himself in seamlessly. He gets along with my brothers, especially Raf, like he's known them for ages. He's kind to my sisters, listening to their teenage chatter with interest and making them feel seen. He and my Papá spent more than a couple of hours discussing how big corporations are detrimental to small business owners. Other than when Teagan reminds her that I'm my own person, Mami gets along great with him. Last night at the rodeo, he patiently listened to Abeulo describe the rodeos he grew up attending while asking questions. And clearly Abuela loves him. When she told him she expected his help with tamales, he didn't bat an eye, just agreed to do whatever she needed of him. I honestly think he's more excited about it than she is.

Quickly throwing on a hoodie over my leggings, I toss my hair up in a messy bun, and swipe some deodorant under my arms before stepping out of my room. After using the bathroom and brushing my teeth, I pad into the kitchen, following the smell of coffee and chorizo. I hear Mami's laughter mingling with the deep timber of Rafael's voice, and hope he's making his special Chilaquiles. He has some secret ingredient that he refuses to tell any of us. It doesn't matter how many times I watch him make Chilaquiles, I never figure it out. As I round the corner, I see that it's not just my mother and brother congregating, but also Teagan and Abuela. The latter are sitting at the kitchen table looking through an old family recipe book. My heart warms watching her talk him through the process of making tamales. He's completely invested.

"Buenos días, mija," Mami greets me and Teagan's eyes lift in my direction. He winks before giving his attention back to Abuela.

"Buenos días." I shuffle over and kiss her cheek before making a beeline for the coffee bar where mugs, creamer, and sugar are waiting. As I doctor my cup, I try to peek over Raf's shoulder. "Are those Chilaquiles, mi hermano preferido?"

"Hey!" He swats at me with a spatula and angles his body to shield what he's doing. "Keep that up and you won't get any, chaparrita. You know the rules."

"Oh come on, Raf! You can't be the only one to know the secret ingredient!

190

What happens if you die? Not only will we be mourning your loss, but we'll never have your Chilaquiles again?"

"Pretty much," he agrees. "Sucks to be you."

"What if you get married and have kids someday? Won't you want your children to pass it down for generations?" I'm being ridiculous, I know.

"Well, if I have kids, I'll worry about it then. Since that doesn't seem likely at the moment, you're SOL, Layla."

I stick my tongue out at him and lift my foot to kick him in the ass when I walk by. He reciprocates slapping my leg with the spatula that makes me yelp. Murmuring curses under my breath, I take my coffee to the table to see where Teagan and Abuela are in their tamales lessons.

"So, why do you soak the husks if you're just going to steam them?" I hear Teagan ask quietly.

"Soaking them makes it easier to fold them over the filling," Abuela tells him patiently.

"Yeah, makes sense. So after soaking them, we make the filling and the dough?"

Abuela confirms that he's correct with a nod and beaming smile. When he grins back at her, she actually blushes, proving that no one is excluded from Teagan's charm.

"Which filling are we making for the tamales?" I ask, sipping my coffee.

"Red chile pork, salsa verde chicken, and bean. I made them yesterday, so all we have to do is fill and steam."

"And eat them!" Marcos comes waltzing through the back door with his sunglasses on, a clear sign that he's hungover, but still chipper. Which is par for the course as far as he's concerned - there's not much that gets my older brother down and out.

Mami slides from the bar stool she's been sitting on to kiss my brother hello before rinsing her coffee mug, then placing it in the dishwasher. Rafael hands her a plate of Chilaquiles before passing one to Marcos, who groans in thanks. I distinctly remember him telling me once that Chilaquiles are his go-to hangover food.

"*Gracias San Rafael.* If you weren't my brother, I'd kiss you," Marcos says, earning a disgusted look from him.

"Where did you two end up last night after the rodeo?" I question my brothers while filling plates for Abuela, Teagan, and myself.

Marcos, between mouthfuls of his breakfast, begins to tell us about a new bar he found downtown. "It's this weird cross between a honky tonk bar and a night club. There are two levels inside. The bottom is the bar with a dance floor and the top is like a VIP area, just not as swanky. And you don't have to be some rich *pendejo* to get in. You just have to pay a cover fee, let them slap a neon bracelet on you, and you're good to go. The best part is that they switch up the music themes every hour or so. When we got there it was two-stepping and square dancing, followed by Salsa hour, then that weird techno music they play at raves."

Oddly enough, the place sounds like a lot of fun. I enjoy dancing to various types of music, so I bet it would be a blast.

"Raf and I were thinking about going back tonight, actually. You two should join us." He points a finger at Teagan and me as I look at Rafael questioningly. That's not his scene, so I'm shocked that he went along with Marcos. He simply shrugs and goes back to eating.

"Yeah, maybe," I reply as I approach the table. "What do you think, Teag?"

When I set his plate down, I feel a hand wrap around the back of my knee, squeezing gently before I sit.

"Sounds deadly. Let's do it."

"Right on," Marcos says. "We're leaving around seven-thirty, so if you want to ride with us, be ready."

* * *

"If I eat one more tamal, I'm going to absolutely burst." Teagan reclines back in his chair, rubbing both hands on his belly.

"I told you to start with just one of each," I chastise him playfully.

"Aye, you did, Lovely. I should have listened, but they're all so good I couldn't stop. Especially those pork ones."

Those have always been my favorite too. Abuela's red sauce is the stuff of legends. However, unlike my brother, she isn't stingy with the recipe and ensured we all have a copy.

"Now it's time to dance them all off. Come on, guapo." I grab his hand and tug in an attempt to pull him from the chair.

Groaning, he stands and lets me lead him back to our rooms. "The idea of dancing right now is not appealing in the slightest. I think I'd rather take a nap. Can we do that?"

Giggling, I send him through the door to his room. "If you don't go, my brothers will never let you live it down, and I promise that's not something you want. Go get dressed while I fix my hair."

I take my time getting ready. With the rodeo, I wanted to look cute, but for tonight? Tonight's destination calls for something edgier. Using my flat iron, I straighten my hair until it's smooth before pulling it back into a tight, high ponytail. I know I'm going to get sweaty while dancing, so I apply light foundation and powder to make my skin look smooth and flawless. Foregoing blush, I brush some bronzer over my cheekbones just to highlight them. A neutral but shimmery eyeshadow, thin swipe of eyeliner, and lengthening mascara is all I do, but it's enough to make my normally boring brown eyes pop. And just because I know it will drive Teagan wild, I apply a bright red lipstick.

Rummaging through my suitcase, I dig out the outfit I purchased with a night like tonight in mind. I feel giddy just thinking about my Irishman's reaction when he sees it.

Chapter Twenty-Nine

Teagan

Jaysus, Mary, and Joséph and all the saints.

Layla prowls into the living room where I'm hanging out with her brothers and we all go silent. Starting from the top, my gaze does a slow descent of her body. She has her hair pulled back in a sleek ponytail and her make-up is subtle apart from those crimson lips. I get hung up on those for a moment before continuing to the black corset top that's pushed her breasts together and up so that they're nearly overflowing. She's paired it with black leather leggings and some red fuck-me heels. The only jewelry she has on are some large silver hoop earrings. I'm about to stand and pull her back to her room to show her just how much I enjoy this look when Marcos cuts in.

"What the fuck are you wearing, Layla? You can't go out in public like that!"

I'm instantly enraged that he has the audacity to try to dictate what she can and cannot wear, but this is one instance where she doesn't need me to fight her battle.

"First of all, *Marcos*, I can wear whatever I damn well please. Second, you are not my keeper. You may be my big brother, but you, and every other man on this planet, have *zero* say in the choices I make pertaining to my own body."

Scoffing, he turns to Rafael for support but doesn't find it. Raf gives him a disbelieving look and shakes his head in disappointment.

"What about you?" Marcos directs at me. "You're okay with your girl going out like this?"

Standing, I square my shoulders and move to Layla, kissing her cheek before sliding behind her and wrapping my arms around her middle. I look pointedly at her brother and say, "Aye, I am, but it doesn't matter what I say. She's right, mate. Her body, her decision. You'll do well to remember that with your lass."

Marcos' eyes narrow at me. He starts to puff up in indignation but deflates quickly when Layla steps out of my embrace and goes to him, curling a hand around his bicep. "Don't be a dick, Marcos. Let's go have a good time, okay? No one is going to mess with me while the three of you are around anyway if that's what you're worried about. Right Raf?" She looks to her other brother who, as usual, has kept quiet this whole time.

"Sí, chaparrita," he says with a wink. "But I don't think Teagan will be taking his hands off you the entire night, so there won't be any question about your status."

"Too right," I agree. My lass can wear whatever she wants, but I will make it known that Layla is *mine*.

* * *

The drive to the club is tense, despite my attempts to lighten the mood. I expected Layla to receive some slagging from Marcos but was surprised by his outburst. From the small amount of time I've spent with him, he's seemed pretty easygoing with a more progressive outlook, but maybe I've pegged him all wrong. Talking to Layla about it now is out of the question since he's currently sulking in the front seat.

After parking the car in the lot across the street, we make our way to the entrance where a decent-sized line has formed. The thump of the bass can be heard, but it doesn't give away what type of music they're currently playing. A group of guys around my age zero in on Layla, leering at her in a way that makes my jaw clench. I'm already holding her hand, but I release it to lay my arm over her shoulders once we reach the end of the line, drawing her closer while staring the wankers down. She must sense the tension in my body because she glances up at me with a questioning look.

Bending my head, I whisper in her ear, "Those tossers keep looking at you like that and I may have to go caveman on you just so they know you're spoken for."

A low, throaty laugh sounds from Layla before she turns inward and slides her hand up my chest to cup my jaw. Before I have a chance to register what's happening, she's kissing me. And it's not your casual shifting—this is full-on lobbing the gob with wide, open mouths, tongues fighting for dominance kiss. The hand not holding my face curls into my shirt, pulling me close. On instinct, my hands grip her hips then snake down to cup her arse. I'm about two seconds away from backing her into a dark alley when I hear someone clear their throat loudly.

"If you two are done tongue fucking each other, can we please move?"

Marcos is eyeing us with disgust when we pull apart. There's a large gap between us and the people we got in line behind, but the fuckers who thought to stare at my lass are no longer looking this way.

"Right, sorry, mate."

Securing Layla under my arm again, we move forward while Marcos grumbles to Rafael about having to pluck his eyes from his head after watching our public display. I'd feel the same if it were my sister, but I can't find it in me to give a single fuck if it means the rest of the world knows Layla is mine.

Once we've paid our cover charges and received our bracelets proving we're of the proper age to drink, we enter the club. I usher Layla in ahead of me, keeping a hand on her at all times. I'm surprised at how bright it is in here. Rather than the dark and hazy atmosphere that's common for nightclubs, it's dimmed just enough to be soft and moody. There are no fog machines or flashing lights, just a large dance floor in the middle of the room full of people line dancing to the country song ringing out. Along the outskirts of the space are tables and booths similar to how Pat has things set up at O'Nelly's. To the right of the entrance is the biggest bar top I've ever seen. It extends along the wall to the right before curving into an L-shape at the back wall. There are four bartenders - two men and two women - evenly spaced along the bar, all with their own fully stocked shelves.

It's amusing to see predominantly women grouped around the first bartender. He reminds me of the male version of Alicia with his jet-black hair, tight black t-shirt, and both well-muscled arms sleeved in tattoos. He knows exactly what he's doing with every smirk and wink if the full tip jar is any indication. The next bartender is a curvy lass with a high blonde ponytail who is just as popular, but the majority of her customers are men. She's clearly as skilled as the counterpart, leaning over the bar to speak to a patron, fully aware that he's looking down her low-cut shirt. She blows him a kiss when he drops a twenty-dollar bill in her tip jar. The other two bartenders are busy as well, but it appears to be only couples at these two stations.

"What are you two drinking tonight? The first round's on me," Rafael calls out over the music, surprising us both.

"You don't have to do that," Layla replies, but he holds up a hand to stop her.

"I know I don't, but I want to. If you don't tell me, then I'll just order you a PBR."

She gasps loudly before glaring at him. "You would not! You're a lot of things, Raf, but cruel isn't one of them. I'll take a Dos Equis with an extra lime."

"Thanks, mate," I tell him with a nod. "I'll have whatever you're having, as long as it's not tequila."

Layla bursts into a fit of giggles that has me regretting my words. Raf just raises a brow and looks between the two of us.

"Ah hell," I groan. "Let's just say tequila and I are not friends, yeah?"

Raf nods knowingly and saunters off toward the bar where a young, male Hispanic bartender is mixing drinks. He looks up as Raf approaches and a shy smile breaks across his face. Raf rubs a hand on the back of his neck while resting the opposite arm on the bar as he says something. The bartender starts blushing, and I catch Rafael running a single finger along the back of the man's hand.

Oh.

I start to ask Layla about it but remind myself that it's none of my damn business and doesn't change a fecking thing. As curious as I am, if he wants to discuss his love life with me, he will.

"Where'd Marcos run off to?" Layla asks suddenly, her head turning from one direction to another as her neck cranes, searching for him.

I follow her lead and begin to scan the crowd. After a moment, I spot him.

"There he is," I tell her, lifting a hand and pointing toward the stairs leading to the VIP level. He's following a young, brunette woman in a red dress, and although I can't hear him, it's evident he's pleading with her. They reach the top of the stairs and he grabs her hand, spinning her so their faces are inches apart. Even from this distance, I can sense the building tension. It looks like he's about to kiss her when a blonde walks through a VIP area straight to him. It's dim enough up there that I can't see her face, but something tickles my brain when she presses her body against his side and runs a hand down his arm. She says something that makes the brunette stiffen and Marcos whips his head toward the blonde, seething. She jerks back in alarm and literally spits in his face before stomping back to the room she came out of. Marcos wipes a hand over his face and hangs his head in defeat.

"Damn, that was brutal," I say with a wince.

Layla nods her head absently before turning to me. "Part of me feels bad for him but the other part of me says it serves him right for having a revolving door of women for so long. It's no wonder she doesn't trust him to continue a relationship after he moves. He can't even go to a bar without some past hookup or wannabe approaching him."

Rafael appears at our sides, holding a whiskey tumbler and two bottles of beer with lime wedges jutting out of the top. We thank him while keeping our eyes on the VIP area.

"What did I miss?" He asks, looking from us to where Marcos is descending the stairs.

I take a long pull from my beer before responding, "There was a confrontation with a couple of lasses that didn't end well."

"Yeah," Layla agrees. "Be prepared for a grumpy Marcos."

Raf groans, tossing back the rest of his drink. "I'll go get a bottle of Tito's."

Layla

"So that's the girl that's changed your life, huh? What's her name?"

I hadn't planned on asking Marcos about it, but as his little sister, it's my job to annoy him. He also deserves my nosiness after all the shit he's been giving Teagan and me. He's been sitting across from me, nursing a bottle of Tito's and pouting like a child.

"Layla," Raf mutters a warning under his breath.

"What? Everyone here saw that debacle take place. Acting like it didn't happen is stupid. And how else are we supposed to help our beloved brother if we don't get the details?"

Marcos groans as he leans forward and buries his face in his hands. I made him go to the bathroom and wash it with soap and water before he could have his liquor—germs are germs.

"Her name is Camila. I met her last year at a post-win after-party. She was friends with my date, but her boyfriend at the time knew the hosts. You could tell she was miserable, but she wasn't my problem, so I went about my night like the *pendejo* I am. After a couple of hours, I went outside to catch some air and she was sitting in a lounge chair by the pool, crying and holding her wrist with the opposite hand. Looking around, I didn't see anyone else, so I made my way over. Come to find out, her boyfriend was drunk off his ass and tried to get handsy with her. She kept telling him no,

HIS SPANISH ROSE

so he got mad, grabbed her wrist, and tried to lead her off somewhere. His grip was hard enough to leave bruises. I guess he caused a big enough scene that some party-goers intervened and hauled him off."

My heart hurts for this girl, and it reminds me of Norah's assault. I'm incredibly lucky to have never had anyone try to force me into sex, so I can't fully relate, but I can imagine how terrifying it would be.

"Anyway, I stayed out there with her, just talking about nothing, until she calmed down enough. I hadn't been drinking, so I offered to take her home. My date was too busy drinking and dancing to notice my absence, and I didn't care enough about her to stay. I ended up spending the night at her place—on her couch, Layla. Don't give me that look. She didn't feel safe, so I offered to stay just in case her asshole of a boyfriend showed up. There are a lot of other details to the story, but the shorter version is that we became friends, even though I was completely gone for Camila. It took months to get her to agree to go out with me, but eventually, she said yes and that's all I needed. We were happy, she felt safe, and I had my forever-date. Then CFC happened and you know the rest."

I'm momentarily swooning at the fact that my womanizing brother referred to a girl as his "forever-date". It's so unlike him that I'm forced to believe he really does love her.

"Okay, so who was the blonde?" Raf asks.

"Ugh," Marcos groans. "That's Ashley. We hooked up a few times over a year ago when she was in San Antonio for an internship. I was there for a conference and we met at the hotel bar we were both staying at. I thought it was done and over, but then she ended up moving down here this last summer thinking we were together."

Teagan suddenly chokes on his beer and we all look at him in alarm.

"Teag, are you okay?" I start thumping his back, even though I know that doesn't actually work.

Once he gets himself under control enough to speak, he sputters, "Please tell me her last name isn't Rogers."

I gasp loudly as my brain catches up and Marcos freezes, eyes wide as saucers. "Yeah, it is. How did you know that?"

200

"Ashley is my ex, mate."

I'm about two seconds away from puking at the thought of both my boyfriend and brother sleeping with the same girl.

Chapter Thirty

Teagan

No fecking way.

"What do you mean she's your ex?" Marcos looks at me like I'm speaking gibberish.

"Exactly what I said. She's my ex. Before Layla. We broke up because she cheated on me last February. With a bloke from Texas."

"No," he says, the blood draining from his face.

"I wish I was slagging you. Really."

I run my fingers through my hair, and even though the last thing I want is to see her, my eyes search the space for Ashley. Layla hasn't said a word, but I can feel how tense she is next to me. Honestly, I'm afraid to look at her. If I found out that she'd been with my sister's boyfriend before me, it would take a hot minute for me to come to terms with that.

"Fuck," Rafael breathes out then stands. "I'm going to get another bottle of Tito's."

Once he's gone, I brace myself and turn to Layla. Her eyes are closed, and it seems like she's practicing some deep breathing.

"Cailín," I murmur as I reach for her hand.

"Don't." She pulls her hand away and tucks it under her leg. "Just...give me a minute."

Her words aren't harsh, which is a relief, so I give her the space to process before turning back to Marcos. He hasn't moved an inch and his face is still pale.

"So. This is awkward, yeah?"

"Teagan, I'm so sorry, man. I had no idea she was with... She never said... I just assumed..." Marcos is grappling for words, but there's nothing for him to apologize for.

"Marcos, mate. Stop," I tell him. "You didn't do anything wrong. This is all on Ashley."

A small retching noise sounds from Layla and she whispers, "Oh my god. What if my brother's..." She absently stares at the table and makes a circle with her finger and thumb before poking a finger from the opposite hand through it. Her head pops up, dark brown eyes darting between my face and her brother's in alarm.

"Please, for the love of god, tell me that you used a condom. Every time. Both of you. Please. If I find out that you both stuck your dicks in the same girl without wrapping it up before Teagan and I..."

Marcos blanches.

Oh shite.

I hadn't even considered that, which makes me a right arsehole, but she makes a good point.

"Jaysus, no! 'Course I used a condom! You're the only one I've ever..."

"Do *not* finish that sentence, amigo," Marcos mumbles from behind the hands covering his face. "We may have unknowingly shared the same girl, but I do not want to hear about you and my sister."

Layla's back goes ramrod straight before a string of Spanish flies from her mouth so fast I can't even pretend to understand it. Whatever she's saying has him looking scarlet. Serves him right, honestly. He's been harping on about our sex life since the beginning, and while I don't blame him for anything with Ashley, it's *his* sex life that has us in this pickle to begin with.

Raf chooses that moment to reappear and by the smirk on his face, I'd bet money that he's loving every second of Layla eating the head off their brother. While his eyes dance between the two of them, he carefully sets some shot glasses on the table, proceeding to fill them with tequila. When he looks at me in silent question. I nod, grab a glass, and toss it back. After this little revelation, tequila might be what gets me through the rest of the night.

* * *

I'm not quite off my head, but I'm sporting a pretty good buzz. By some unspoken agreement, we all decided that taking shots was preferable to discussing Ashley, and made quick work of the bottle of Tito's. Layla clumsily rises from her seat, declaring she has to pee. When I offer to escort her, she says she's got it under control but to come looking for her if she's not back in five minutes. Her brothers don't see the wink she gives me, or the exaggerated sway of her hips, as she walks away. I'll give her seven just to make her sweat it out.

Until then, I talk football with Marcos and Rafael. We discuss the upcoming Women's World Cup and I tell them about little Gabriella from my after-school group. Marcos has connections to the US Women's National Team and offers to pull some strings to see if he can get at least one of them to make an appearance for my class.

"Go on! Are you serious?" I'm absolutely delighted not just for my kids, but for the facility as a whole. It would do wonders for us.

"No promises, obviously, but I'll make some calls this week." Marcos tosses back another shot of tequila before looking around. "Is Layla still in the bathroom?"

Ah fecking hell. I check the time on my phone. It's been exactly seven minutes.

"I'll go check on her. Need to visit the jacks myself." Without another word, I wind my way through the people milling around the bar and the dance floor until I find the hall with the bathrooms. My mission is easier when I discover they're single-person restrooms rather than multiple stalls. I find the ladies' room, and rap my knuckles on the door.

"Layla? You in there, Lovely?"

The lock clicks and the door opens a crack. My favorite brown eyes peek through before a hand darts out and grabs my wrist before pulling me inside. I chuckle as Layla shoves my back against the closed door and locks it as she starts placing kisses along my neck and jaw. Before I can even get my hands on her, she's palming my cock through my jeans. I groan at the sensation, my hips jerking in response. I cup her arse in my hands pulling her in.

"Mmmm. Took you long enough," she breathes into my ear, grinding against me.

"Sorry, love." Moving a hand to her neck, I find her long ponytail and wrap it around my hand, yanking her head back, earning a moan from her. "I'm here now though. Why don't you tell me what you need, Cailín."

I don't give her a chance to answer before I capture her mouth with mine, plunging my tongue in to lay claim. Her fingers find the button of my jeans and pop it open then slide the zipper down. She thrusts her hand under the band of my briefs and pumps me a couple of times.

"Fuck, baby," I growl into her mouth.

Layla arches into me. Reluctantly letting go of her arse, I pull the edge of her corset top down so her tits pop out. Angling my head, I flick the tip of my tongue over a peaked nipple a few times before sucking it into my mouth, rolling the stiff bud between my teeth.

"Ay, Teagan. I need you to fuck me. Right now!"

She's rocking desperately against my leg. If I add enough pressure I know I can get her off this way, but I know my Layla. She needs to be filled. Gently pushing her off of me, I hold her at arm's length. Her beautiful face is flushed, eyes shining with lust. Her chest is heaving, breasts still exposed, and she looks so fucking hot right now. I want to spend hours doing the dirtiest things to her. When she reaches for me, I hold up a hand.

"Wait, Cailín," I command. "Go to the sink and face it."

Once she obeys, I prowl behind her, pressing my chest into her back and my hard cock into the curve of her arse. Gripping her hips, I walk her forward until the edge of the sink is pressing into her lower belly then slide my hands up to cup her tits, squeezing them roughly. Her head falls back to my chest, just under my chin. Unable to resist that column of skin, I dip my mouth to her neck, licking a path to her ear.

"Here's what's going to happen," I murmur. "I'm going to pull your pants down and you're going to lean over the sink, holding the sides. Then I'm going to fuck you hard and fast from behind." I catch her gaze, holding it as I nip the delicate skin just under her ear. "And you're going to keep those beautiful brown eyes open, watching me do it, understand?"

Layla whimpers, but holds my gaze in the mirror as she breathes out, "Yes, *Papí.*"

My cock strains painfully against the fabric of my briefs, urging me to get on with it. In one swift move, I hook my fingers into Layla's pants and the string of whatever knickers she has on, yanking them to her knees. When the air hits her naked skin, goosebumps erupt all over. I rub my hands over her arse, then give her a quick slap. She gasps.

"What are you supposed to be doing, Layla?" I lift a brow at our reflections.

Realizing her mistake, she bends over the sink and grips the side of the porcelain, never taking her eyes off of mine.

"Good lass."

She watches as I drop my jeans and briefs, cock springing free to slap my stomach. I grip it and give a good tug. Layla's hips start shifting and I realize she's pressing her thighs together, searching for release. If we were anywhere but at the club, I'd take my sweet time with her, edging her until she screamed. The best part is that I know she would be into it. She'd probably cuss me in Spanish, but she'd love it all the same.

I wrap her ponytail around my hand again, pulling so she has no other choice but to keep her head up and eyes on us. I line myself up with her pussy and punching my hips into her, filling her in one quick thrust. She screams out, and I don't think either of us cares if there's someone on the other side of the door. Keeping my word, I fuck her hard and fast, holding her still with a hand on her hip and the other in her hair. The harder I pound into her, the more noise Layla makes, begging for me to fuck her harder. I'm moments away from blowing my load, but I'm here to take care of Layla. I slide the hand on her hip around her body until I find the juncture of her thighs. It doesn't take more than me pressing her clit for her to come. She practically screams my name, and as I watch her skin flush with the orgasm, I find my own. The garbled sound falling from my throat is loud as my body stills, filling her with my release.

We're both panting heavily when a knock sounds at the door a muffled voice yelling, "Go find somewhere else to fuck so the rest of us can use the bathroom!"

Layla and I look at each other before a rush of quiet laughter flows from us. We might have been in here a little longer than intended, so we hurry to clean ourselves up and readjust our clothes. We consider trying to sneak out one at a time, but the gig is up. Whoever is waiting outside knows exactly what we just did, so we decide to own it. I open the door, Layla one step ahead of me, and come face to face with none other than Ashley.

She opens her mouth to scold us, eyes immediately pinning on Layla, then she glances up at me doing a double take, her blonde hair swinging behind her.

"Teagan?" She asks in astonishment.

"Ashley," I say in greeting, making a point to wrap my arms around Layla's waist, relishing in the way she relaxes in my hold.

"What are you doing here?" Her gaze darts to Layla, eyebrows climbing her forehead.

"I'm here with my girlfriend and her brothers." It's so tempting to add their names, but I don't want to cause a scene. I just want to get out of this hallway.

"Your girlfriend. This..." she scoffs, "is your girlfriend?"

My temper flares, but before I can utter a word, Layla sticks out a hand towards my ex. "Yeah, I'm Layla Diaz. You're actually *intimately* acquainted with *my brother,* Marcos."

Chapter Thirty-One

Layla

I try to keep my head down when it comes to tense situations, but right now, the way Ashley is looking at me? Speaking to Teagan like I'm not *right here* in his arms? It has me seeing red. So, when I tell her who exactly I am, the look of terror on her face is worth it.

"Marcos Diaz… is your… brother?"

The way she stutters over the words is so satisfying. I like to think I'm a kind person, but sometimes my inner bitch comes out.

"Yep," I say, popping the 'p'. "In fact, we just realized how connected we all are. Small world, isn't it? I mean, what are the chances that the man you betrayed would be the love of my life? And the man you cheated *with* is my brother - who didn't know you were already dating someone, by the way." I roll my eyes, sarcasm dripping in my voice. "*Such* a crazy coincidence!"

Teagan stiffens behind me, his hand splaying across my stomach as his thumb brushes the underside of my breast—either in warning or to piss her off. Ashley notices, so I draw my fingers along the veins of his forearm. Color stains her cheeks as she gapes, open-mouthed at us.

"Anyway," I say, untangling myself from Teagan. "We're done in the bathroom now, so it's all yours. And don't worry, we cleaned up our mess."

Winking at her, I pull Teagan away from the bathrooms and back to my brothers.

Once we're out of her line of sight, I veer toward the bar, desperate for a drink that isn't Tito's. The bartender is busy, so I lean with my back against the bar, elbows propped on top behind me. Teagan is staring at me with an unreadable expression.

"What?"

Closing the small gap between us, he snatches my chin between his finger and thumb, lifting my head so our eyes meet. "Are you alright?"

Confused, I ask, "What do you mean?"

A soft smile tugs at the corner of his mouth. "I've just never seen you so…"

"Bitchy?"

He drops his hand, giving me a wry look. "I was going to say confrontational. I've never seen you so confrontational. And to be perfectly honest, I'm rather turned on by it."

A sharp laugh escapes me. "Was what we just did in the bathroom not enough for you?"

Bending so his lips brush my ear, he whispers, "It will never be enough for me, Cailín."

I can't even tease him because I feel the same - I always want him. He stirs up desire so strong, it can barely be contained. Words are powerful, so telling him that I love him is enough, but showing him with my body connects us on a deeper level. Touching him is addicting. I love the feel of his skin and those sculpted muscles under my hands, my tongue. I love the way his hard edges sink into the cushion of my body, how his strong hands hold me to him. Teagan makes me feel safe and confident, shielding me from anyone or anything that makes me question myself, all while empowering me to go after what I want from life.

Overcome by these thoughts, I fling myself at him, hugging him tight. He doesn't even hesitate to fold me into his arms.

"What's this for, Lovely?" He lets out a small laugh.

"I love you," I whisper into his ear. "So much."

He tightens his hold and kisses my neck before murmuring against my skin, "I love you too, Layla."

"Are *you* okay? Is this the first time you've seen her since she left?"

I'd be okay to never talk about Ashley again, but he has to be feeling some kind of way after not only learning who she'd been cheating with but also coming face to face with her.

"Aye," he says, leaning back to look at me. "I can't say I enjoyed seeing her, but it was only painful in the sense that it was awkward as fuck."

Tilting my head to the side, I ask, "Awkward because we got caught fucking in the bathroom?"

A low chuckle sounds from his throat. "No, lass. I have no shame when it comes to you and the things I like to do to this body."

He emphasizes the words by coasting his hands from my hips to just under my breasts. To anyone watching, it looks like he's holding my sides, but in the pocket of space between us, he's brushing his thumbs over my nipples. Inhaling deeply through my nose, I attempt to quell the fire burning in my core. God bless those large goalie hands.

"Honestly," he continues, "I mostly felt embarrassed for her. She fancied herself in love with a new bloke, only to uproot her life and find he didn't feel the same. How's the saying go? 'What goes around comes around?'"

"Or 'Karma's a bitch,'" I supply.

Teagan laughs and the smile that accompanies it lights up my entire world. Yeah, he's the sexiest man I've ever met, but he has a genuinely beautiful soul. Never have I encountered anyone who radiates so much goodness. He's kind, thoughtful, caring, and sincere. He's funny but knows when to be serious. I love how he reads my every move and knows exactly what I need, whether it be words of encouragement, squeezing my hand to let me know he's there, or a quick and dirty fuck in the bathroom of a club.

* * *

It's the last full day with my family before we fly back to North Carolina. Although the trip has been better than I could have ever imagined, I'm more than ready to be home in my normal routine, around my friends, and able to unwind with Teagan in the comfort of a quiet and *empty* house.

I've just sat down to join my parents and sisters for breakfast at the table, a cup of coffee in hand when my phone rings. The screen lights up with Norah's name.

"Hey, chica," I answer quickly.

"Hey! How's your trip going?"

I know Norah's voice and right now she sounds distracted.

"It's been a lot of fun. What's up? Is everything okay? You seem frazzled."

"Ugh. I'm really sorry. I wasn't going to bother you, but I need a huge favor," she says, the words rushing out of her.

"Okay, lay it on me."

"We need help with the makeup for the drag show. The cast is huge and we don't have enough artists to handle it all. Please, please, please will you join the team? I'll make you dinner every night for a week!"

My first instinct is to decline because I've been doing it for years with my parent's voices in my head telling me it's not realistic, but there's another voice—with a warm, Irish accent—reminding me to not let anyone hold me back from my dreams. For the first time in my life, I feel empowered to stand up for what I want. If it backfires, then at least I learned and can say that I tried.

"We could even just use this as a trial," Norah says quickly, thinking my hesitation is because I'm turning her down. "If you hate doing the drag show, then no harm, no foul, but if you love it, I'm pretty certain Dr. Andrews has a paid position open that I guarantee he'd hire..."

"I'll do it," I cut in. I need my best friend to breathe, not talk a million words a minute.

"Wait, really?"

I laugh at the shock in her voice. "Yeah, send me the details so I can ask off at the store. And if it's a good fit, I'll happily take that job."

"Oh my god, Layla! Thank you!" Norah squeals so loud I have to hold the phone away from my ear. "I can't wait to show you what I have in store for the guys. Teagan will hate me, but it will be worth it!"

This gets me laughing, remembering the bet he lost and how he'll be modeling Norah's designs for the cast and crew. I can't wait to remind him when he gets back. Marcos and Rafael invited him to join some friends for a pickup game early this morning, so he was gone before I woke up.

"I literally cannot wait to do Teagan's makeup," I tell Norah. "Highlighting those cheekbones of his is a secret dream come true."

"Right? What is it with these Irishmen and their perfectly chiseled faces?" The amount of conversations we've had about Eamon and Teagan's physical appearance is borderline obsessive.

"And bodies," I add, because, well, they're works of art.

"Girl, that is no lie," she sighs longingly. "Alright, I need to get back to the drawing board, but thank you a million times!"

"I still expect dinner for a week, Norie."

"Duh. You know I'm good for it."

We say our goodbyes and as I'm setting my phone down, I glance up to see my parents staring at me.

"What?"

"What was that about?" Mami demands.

"Oh, Norah needs help doing the makeup for the spring play. Since she knows how much I love doing that, she asked if I could help." I pause, taking a deep breath before telling them the rest. "And, if it's something I enjoy, there will be a job waiting for me in the department. Which means I can finally quit the grocery store."

Papá looks at me thoughtfully, but Mami purses her lips, disapproval coloring her face.

"Mija, do you think that's a good idea? The makeup industry isn't reliable. And what about your degree?"

"What about my degree?" I challenge. "I'm still going to have it regardless of where I'm working. This is my dream, Mami. I would love to be a professional makeup artist. This could be the start of something great."

"Baby, you know that I want you to be happy, right? Makeup could be a good hobby for you, but it's not a serious job. How will you provide for your babies?"

"Por favor, Mami. I don't have babies. And I don't want babies."

She gasps loudly, slapping a hand to her chest in horror.

"At least not for a long while," I amend. "I'm only twenty-three. There's so much life I want to live, things I want to explore before I dedicate myself to raising children. I need you to be supportive of this."

"How can you say I'm not supportive?" Her hand slaps the tabletop and the twins' heads snap up from their phones, eyes wary. "I'm your mother, of course I'm supportive! I'm also trying to be realistic! All I want is for you to be successful and happy."

"Who's to say that I can't be both doing something different? Are my only options to be a wife and mother or a businesswoman? What if I just want to be *me*? What if the thing that makes me happy is following a dream that's different than yours?"

Tears fill my eyes, but I'll be damned if I let them fall. I've never raised my voice at my mother until today, and if the shock on her face is any indication, she's just as upset over it as I am.

"Mami, I don't want to fight with you, but I need you to give me the space and freedom to make my own choices. And mistakes. That's what life is all about, right? I'll never know the potential I have until I try."

"She's right, Raquel," My father's gentle voice says, leaving me at a loss for words.

"Roberto!"

"*Mi amor*, don't you remember how our parents told us we were too young to get married? Your mother even told you to not waste your life with a '*vaquero* like Roberto Diaz'. Aren't you glad we didn't listen? Look what we would have missed out on." He gestures toward me and my sisters.

She softens as she surveys us, contemplating my father's words. A tear spills onto her cheek as she looks over at him. "You're right. All I wanted was to be a wife and mother, specifically *your* wife and the mother of *your* children."

He slides his hand over hers on top of the table, squeezing gently. "You worried about the boys too, remember? Especially Marcos."

Mami scoffs while my sisters and I titter at the memory of the fight they got into when he said he wanted to pursue a career as a professional footballer.

"That boy," she shakes her head. "So stubborn. But he proved me wrong, didn't he?"

"Yes, he did. Now, let's give Layla the chance to do the same."

The tears I've been holding back escape at my father's words. I always thought he felt the same as Mami.

"Papá," I choke out. "Thank you."

"Oh, princessa." He slides from his chair and comes to my side, squatting so that we're at eye level. He cups my cheek, making me feel like a little girl again. "Your mother and I want the best for you, but sometimes we forget that what we think is best isn't actually the best for you at all. At the end of the day, the decision is always yours. What's important is that you feel not only loved and valued for who you are, but supported with the decisions you make as well."

Mami joins us, running a hand over my hair. "I'm sorry, Layla. It wasn't fair of me to expect you to live the same life I did. Why did you never talk to us about this before?"

She's still stroking my hair in a soothing manner and the words tumble out. "I didn't want to disappoint you or ruin our relationship."

"Oh, Layla." She squats next to my father and cups my face in her hands. "Listen to me. There is nothing—*nothing*—you could do to disappoint me or push me away. I may not always agree, and we may have our fights and need some space, but I'll always be your Mami. You'll always be my chiquita. I love you so much, and that will never change."

"I love you too," I murmur.

When my parents wrap me in their arms, hugging me tight, the tears I've been keeping at bay break free.

I wasn't going to cry, dammit.

"So," Jazmina interrupts. "Does this mean that Cori and I can just skip this part when we're older? Since you've already learned where you went wrong with the older three?"

"Absolutely not!" Mami nearly shouts. "You'll go through as many, if not more, life lessons than your siblings combined, *pequeñas divas!*"

The girls grumble in annoyance which makes our Papá chuckle. They don't realize how good they've got it, but then again, neither did I at their age. They don't have the extra task of raising their three year old selves like I did though.

While we wait for Teagan and the boys to come back, I catch my family up on the theme of the spring play, telling them how Teagan lost the bet with Norah. The girls are giggling and my parents are howling with laughter. When I tell them that Norah has a red Devil costume planned for him, I'm slightly concerned that Papá is going to pass out with how hard he's laughing. His face is beet red and tears stream down his cheeks. I've never seen him get this tickled over anything.

"We're back!" Marcos calls out from the front of the house and we try to school our features before they enter the dining area. "Layla, your boy can do more than just protect the net. Why didn't you tell me that he…"

He stops short when he sees our father's face.

"Aye, I'm more than just a pretty face who's good with his hands," Teagan's voice enters the room before his face does. He's sweaty and red-faced, but has the biggest smile on his face. "You just ask your sis…oh. Hiya, love."

"Speak of the devil…" Cori mutters, and all of us at the table hold our breath to see who will break first.

To absolutely no one's surprise, it's Papá.

216

Chapter Thirty-Two

Teagan

"No. Absolutely no fecking way am I wearing that. Forget it, Grady."

It's the first time we've gone out to Paddy's since coming back from visiting Layla's family. We had a great time, but I'm delighted to be back home. Or I was until this grand reveal.

"Don't be such a baby, O'Brien," Norah laughs, pulling the sketch of me in a shimmering red Devil outfit, fishnet stockings, and matching high heels back to her side of the table. "Yours isn't even that bad! Ro's is the worst, and even that isn't horrible."

Not that horrible! I beg Eamon to talk some sense, or at least some compassion, into his lass, but he's clearly siding with the chance of getting laid tonight. Wanker.

"Besides," Norah continues. "If you had won, you know you wouldn't let

Layla and me out of doing our cheer. It's not like you're performing on stage. You're just modeling the costumes for the actors."

Scoffing, I glare at the fire sprite. "Oh, is that all? Just my arse exposed and in fucking high heels? I could break my ankle and never be able to play football again!"

Norah winces then concedes, "Okay, no high heels. Just the rest of it! And the makeup will mask your face, so no one will even really know it's you."

Eamon groans loudly, "Fuck, I forgot about the makeup. Teagan, you arsehole."

I'm the arsehole?

Apparently so, because Ro chooses that moment to approach the table and accuse me of being as such. He's not so cheeky when I show him his costume—a denim Western-themed bustier and matching denim knickers covered in glitter. Oh, and a denim cowboy hat and *chaps*. His attempt at bribery for Norah to forget the whole deal falls on deaf ears, but when Alicia arrives with a pitcher of water and tells him to suck it up, he changes his tune.

"What the feck is that supposed to mean?" Ro asks indignantly. "Aye, I may know that my body is in pristine condition, but that doesn't mean I want to go flaunting it in front of Jesus, Mary, Joséph, and the entire drama department!"

For once, I'm in firm agreement with him. There's a difference between knowing one is fit and showing it off.

"Welcome to the world of women, where we're expected to look a certain way and dress accordingly to please the male species," Alicia snaps. "But God forbid something happens to us in those clothes. Then, it's clearly our fault for dressing provocatively."

We fall silent, because, not only is she right, but the bitterness lacing her voice implies she has personal experience with this.

"Sorry," she sighs. "Sensitive subject. Anyway. The point is, don't be such a baby. Embrace the opportunity and give it your all like you do on the pitch."

Without another word or even a look at any of us, she pivots and heads back toward the bar. Rowan watches her carefully, his jaw clenched tight. He may try to hide it, but we all know he's got it bad for Alicia. If anyone hurt her, there's a good chance he'd fly off the handle. He's pensive when he turns back to the table and folds his arms across his chest. His mind is working overtime, trying to discover whatever unspoken meaning lies in Alicia's outburst.

Layla and Norah excuse themselves to go check on their friend, so I take advantage of their absence.

"Ro, you should go talk to her," I suggest to him.

His amber eyes lock onto mine as his ginger eyebrows furrow. "She's not going to tell me shite. Alicia is more likely to toss a pint in my face than actually open up to me."

"I'm not saying to go storming up there, demanding an explanation, mate. Maybe just tell her that if she needs to talk, you're here for her. And casually mention that if you need to go take care of some arsehole, you will."

"Right," Eamon agrees. "And you know we'd help you out. Men who can't take no for an answer from a woman deserve a proper knuckle supper."

"Aye, thanks, mates." Ro rubs a hand through his red hair and releases a long breath. "Here goes nothing."

Eamon and I watch as he saunters to the bar, leaning his forearms across the top, and mutters something to Layla and Norah. The lasses say their goodbyes and return to our table, relaying what information they gathered. Eventually the conversation shifts to Mac and Myra and the baby girl that will be joining them soon. We all agree that they've come a long way, but Mac will need to rethink the way he views women if he's to be a good father to their daughter.

I angle my body towards Layla, bumping my knee with hers. She glances at me, pulling her long braid over her shoulder. I follow the movements of her fingers as they glide over it until she reaches the end and starts rolling it between her thumb and forefinger. Reaching out, I gently tug the braid from her grasp and twist it around my finger absently. I love the feel of her hair in my hands, whether it's running my fingers through the strands as we cuddle, winding it around my hand while I take her from behind, or burying my fingers into the roots while she's on her knees before me like she was last night.

Layla clears her throat, breaking me from my fantasies. When I meet her eyes, she has one brow raised and pointedly looks down. Unknowingly, I've wound her braid around my palm, and my cock is noticeably hard. Rather than being embarrassed, I grin and wink at her, give her hair a gentle tug, then release it before shifting in my seat to hide the evidence of my thoughts. She snorts in amusement, shaking her head slightly.

Eamon and Norah are oblivious to what's happening across the table from them because they're clearly in their own world. He's whispering in her ear and, whatever he's saying, has her cheeks turning the same shade as her hair. His arm shifts under the table and if I'm not mistaken, I'd say he's sliding his hand to her inner thigh because she squirms and her arm darts under the table.

A handful of months ago, after Ashley left me, I would have been a miserable bloke watching these two, but now all it does is give me ideas and a strong urge to usher Layla somewhere private. Not tonight though. We've been at it like rabbits since getting back from Texas, and I promised to keep my hands—mostly—to myself when we get back to her place. I'm allowed to hold her while we watch a movie, but I'm under strict orders to keep my fingers—and other body parts—above the belt.

As soon as we walk in the door, she's off to her room while I amble into the kitchen to make a snack. Unwrapping the packet of popcorn, I toss it in the microwave and set the timer, grabbing a beer and filling Layla's monster-sized water cup while it cooks.

"What do you want to watch, Lovely?" I call on my way to the living room, snacks in hand.

"Something funny, please!" She hollers back. "I think tonight was serious enough with Alicia. We could use something lighthearted."

"Aye, good call." Settling into the corner of the couch, I flip through the comedy section on Netflix until I find one we haven't watched together yet, queuing it up.

The sound of her bare feet padding down the hall causes me to look her way and *fecking hell*. How am I supposed to keep my hands to myself when she looks good enough to eat in my Seahawks hoodie, that little pair of sleep shorts, and her hair in a knot on her head? I must be staring at her in some sort of way because she stops short and glares at me.

"No."

"What?" I ask innocently.

"Teagan O'Brien, do not look at me like that." She pops a hip out, resting a fist on it, and looks pointedly at my cock. Grey sweatpants do nothing to hide an erection. "We are not fucking tonight. My body needs a break!"

I stick my bottom lip out, pouting like a petulant child. "But you look so good in my jumper, love. Seeing you in my clothes gets me heated up."

Layla closes her eyes and inhales deeply like she's searching for patience. Her lips move silently, counting to ten before exhaling. God, she's adorable.

Finally, she looks at me. "Do you need to go take a cold shower?"

"Fuck no," I exclaim. "That sounds brutal."

"Then get yourself under control. I was really looking forward to just cuddling and watching a movie with you."

The corners of her lips turn down and her eyes fall. She looks so disappointed and I can't stand it.

"You're right," I concede. "I'm sorry, love. What you're wearing is not an excuse for me to misbehave. Now, get over here so I can hold you."

Layla fights a smile, but loses the battle. She rolls her eyes before closing the distance and sinking onto the sofa beside me. I slip my arm around her, tugging her closer to burrow into my side, kissing the side of her head now resting perfectly in the crook of my neck. We get a good laugh out of the movie, but it's also a peaceful experience. Doing something mundane with Layla is just as enjoyable as feeling her naked body writhing beneath mine—just a different type of enjoyment.

* * *

I'm completely shattered. It's been a long week, between classes, football, and work; it feels like I've been up to ninety. Graduation is looming and I still haven't figured out what I'm going to do. I've been in communication with the North Carolina Independent Colleges and Universities nonprofit organization regarding a couple of positions they have open, but nothing concrete has come from it yet. It's not my dream job, but it will be a good way to get my foot in the door for other opportunities. If all else fails, I talk to my manager about working full-time with the kids at the gym. They're a good time and I hate the idea of leaving them. Chances are that even if I do get hired on at NCICU, I'll still work part-time, or at least volunteer, for the after-school program.

It's Friday, and I just finished a scrimmage at the campus pitch. It's been unseasonably hot the last few days and today was no exception. Tearing my goalie gloves from my hands, I tuck them under my arm as I make my way to the bench where my water bottle sits. Coach is talking to a man I've never seen, but his attire suggests he's a scout of some sort. Following their line of sight, I realize they're watching Eamon. And for good reason. He was on fire today. Not that he doesn't always give his all, but he played fiercely, scoring a goal on every attempt. I'm just glad we were playing on the same side or my status as a goalie would have gone down the jacks.

"Kennedy!" Coach barks out.

Eamon whips his gaze their way and nods when Coach beckons him over. Lifting the bottom of his practice jersey, he wipes the sweat from his face before jogging across the field. Coach tosses him a bottle of water as he approaches, then introduces him to the other man. This isn't any of my business, so I gather my belongings and head for the locker room to shower. Pulling my phone from the front pocket of my bag, I check to see if I have any missed calls or messages, smiling when I notice that I have a text from Layla.

Layla: *I got called in to close tonight, so I won't be home until late. Hope the scrimmage went well. Love you, guapo.*

Disappointment seeps in knowing that I won't get to see my lass tonight, but it's probably for the better. I have a mountain of homework to catch up on, and if I go to Layla's, the last thing I'll be doing is homework.

Teagan: *Sorry, Lovely. I'll miss you. Let me know when you get home, yeah?*

222

Love you more, Cailín.

I stuff my phone back in my bag before shutting it in my locker and hitting the showers. If I hurry, I can maybe swing by to give her a quick kiss before her shift. That's all the motivation I need to race through, washing my hair and body at lightning speed. Shutting the water off, I grab a towel and tie it around my waist. Realizing I left my clothes in my bag in my rush, I head for my locker to retrieve them.

"Teag, mate, c'mere till I tell ye," Rowan appears on the other side of the door, making me jump.

"Bleeding Christ, man, you scared the life out of me! Give a bloke some sort of warning, will ya?"

"I will, yeah, but listen," Ro says hurriedly. "That oul fella out there with Coach and Eam is a scout from Inter Miami! Overheard them talking about bringing our mate out for a week or so. Think he'll sign with them if they offer?"

I pause to consider. Eamon is good enough, but I don't think his heart is in it. Especially with Norah at his side. The lass would move wherever he goes, but would he be up for traveling? Leaving her for weeks at a time?

"Nah, I don't think he will."

"He'd be a fucking eejit to turn that down. He could be set for life there," Rowan argues like he's trying to win me over to his side.

"He won't go because of Norah and you know it."

"Ach, that's rubbish. She's not the type to hold him back."

I'm a little shocked that he's defending her, rather than putting the blame on the lass.

"Yeah, mate, I know. She'd follow him to the moon and back. That's not what I'm saying. Eamon won't want to travel regularly. He's so gone for Norah I don't think he could handle being away from her for a few days, let alone weeks."

Rowan purses his lips as he takes in my words, then finally agrees. "Aye, as much as I hate to admit it, I think you're right. Both of you are tied down tight by your mots."

I grin at the thought of Layla tying me down. It doesn't sound half bad, honestly.

"Better you lot than me though. I'm not giving up my life for a lass."

Clapping a hand on his shoulder and squeezing, I say, "Rowan, one day you're going to eat those words and I, personally, cannot wait to watch from the front row. Now, if you'll excuse me, there's a Spanish rose I need to go kiss."

Chapter Thirty-Three

Layla

My nerves are frayed, which is ridiculous because this is just a practice run. All I'm doing is putting stage makeup on the Irish trio—transforming them into a black cat woman, denim cowgirl, and a red devil. No big deal. Except that I really want the department head to like my work enough to offer me a job. Not only would it be something I'd love, but the pay and benefits will be better as an official employee of UNCW than as a grocery store clerk. The position requires experience, and preferably a degree in theater, but having your best friend as one of the most beneficial members of the department holds a lot of weight.

Norah's designs for the guys are brilliant, tailored perfectly to their personalities. Eamon is more mysterious—keeping out of the light, while Rowan is flashy and loud. Teagan may not appear so devilish to the outside world but behind closed doors? He's deliciously wicked. And if I'm being honest, the idea of seeing him in his costume has me more than a little excited.

"You're going to do great," Norah assures me, gripping my shoulders and forcing eye contact. "Promise. Dr. Andrews is going to love your work."

Blowing out a breath, I nod. "Okay. I can do this."

"Hell yeah, you can. Now, who's your first victim?"

That gets a laugh out of me as I contemplate which of the guys I want to work on first. I'm inclined to choose Teagan, but he's more nervous than I am. He tossed and turned all night last night. Even after my attempts to distract him and tire him out with my body, he still remained restless. I would have slept like the dead if not for all of his movement.

At around four o'clock this morning, I gave up on sleep and rolled to face him. He was wide awake, staring at the ceiling.

"Hey, Papí," I whispered, knowing that name would get his attention the quickest.

"Hey," Teagan murmured, rolling to his side. "Did I wake you?"

I nodded, reaching out to brush his hair from his forehead.

"Fuck. I'm sorry, Cailín." He slid his arm around my waist, pulling me flush against him, and tucking my head under his chin. "Go back to sleep."

"I can't." Even though the feel of his fingers gliding up and down my spine had my eyes drifting close. "Not when I know you're freaking out. Want to talk about it?"

He released a heavy sigh. "I'm not sure there's anything to talk about. I'm nervous as fuck and feel like a right eejit over it."

I pulled back to meet his gaze. "Walk me through it. I understand stage fright, because if you'd won the bet, I probably would have moved back to Texas to avoid cheering in front of a crowd. But you play on the field regularly and perform at Paddy's often. What, specifically, scares you about this?"

"You mean other than being half naked, on a huge stage, with all the lights and actual drag queens watching me? Sure, there's nothing remotely terrifying about that. Nothing frightening at all about feeling like an imposter who will, at anytime, do something that offends them."

I pressed my lips together, attempting to stifle the laugh that's trying to break free.

"Would it help to know that Norah talked to them beforehand to make sure they were okay with the fitting?"

Teagan's eyes widened a fraction, but he shrugged his shoulders. "Aye, a little."

"And you won't be up there long at all," I promised him. "It will take longer for me to do your makeup and get you dressed than it will to model it."

Groaning, he rolled to his back, eyes going to the ceiling once more.

"Do you need me to help you sleep again?" I purred, running my hand down his bare chest and the planes of his stomach until I palmed his cock through his briefs.

His hips jerked at my touch and I could feel him harden under my hand. When I met his eyes, I slipped under the fabric to cup his balls. His head fell back into the pillow, exposing the column of his throat. He swallowed thickly as I began pumping my hand along his length.

"Bloody hell, you do things to me, Layla," he bit out through clenched teeth.

"I'm about to," I countered, raising myself with my other arm to flick my tongue over his nipple.

Suddenly I felt his fingers knot into the hair at the nape of my neck and yank my head back before his mouth crashed to mine, tongues twining and fighting for dominance. When his free hand slid into the front of my panties and a finger pressed my clit, I moaned into his mouth, but pulled away quickly.

"No," I told him sternly, moving to the lower end of the bed, and straddling his legs. "I'm taking care of you, Papí, so be a good boy and let me."

Teagan's eyes darkened and his nostrils flared as he watched me bend to run my tongue along one side of his Adonis belt, and then the other. "Go on then, Cailín."

In answer, I rolled the band of his briefs down before lowering my mouth to just above his cock. Brushing my lips over his warm skin, I lifted my eyes, peering at him through my lashes to make sure he watched as I sucked the skin roughly into my mouth, grazing it with my teeth, intent on marking him. A strangled sound fell from his lips, hips bucking against me.

"Layla," Teagan gasped, hands fisting the sheets at his sides. "I need to touch you. Please let me touch you."

"No," I answered simply, undressing him fully. "You can touch me after I make you come."

"Fuck, this is so hot."

"Close your eyes and don't open them until I tell you to." I'd never done this before, not once been the one to give orders in bed. It was exhilarating.

I teased him with my hands, my tongue, my lips, the tip of my nose, but waited to take him fully into my mouth until he was panting and begging to come. The moment my lips closed around him, a string of curses filled the air around us, getting louder the more of him I consumed. With hollowed cheeks, I withdrew slowly, making sure to flick the underside of the head of his cock with my tongue.

"Baby, please. Please let me come. I need to come."

I lowered my mouth again, gaining speed, and wrapping my hand around his girth. His groans grew louder, my name mixed in. Finally, I cupped his balls with my other hand and applied slight pressure at the same time the tip of my tongue ran across that sensitive line under the head.

"Fuck!" Teagan yelled as he spilled his release down my throat.

He slept soundly after that.

"Layla, yoohoo!" Norah's voice pulls me back to the present.

"Sorry, spaced out there for a minute." I'm sure she notices the way my cheeks flush, but doesn't mention it. "Um, let's start with Eamon. I feel like he'll be more forgiving of my nerves than Ro."

"Good call. I'll go get him."

While Norah seeks out her fiance, I arrange all of the makeup and brushes along the vanity in the order I'll need them. Eamon's look will be a little easier because I'm essentially painting a black eye mask and red lips on him. Simple enough.

"Hiya, Layla," Eamon's deep voice greets me. I wouldn't classify him as broody, but he's definitely less inclined to start up a conversation than his Irish counterparts.

"Hey, you ready for this?" I motion for him to sit in the chair opposite me, only slightly worried that his larger form won't fit. He's not big and bulky, but the guy is tall, lean, and muscular.

"Not in the least, but here we are."

"You're a good sport," I tell him while I search through the tubes of foundation to find one that best matches his skin tone.

228

A low chuckle sounds before he says, "It makes her happy, so of course I'll do it."

Norah really could not have found a better match.

"I don't think I ever really thanked you," he says, startling me.

"For what?"

"For sticking by Norah while I was being a proper arsehole. And for being so good for Teag. I realize neither of those things were done specifically for me, but I appreciate them all the same."

Tilting my head to the side, I tell him, "You're right. I don't do either of those for you, but you're important to two of the people I love most. That means you're important to me too, Eamon. I understand why you sent Norah away. It absolutely was *not* the right decision, but I get it. You were trying to put her first, and I admire that."

Eamon looks down at his lap and clears his throat. "Thanks, Layla. That means a lot. You're uh, you're important to me too."

It's a sweet, but awkward moment for us, so I clap my hands together and reach for a brush. "Let's get started. I only have so much time to transform you three."

* * *

"All done, Ro. Are those lashes bugging you?"

"No, love, they're okay. I think. A little heavy, but nothin' is poking my eyes out. When can I look?" Rowan cranes his neck in an attempt to peek in the mirror.

"Wait!" I order. "Let's at least get the wig on."

"Ach, I forgot about the bleedin' wig." He rolls his heavily lashed eyes, the overhead lights catching the sparkles in the shimmery fibers.

"Hey, you've done so great today. Don't start whining now."

Rowan has been an absolute delight. He's cracked jokes and followed instructions perfectly. Unlike the other two.

"Have you seen it, lass? It's godawful! It doesn't even look real!" He's so indignant I can't help but laugh.

"That's the point, Ro," Norah sing-songs from across the room. "Now come here so we can get your chaps on."

"Right-o, fire sprite!" The tall, redhead springs from the chair and sashays toward Norah as if he's on a runway, the sparkly, denim boy shorts barely covering his ass. He is, without a doubt, the biggest diva I've ever met.

Now that the three of them have their makeup and hair done, I start packing up the items I brought with me and organizing the department's products. Glancing in the mirror, I catch Teagan's reflection. He's perched on the edge of a chair, and even with the thick layer of makeup, I can tell he's pale. Sweat beads on his brow as he breathes deeply, inhaling through his nose and exhaling through his mouth.

"You okay over there?" I ask cautiously.

"No," he groans as his blonde, wig-clad head drops between his shoulders over the small trashcan between his knees that I didn't notice earlier.

"Fecking hell, Norah. These chaps are heavy!" Rowan blurts out.

"You look great, Ro. And you're a good sport," Norah assures him. "You've complained the least out of the three of you."

"Ach, well if we *have* to do this, we might as well give it our all! Plus," he declares, turning his backside to the mirror, "these knickers really make my arse look good."

A snort escapes me just as Teagan says, "I'm going to hurl."

Chapter Thirty-Four

Layla

"Teag, let me in," I plead.

"Just…give me a few minutes, okay?"

I pause, not wanting to leave him alone. "Do you want me to stay in here?"

After Norah checked his costume to make sure everything was where it should be, Teagan clomped down the hall in his platform boots to the bathroom. I followed him in, and he all but threw himself into a stall, closing and locking the door in my face, before vomiting in the toilet.

"No, you can go…" he barely gets the words out before he's heaving again.

"Okay. I'll come check on you in a few minutes."

As I exit the bathroom, a large black-haired cat woman slinks toward me. It takes me a second to realize it's Eamon in full costume. All three Irishmen are good-looking, and obviously, Teagan is the only man for me, but it would be an outright lie to say Norah's fiancé doesn't look damn fine in his attire. The black, leather bodysuit clings to him like it was painted on.

I let out a whistle. "Looking good, Kennedy!"

"Thanks," he says dryly. "Remind me to never let Norah and Teagan challenge each other again. And no tequila. Ever."

"Deal. Though after today, I don't think Teagan will even consider it." I throw a thumb over my shoulder toward the bathroom door. "He's riding the struggle bus at the moment."

"Aye, that's what Norah said. I came to help." He starts to rub a hand over his face.

"Ah-ah! Hands off!"

"Fuck. How do you lasses wear this shite? It's suffocating." The scowl on his made-up face just adds to his Grumpy Cat persona, making me giggle.

"Good luck with Teag."

"We'll see," Eamon says doubtfully, pushing open the door. "He may not be very keen to listen if he's this worked up."

It's so baffling to see Teagan in this state since he usually welcomes a challenge with open arms. I've never even seen him lose his temper. Shaking my head, I make my way back to Norah to see if she needs help with anything else. I find her talking to Dr. Andrews, the department head. He lifts his eyes when he sees me, waving me over.

"Miss Diaz! You've done some extraordinary work today!"

My face heats at the praise. Compliments always embarrass me.

"Thank you, sir."

"Ms. Grady tells me you're hoping to pursue a career in makeup application. How would you feel about joining the department? We could use your talent on the team."

Norah told me this was a possibility, but having the confirmation is still a shock to my system. I never thought that my dream could become a reality.

"I would be honored, Dr. Andrews. Thank you!"

"Excellent!" He claps his hands together before extending one to me. "Come see me next week and we'll discuss the details."

"Of course," I say, accepting the handshake. "Thank you so much!"

He smiles warmly. "Alright, it's almost showtime. I'll be out in the audience if you need me."

Norah reaches over to squeeze my hand. "See? I told you he'd love your work!"

My cheeks hurt from grinning so hard. I can't believe that my dream is becoming a reality. Even if this just becomes a side job, it's still more than I ever thought possible. And now that my family is learning to be more supportive, it's just that much sweeter.

"Thank you, Norie, for pushing me to do this," I tell her sincerely. "I wouldn't have done it on my own."

She smiles sweetly at me. "All you needed was one open door. You did the rest. Now, let's go check on your man and get him on stage."

We don't have to go far. Eamon and Teagan are walking toward us, the former draping an arm over the latter's shoulders. Catwoman is murmuring something to the devil, who is nodding his head weakly. He looks so sullen, but not nearly as queasy.

"You've got this, mate." I hear Eamon say.

"We good?" I ask once they are within earshot.

Teagan blows out a breath before meeting my gaze. "Aye, Lovely. Or at least, we will be."

"Kennedy and O'Brien!" Rowan hollers as he stalks toward the group. "Huddle up! Just like before a match. Let's go!"

Teagan and Eamon look sideways at each other before shrugging and following orders. They form a small circle, arms hooked over each other's shoulders, heads bent together.

"Alright, listen up, boyos. This isn't like a regular match, yeah? This is bigger. Our opponent is unlike any we've ever faced. But do we back down from a challenge?"

The other two mutter a weak "no".

"Ach, c'mon, you can do better than that! Do we back down from a challenge?"

"NO!" They roar.

"Fuckin' right, we don't! Because who are we?"

"Seahawks!"

They're swaying back and forth in their little circle, chanting and yelling. It's ridiculous, but it's working. Teagan is no longer sulking, but grinning from ear to ear. Eamon's eyes are bright with determination. Norah and I, however, are laughing our asses off.

"Now let's get out there and show them that it takes more than some face paint and tight costumes to keep us down!" Rowan challenges, putting an arm in the middle of their circle.

Once they've all stacked hands, they roar "Seahawks" one last time, and break. Norah snorts and then ushers them to stage right.

"Alright, Seahawks, don't forget to smile your biggest smiles, bat those lashes, and sway your hips for all you're worth."

Rowan gives her a haughty look before prancing onto the stage, blowing kisses and twerking while spinning the lasso over his head. The tassels on his costume bounce with his movements, scattering a kaleidoscope of color over the floor. He gives the audience quite the show and they're eating it up. By the time he reaches his marked spot, Teagan is taking his position. He looks over at me, so I blow him a kiss. With a wink and a wicked grin, he squares his shoulders and struts onto the stage, twirling his long devil tail. He took Norah's instructions seriously, and is swinging his hips so hard I'm afraid they'll dislocate. He stops and pivots, angling his body to show off every aspect of the costume. Someone in the audience whistles loudly, causing him to quirk a brow before shaking a finger at them. I dissolve into a fit of giggles so hard, I'm crying.

It's not until Eamon takes his place that I compose myself, but that only lasts a moment because he grabs Norah's face, planting a hard kiss on her mouth. He releases her and swaggers to join the others. While slinking his way across the stage, he claws at the air and hisses at the crowd. Then, without warning, he drops his body low, rolls back up seductively, and slaps his ass. Norah is holding her stomach and crowing with laughter. I think we all expected Rowan to rise to the challenge, but the other two killed it. I'm so proud of them, but mostly Teagan. He faced a fear, and in true Teagan fashion, made it a joyful experience.

I watch as the trio of Irishmen take a bow to a standing ovation. Ro is still blowing kisses and circling his lasso, while Eamon and Teagan hold up their tails and flip their long wigs over their shoulders. Norah catches my attention and rolls her eyes at their antics, but there's nothing but love and affection in her gaze. Not just for Eamon, but all of them. She doesn't have biological relatives anymore, but she's proof that people don't have to share DNA to form families. Family can be found in the group of people that love you for who you are and encourage you to be the best and most authentic version of yourself.

And I'm lucky enough to have two.

Chapter Thirty-Five

Teagan

"Ma, I know you want me to come home after graduation, but I can't do that now *and* come back in September."

I've been on the phone with my mum for nearing an hour now, trying to tell her that I'll be back in Ireland in September for Eamon and Norah's wedding, but all she heard was me saying I wouldn't be coming over the summer.

"In September?"

"Aye, that's what I've been trying to tell ya, but you've been eatin' the head off me this whole time. Eamon and Norah are getting married in September." I finally explain, rising from the sofa in my flat to make a cuppa.

She hums as if contemplating my words before asking, "They're getting married in Ireland?"

"Yeah, in Kilkenny."

"I see. I suppose that's your only reason for coming back, is it?"

Christ. I love my mum, but sometimes she makes things unnecessarily difficult.

"No, Ma." I pinch the space between my eyes. "I'm not coming back just because of their wedding. If they weren't getting married, I'd come this summer. No matter what, I was still coming home for a spell."

"Just a spell?" She sounds genuinely shocked. "Are ya not coming home for good now that you've gotten your degree and played football?"

"For good? What? Do you mean back to the farm?" Now I'm the one in shock.

"Aye, 'course that's what I mean, Teagan. What else would I mean?"

A soft knock sounds at the door and Layla enters right after, smiling. I point to the phone and mouth, "my Ma", and she nods knowingly before heading down the hall to my room. My eyes trail after her, enjoying the way her arse looks as she walks away.

"I was thinking maybe you were codding me since I've made it pretty fecking clear that I'm staying in the States," I say sharply. "Where the bleedin' hell did you get the notion I was coming back for good?"

"You'll mind your tongue when speaking to me. Your Da said once you were done dossing about overseas, you'd be coming home. Said you just needed to get it out of your system and then you'd be back."

I scoff. "Will I, yeah?"

At this point, I've lost interest in talking with her. I stalk back to my room where I know my lass is, and freeze in the doorway. Laying stomach down on my bed, she's reading a book. In just her knickers. I'm vaguely aware of my mum prattling on.

"Ma, listen," I start, eyes never leaving Layla. At the sound of my voice, Layla angles her head to peek over her shoulder at me, batting her lashes. "I've gotta go. Something urgent just came up. Talk later, yeah?"

"Teagan, this is important..."

"Love you too. Ta." Ending the call, I place my phone on top of my dresser. I step into the room, closing the door behind me.

Layla starts to turn over, but I want her just like this. "Stop. Stay right where you are, Lovely. I want to admire the view."

She giggles but obeys. Reaching behind my head, I grab the collar of my shirt and tear it off, dropping it to the floor. Propped on her elbow, Layla's long hair cascades over her back in an ebony waterfall. I can't tell if she has a bra on or not, but appreciate the deep purple satin knickers that only cover the upper half of her peach of an arse.

"To what do I owe the pleasure, Cailín?" I keep my voice low as I pop the button on my jeans, stepping out of them when they fall.

She glances over her shoulder and purrs, "You seemed a little tense. Thought I could help you relax."

Because we both know this is going to lead to us naked, I remove my briefs and approach the end of the bed. Bending at the waist, I lean over, caging her in with an arm on either side of her torso, and whisper against the shell of her ear, "You're such a good girl for me, aren't you?"

Goosebumps erupt over her skin as she nods. "Sí, Papí."

I bring a hand to her hair, scooping it up and laying it over her shoulder. No bra. With a single finger, I follow her spine from the base of her neck to the top of those plum-colored knickers. Hooking my finger under the elastic band, I pull until it snaps back into place. She flinches, sucking in a breath.

"How are you going to help me, Layla?"

"However you want." Her voice is just a whisper now.

With a kiss to the small of her back, I trace the line of fabric with my nose down one cheek, biting the fleshiest part not covered with satin. Layla squeaks as she attempts to rub her thighs together.

"Don't move," I command, voice low with desire. "Do not seek relief of any kind, understand? You'll come when I say so, and only by my touch."

"Fuck," she breathes out. "Sí, Papí."

Climbing onto the bed, I trap her legs with my knees and sit back, careful to not put my full weight on her.

"Arse in the air, Cailín. I want it right in my face."

There's no hesitation as Layla slides her body onto her hands and knees, but I press my hand between her shoulder blades—a silent order to put her chest flat on the bed.

"Arms extended above your head." She complies instantly, so I reward her with a bite to the other cheek.

"Teagan," she whines, wiggling her hips.

I slap her arse sharply, making her gasp. "I said not to move."

"Sorry, Papí."

A crimson handprint starts to bloom on her skin, so I rub it soothingly as I contemplate where I want to start with her. My cock is so hard, I know I won't last long once I sink inside of her. I never miss an opportunity to taste her though.

"How attached are you to these knickers?"

"Right now? Not at all." Her voice is muffled by her arms.

"Good," I say, then grip the fabric with both hands and literally tear it from her body.

Layla gasps, but it quickly turns into a moan when my tongue reaches her pussy. I lick her slowly from front to back, lingering where she's the wettest. She tastes so fucking good. Her hips start to grind, so I stop, smacking her arse.

"Cailín…" I growl in warning.

"I can't *not* move, Teagan," she whimpers, turning her head to stare at me. "It's impossible."

"You can do it, Lovely." My words fall against her golden skin like a caress. "Just a little longer for me and I promise you can move as much as you want, yeah?"

With a deep inhale, she exhales her reply. "Okay, Papí."

"I love it when you call me that," I tell her before diving back in, spearing her with my tongue as my hands squeeze and knead her arse.

Devouring her vigorously, her sob filled moans and heavy panting ricochet around the room until she's begging, pleading for me to fuck her.

"*Please*, Papí. I need you."

With a final languid lap, I relent, nipping her inner thigh gently. Rocking back to sit on my heels, I take in the sight before me with satisfaction. Her legs quiver, pussy swollen and glistening.

"Teagan, either fuck me or let me move. I'm aching."

"You did so good, darlin'," I praise her.

Sliding a palm up her spine, I fist it into her hair. Tugging gently, I coax her into a kneeling position between my legs, her back to my chest. One arm wraps underneath her breasts while I grip her chin with the other so I can turn her face to mine and kiss her deeply.

"See how good you taste?" I murmur against her mouth. "It's no wonder I can't get enough of you."

Layla slides her hand into the hair at the back of my head, pulling my mouth back to hers for another kiss. As she sucks my tongue into her mouth, her free hand grabs mine from under her breasts, moving it to cup her. I love the heavy weight of her in my palm, the way her softness rests against me. Releasing her chin, I walk my fingers down her body until I find her clit. When the pad of my middle finger rubs circles over it, she pushes her hips back, grinding against me.

Her lips tear away from mine. Layla spins to face me, reconnecting our mouths, tongues battling for dominance. Nails scrape against my scalp, making my cock twitch between us. Carefully, we shift until she's on her back, those sinful legs wrapped around my waist. I hate to leave her mouth, but the rest of Layla's bronze skin is begging to be kissed and licked. When I move to the juncture where her neck and shoulder meet, her body bows against me.

"So needy, Layla," I mouth against her chest before moving down to those dusky nipples. I pause, taking one in my mouth while tweaking the other between my thumb and forefinger.

"I need you," she pants, body rolling beneath mine. "Please."

"Aye. I've got you."

The promise comes so easily. I will always take care of her in any, and every, way she needs or wants. When her body is aching for release, I'll be the first—and only—to provide it. When she needs support or encouragement, I'll be the one to remind her that she's capable of anything she sets her mind to. When she needs protection, she'll find it in my arms, or standing behind my back as I take the blow for her.

Without taking my mouth from her body, I guide my cock into her heat slowly, savoring the way she feels, how perfectly crafted she is for me. Every time I sink into her feels like our first time together. The way our bodies meet, paired with this emotional connection, lights me up in ways I never expected. The physical attraction has been there since day one, but it's morphed over the last months, turning into something vital to my very existence. I *need* Layla. I need her physically, emotionally, and spiritually. She is the other half of me.

Is there a feeling or action bigger than love? If so, that has to be what I'm experiencing. My heart swells in my chest, beating desperately for the beauty beneath me. Lifting my gaze, I find her dark brown eyes boring into my own with an intensity that matches the thoughts in my head.

Each thrust is punctuated with a kiss—to her lips, her neck, her shoulder, wherever I can reach while staying inside of her. Her gasps turn to moans as her fingers grapple for purchase in my skin as she edges closer to release.

"Deeper," Layla orders breathlessly. "I need you deeper, Teagan."

My hips punch forward in compliance, earning me her screams of approval. I need more. Sliding my arms beneath her, I scoop her up into a sitting position, legs bracketing my thighs. Her arms wrap around my neck while I latch onto her full hips with a bruising grip. This angle keeps her fully seated to the hilt, making every thrust that much deeper.

"Fucking come for me, Layla," I grit out between clenched teeth. I'm so close that it's painful.

"Come with me, Papí."

She doesn't have to tell me twice. Pressing the pad of my thumb to her clit, I move it just the way I know she likes.

"Yes!" Layla screams, tossing her head back as her inner walls clamp around my cock, her orgasm barreling through her.

"Fuck, yes." Growling, I thrust one more time and spill into her.

My body falls back onto the bed and Layla collapses on my chest. We're covered in sweat and panting harshly. Layla traces idle designs on my pec, while I lazily run my fingers through her silken hair.

"I love you," she whispers.

It's not the first time she's said those words, and it won't be the last, but it still gives me a thrill. The sincerity behind them makes my heart swell even more. I tilt her chin up so I can look into her eyes.

"I love *you*, Layla," I tell her earnestly. "So much that those words don't feel like enough most of the time. That probably doesn't even make sense."

"No," she says quickly, cupping my jaw. "It makes perfect sense because I feel the same way. You're everything I didn't know I wanted or needed. Or even thought I could have, if I'm being honest."

My eyebrows pull down in confusion. "What do you mean, love?"

Pulling herself up slightly, she folds her arms over my chest and rests her chin on them. "Before you, when I envisioned my future? I saw myself with someone my parents picked out, married much younger than I wanted to be. I'd have a bunch of babies, all while working a job I didn't love. Never, in a million years, did I ever imagine I'd find someone on my own. I never dreamed of finding someone who not only respects my dreams, but encourages me to go after them. Someone who will stand up for me, making it known that I'm my own person; I don't have to repeat history just to leave a legacy. Teagan, I know, beyond a shadow of a doubt, that we'll spend the rest of our lives together. But I love that there's no pressure to get married and start a family."

A lump forms in my throat. It's nothing I haven't come to realize myself, but hearing the words come from her mouth is a beautiful sound. Brushing her hair behind an ear, I respond with a whispered, "Aye."

Her eyes soften. "I know that you want that someday, though."

"Layla," I breathe. "My lovely Layla. I'll be honest. I would marry you right this very second and give you a million babies... *if* that's what you wanted. Yeah, I want that someday, but only with you, if and when you're ready. If that day never comes, then so be it. I'm not going anywhere. If I can't do life with you, I sure as fuck don't want to do it with anyone else. If we never get married, and only have a dog, I'd still be the happiest bloke on the planet."

She giggles. "God, you say stuff like that and it makes me want to forget everything I just said. Just marry you and have your babies right this second."

A grin spreads slowly across my face. "And hearing you say that makes me want to practice putting babies in you right this second."

Layla's squeals turn to soft groans when I suddenly roll us over, taking her mouth with mine, and sliding my cock inside her again to show her how dedicated I am to practicing.

Chapter Thirty-Six

Three Months Later

Layla

I thought Teagan meeting my family was nerve-wracking. It doesn't hold a candle to me meeting his. Every time I think about it, I break out into a cold sweat.

In just a few short weeks, we'll be flying over the Atlantic Ocean to not only meet his family, but to celebrate Norah and Eamon's wedding. It's been a whirlwind of activity since they set the date. Luckily, I had enough money saved to buy my plane ticket, much to Teagan's dismay. He was more than a little irritated when I told him he wasn't allowed to pay for my airfare. He didn't have a good enough argument, so I won that battle only to lose when it came to rental cars and lodging. Behind my back, he booked everything else, even going as far as pre-paying for my portion of the spa day I had planned with Norah and the other girls.

Teagan began working for NCICU as their Director of Communications about a month after graduation. He had applied for the position on a whim, not believing that he'd have a shot at it with little experience under his belt. Apparently they took a look at his transcript, resume, and work history, liking what they saw enough to offer him the position. He accepted, on the condition that he'd still be able to work a couple of days at the Children's Department as well. His superiors didn't have an issue with that at all, so Tuesdays and Thursdays are spent with the kids. Which is where we are now.

It's the first time I've ever accompanied him, and it feels like I'm intruding on a sacred place. We arrive before the kids, so I climb to the top of the bleachers in the rec room, ensuring I'll be out of the way. Teagan goes about setting up for today's class, placing small, orange cones in patterns across the court. Do I spend more time admiring the way his tight t-shirt and athletic shorts move with his body than where he's putting cones? Absolutely.

The fall soccer season has started back up and he's doing a refresher course to see who might be a good candidate for a local team. Teagan claims he doesn't have favorites, but the same names keep coming up every time we talk about it. If I'm being honest, I'm really excited to meet the kids he's spent so much time with. Especially Gabriela.

"Whatcha starin' at, love?" Teagan's voice floats to where I'm sitting, breaking me from my thoughts.

Not ashamed to be caught, I shrug and say, "You, obviously."

His eyes darken, and he starts to climb the first step toward me when the gymnasium doors squeak open.

"Mr. Teagan!" A small voice calls out, drawing his attention to where it should be.

"Gabriela!" He holds a hand out for a high five, but she crashes into him, wrapping her little arms around his legs in a hug.

My heart is officially a puddle in my chest when he places a gentle hand on the back of her head.

"Hello there," he says bewildered, casting a glance up at me.

"Mr. Teagan, I've been practicing my lion pounces all year! Do you wanna see?"

Without waiting for a reply, she runs to the nearest soccer ball, scoops it up, and runs back to place it before him. Then she falls on top of it with a pretty impressive roar. I laugh louder than I intended, causing everyone to whip their heads my way. Blushing, I smile sheepishly at Teagan, but he's grinning. None of the other kids are interested enough to find out who I am, but Gabriela is curious enough for all of them.

Her brow scrunches, creating little lines on her forehead. "Who's that, Mr.Teagan?"

"That," he says, "is Layla Diaz, my girlfriend."

Little Gabriela's eyes widen at first, then narrow at me.

Uh oh.

"You didn't tell me you had a girlfriend." Small hands ball into fists at her sides.

"Didn't I?" Teagan asks sheepishly, a pink hue gracing his cheeks.

"No. I would remember."

In an attempt to smooth things over, I stand and carefully make my way down the bleachers. Once I reach them, I squeeze Teagan's arm before squatting down to the little girl's level.

"Hi, I'm Layla. It's nice to meet you, Gabriela. Mr. Teagan has told me so much about you."

This takes her by surprise, and she asks in Spanish, "He has?"

Continuing in Spanish, I reply, "Yes, he's told me how great you are at football, and that you'll be the next Marta Viera da Silva!"

Gabriela gasps, cheeks flushing with delight as she looks over her shoulder at Teagan. When he smiles at her, that blush deepens. It's so cute. I want to tell her that he has that effect on me too.

Again, in Spanish, she asks, "Are you and Mr. Teagan in love?"

I'm about to break her precious heart. "Yes, sweetheart, we are."

She frowns. "Are you going to get married?"

Tilting my head to the side a little, I ask, "Do you think we should?"

Her little shoulders shrug. "My mommy says when two people are in love, they have to get married."

"Ah. My mommy says that too, but you know what?" I whisper conspiratorially.

"What?"

Not wanting to overstep boundaries, but still encourage her independence, I tell her, "When you're a grown-up, *you* get to decide what's best for you. So right now, listen to your mommy because she loves you. But when you become an adult and find someone you love? Getting married is up to the two of you, not your family."

I can see the wheels turning in her head at my words. "Do you want to get married to Mr. Teagan?"

Smiling softly, I take her small hand in mine. "Someday, and definitely to Mr. Teagan," I toss him a wink when he perks up at his name. "But right now I'm happy to just be in love like we are. One day, when the time is right, we'll get married."

"Can I tell you a secret?" She leans in.

"Sure."

She casts a quick glance at Teagan, who is pretending not to listen. The rise of his cheeks as he tries not to smile is a dead giveaway that he's hearing every word.

"Mr. Teagan called me *love* once."

Biting back a laugh, I ask, "He did? Should I tell him to stop?"

"Nah, it's okay. As long as you don't mind."

I do chuckle at that. "No, I don't mind. Do you want to know what my sisters call Mr. Teagan?"

She nods excitedly.

Leaning in, I whisper in her ear, "*Vaquerito guapo.*"

"Handsome cowboy?" she gasps out in English before dissolving into a fit of giggles.

"Oi! You're not talking about me, are ya?" Teagan fakes outrage as he crosses his arms over his chest. "I'll be makin' ya run laps if ya keep it up, lasses."

I join Gabriela in her laughing fit because she and I both know he won't.

"Miss Layla, you're fun. I'm glad you and Mr. Teagan are in love." She loops her arms around my neck, squeezing me tightly before running off to join the other kids.

Teagan extends a hand to help me rise from the floor, but instead of releasing me, he drags me into his embrace, kissing the top of my head. "Make a friend, did you?"

"Seems like it. I was worried there for a minute. Not sure I could take on a jealous six-year-old and feel good about it."

A chuckle rumbles through him. "What did you two talk about anyway?"

"Just girl stuff." I shrug, then kiss him at the edge of his jaw. "Get back to work, Mr. Teagan. The kids are waiting."

* * *

"You ready to go, Lovely? The Uber will be here in just a few."

"Coming!" I call from the bedroom, where I'm frantically ensuring I have everything we'll need for our trip to Ireland.

"Without me, Cailín? I'd like to at least watch."

I roll my eyes and snort. "You're cute."

"I know. That's why you keep me around, yeah?"

His voice sounds from the doorway, and I look up from my suitcase to find him leaning against the door frame, hands stuffed in his jean pockets. He really is cute in his Seahawks hoodie and ball cap. It's one of my favorite outfits of his.

"One of the many reasons, actually," I tell him truthfully. "Okay, I'm ready. I think."

Teagan pushes off the frame and enters the room. I'm fidgety with nerves and we haven't even left yet. Wringing my hands, I shift from foot to foot until his warm fingers pry mine apart.

"Hey," he says, waiting until I meet his gaze. "What's making you the most nervous? The travel or my family?"

I laugh nervously. "Both?"

"Ach, love, it'll be grand. The travel bit is long, but it's fun. And hey," he puts me at arm's length and wags his eyebrows. "Maybe we'll finally be able to join the Mile High Club."

"Oh my god, stop!" I lightly slap a hand to his chest, but he catches it, bringing my knuckles to his lips.

"And as for my family? Da and Tarrah can come across as cold, but don't take it personally. My mum and brother will absolutely love you though. Honestly, I couldn't give a single fuck if they don't. I love my family, but I don't plan to spend the rest of my life building a future with them like I do with you."

"I know," I sigh. "I just *want* them to like me."

"They will," he says, kissing my forehead. "Now, the Uber is here. Time to go."

Surprisingly, the airport is relatively empty, so getting through check-in and security is quick. We spend the extra time looking at pictures of Teagan's hometown on his phone while he regales me with stories of his childhood. He and his brother were quite the trouble makers, and it reminds me of my brothers. No wonder they all get along so well.

Once it's time to board, the nerves that had been dormant flutter to life. I'm not scared of flying, but I've never flown over an entire ocean. Sensing my unease, Teagan links his fingers with mine, rubbing soothing circles on the back of my hand with his thumb. It helps a little, but not nearly enough to keep me from fidgeting. Take-off is smooth, and after a few hours I drift off with my head on Teagan's shoulder. I wake up in time to see the hills of Ireland come into view below us. The emerald landscape is threaded with sprays of red, orange, and yellow. More details appear the closer we get to the airport, and it's breathtaking. I can see now why Norah is so enamored with the country.

I turn to see Teagan's reaction to seeing his homeland for the first time in years, but he's not looking out the window. He's looking at me.

"Welcome to Ireland, Lovely."

Chapter Thirty-Seven

Teagan

"There he is!"

We've barely exited the car before my brother's gangly form is approaching, arms open wide. All negative feelings aside, I can't help the grin that spreads across my face. He's a right pain in the arse, but fecking hell, it's good to see him. Thomas and I resemble one another, but he has a good three inches on me. He may be taller, but I've got him beat on muscle. He's always been lanky. My hair is a bit lighter from the consistent sunshine of North Carolina's coast, but we have matching green eyes that we got from our Ma.

"What's the craic, Tommy?" I say in greeting as we embrace each other warmly.

"Ya look good, Teag! The States been treatin' ya well, yeah?" He holds me at arm's length, eyeing me up and down.

His gaze shifts to over my shoulder and his eyes widen with mischief. Without turning, I know that he's spotted Layla. Christ, here we go.

"Well, well, well! Ya said you were bringing yer mot with ya, but ya didn't mention what a ride she is!" Bounding around me, he stops before Layla, extending a hand. "Pleasure to meet ya, love. I'm Tommy."

"Layla," She provides, giving him a dubious look as she offers her hand in return. "Nice to meet you."

The fecker kisses her knuckles, and the urge to tackle him to the ground is so strong, I actually shift on my feet.

"Feckin' eejit, keep yer filthy hands to yerself," I grumble, my accent thickening with annoyance. Not even five minutes in, and he's already being a miserable little pox.

"Ach, c'mon now, don't be a craic vacuum!"

Stepping around my brother, I plant myself next to Layla and slide an arm around her waist, pulling her tight to my side. A deep sense of satisfaction blooms in me when she nestles in. Obviously I'm not worried about my brother making moves, but I like that she feels safe in my arms.

"Ma and Da inside?" I ask, hoping to get this initial reunion over with.

"Ma is, yeah. With Tarrah."

Tommy turns back toward the house, gesturing for us to follow. The house and front garden look exactly the same as when I left—the same doormat on the front steps, the same purple primrose planted along the side of the house.

"Da's out with the sheep. We both know the oul fella won't change routine for anything. I think a dog would have to chew his leg off before he'd change things up. Even then, he'd probably use that leg as a walking stick, he would."

Layla chuckles softly. To anyone else, that would be an amusing mental image. Tommy's tone is teasing, but we both know it's God's honest truth. According to our Gran, Da even worked the ewes on his wedding day, scheduling the event around his daily chores.

Tommy opens the door, ushering us both inside. I give Layla's hand a gentle squeeze, knowing that she's probably already overwhelmed. Entering the house first, I'm not surprised to find that the interior is just as unchanged as the exterior.

Spick and span like always, the sitting room to my left still holds the brown sofa and two matching recliners. The end tables by the recliners have the old, tarnished picture frames right where they were the day I left. One holds Gran and Granddad's wedding picture, while the other holds Ma and Da's. Centered on the mantle above the fireplace is the crucifix, flanked by the three patron saints of Ireland and a family photo from fifteen years ago. It might be the only picture of Da smiling I've ever seen.

There's clanging and muffled voices coming from the kitchen, so I lead us back that way. The closer we get, the clearer the voices become.

"Tarrah, hand me the tea cozy, will ya, love? Thank you."

My brother's voice booms behind us. "Ma! Look who finally made his way home!"

I cringe, not only because he's so loud, but because he makes it sound like I'm back for good.

Rounding the corner, I see my mum standing at the counter, adding tea to the kettle, and my sister, Tarrah, sitting opposite on an old wooden stool. Both of their heads whip in our direction. Tarrah is the spitting image of our Ma, down to their blonde shoulder-length bobs. The only difference is that Ma now has silver streaking through the strands. This sends a pang through my chest. She's getting older, and signs of age are more noticeable than the last time I saw her.

"Teagan, love!" Ma wipes her hands on a dishtowel, rounding the counter. Her hands grip my face as she takes me in momentarily before pulling me into her embrace. I return the hug tightly, placing a kiss on the top of her head.

"Hullo, Ma. It's good to see ya."

"Oh, my boy. You've no idea how good." Like Tommy, she holds me at arm's length so she can get a proper look at me. "You've always been my handsome lad, but you're even more so now. Tarrah, come greet your brother."

My sister grins as she moves in for her own hug. "Hiya, little brother.

252

Welcome home."

Ignoring the last part, I kiss her cheek. "Hiya, Tar. How's she cuttin'?"

Ma doesn't give her the opportunity to answer. "Are ya hungry? I've just wet the tae and have biscuits cooling on the rack."

"Sure, Ma, that sounds great," I say with a smile. "But I'd like to introduce you to someone first."

Gently tugging Layla out from behind me, I place her in front of me proudly. "This is my lass, Layla Diaz."

Ma knew she was coming, but she still acts surprised, reaching to take Layla's hand between both of hers. "Oh, hello there, dear! I'm Siobhán. It's lovely to meet you! This is my oldest, Tarrah."

"Hi," Layla says shyly. "It's nice meeting both of you. Thank you for having me."

My sister's gaze lingers on Layla, no doubt finding something to scrutinize. If there's one thing she's good at, it's being a judgmental harpy. I wrap my arms around her middle possessively, giving Tarrah a look that clearly says to keep her fecking opinions to herself. She pretends not to see it.

Layla

It's official. Teagan's sister is a bitch. Between the dirty looks and the underhanded comments about my size, I'm ready to go off. She's tall and thin while I'm shorter and round. However, my tits are bigger *and* my man can't keep his hands off of me. This is evident by the way he pulled me down onto the couch with him, nearly on his lap when we relocated to the living room for tea.

Shortly after our introduction, Tarrah's fiance, whose name I can't—and don't care to—remember showed up. The two of them together are awkward, at best. He's a nasally dickhead who treats Tarrah like his personal servant. She caters to his every whim out of sheer obedience, some archaic desire to be the doting housewife. He doesn't touch her at all, not even sitting directly beside her. Every time Teagan strokes the back of my hand with his fingers, or kisses my temple, or slides his hand over my knee, the sneer on her face grows. She doesn't think I see the longing in her eyes though. Under all of that holier-than-thou complex is a woman who wants to be loved the way her brother loves me.

I tried to make conversation with her regarding their upcoming wedding, but it was a failed attempt. She'd open her mouth to answer, only to be cut off by fiancé Dickhead. Each time, her eyes would drop to her folded hands in her lap. And because I'm me, I ignore him, not looking away from Tarrah. I can feel Teagan shake with silent laughter because he knows exactly what I'm doing.

"Do you have your dress picked out?" I ask.

"Yes," Dickhead answers.

With a saccharine smile, I pin him with my gaze. "Oh, how progressive of you! I love when men can be in touch with their feminine side. In fact, there's a gay couple I know where both men wore wedding dresses when they got married. They just loved how magical it made their special day."

Tommy explodes into a fit of laughter while Siobhán blushes. Tarrah is even more pale than what I thought possible for an Irish girl. Dickhead is red-faced, and not at all amused.

"I beg your pardon!"

"Oh," I say innocently. "I just assumed that since you answered the question meant for Tarrah, you were excited to share with us about your dress."

"Cailín," Teagan mutters in playful warning against my ear.

"Teagan, you really ought to get her under control, mate," Dickhead sniffs. "Otherwise, she'll be wearing the pants in your family."

We both go rigid. My first instinct is to make some comment about how neither of us wears pants when we're together, but I really do want his mom to like me, at least. Pinning the asshole with a glare, my lips part as I prepare to put him in his place but Teagan beats me to it.

"First of all, *mate*," he says icily. "Layla looks fecking gorgeous in and out of pants, so I really don't care either way. Second, a man doesn't control a woman at all. Not sure what century you've been living in, but women are allowed to speak for themselves. As they bloody well should be. And finally, if ya want to keep my sister happy, you'll pull yer head out of yer arse, and start treating her with love and respect, yeah?"

The room goes silent. Siobhán is wide-eyed, Tommy looks delightfully entertained, and Tarrah is slack-jawed as she stares at her brother in disbelief. I'm so fucking proud of him *and* turned on by his outburst. I want to pull him into any empty room I can find and let him put me in my place—under him, on top of him, or on my knees before him.

It's at that moment that an older gentleman, who I'm assuming is Teagan's father, chooses to stomp through the front door. He wears a tweed flat cap over graying hair and his skin is slightly wrinkled and weathered, likely from working outside. He pauses on the threshold, sensing the tension in the air. His gaze goes to his wife first, brows furrowing as he looks from her face to Tarrah's, then to Dickhead's. He turns his head in our direction, hard eyes landing on Teagan, who tenses beside me. I smoothly prop my elbow on the back of the sofa and slide my hand to the back of his head, wishing he wasn't wearing a hat. I want to thread my fingers through his hair, letting him know he's not alone. Neither man makes a move toward the other. No hugs or happy greetings.

"Son, nice to have ya back." His voice is a slightly deeper version of Teagan's lilting accent.

"Hiya, Da. Good to see ya." Teagan says without emotion.

It's so bizarre to hear him speak like that after months of his lively voice, sparkling eyes, and affectionate hands. He feels nearly lifeless as his father assesses him.

"Are you going to introduce me?" His dad nods in my direction, and I avert my eyes.

"Right," Teagan finally stands, pulling me up with him. "Da, this is my girlfriend, Layla Diaz. Layla, this is my father, Martin."

I extend my hand towards him. "It's nice to meet you, sir."

His eyebrows climb his forehead as he looks from my face to my hand. I'm about to pull my hand back awkwardly when he reaches out, shaking it. His palms and fingers are calloused, but his grip is soft. I expected the work-worn hands, but not a gentle touch.

"Pleasure, lass," he says gruffly, then gives his attention back to Teagan.

They clasp hands, but still no hug. "How long are you here for, son?"

"Not long, I'm afraid." Teagan stuffs his hands into his pockets. "We've a wedding for some friends in Kilkenny to attend in a couple of days and will have to head back to the States not long after."

"I see. Could use yer help with a few things while you're here."

"Martin, please," Siobhán begs. "Can we not just enjoy our time with him? Who knows when we'll see him again."

"The work doesn't stop just because the prodigal son returns."

"Christ," Teagan mutters, cupping the bill of his hat with a hand.

"Watch yer language, son. I'll not have ya takin' the Lord's name in vain under my roof." Martin gives him a withering look.

Teagan's jaw clenches as he glares right back. The pressure is building, and if he doesn't get some sort of release soon, he's going to blow.

"Hey, babe?" I say soothingly, waiting for his eyes to meet mine. His face is set in hard lines but softens when he looks at me. "Can you show me where the bathroom is?"

"Aye, Lovely. C'mon." He laces our fingers and begins to lead us from the room. "Then we'll take a walk when you're done. I want to show you something."

Chapter Thirty-Eight

Layla

"If I would have known you were going to take me traipsing through the mud, I would have worn different shoes," I complain as I try to maneuver around a mud puddle in my tennis shoes.

Teagan chuckles, then turns to grip either side of my waist before lifting me over the puddle. "We're in Ireland. What did you expect?"

"It's the *Green* Isle," I remind him. "Not the brown one."

He laughs again, the concern that's been knotted in my chest loosening. I was worried that my normally happy-go-lucky Irishman was going to be as gloomy as the autumn sky above us for the rest of the day.

When Teagan showed me to the bathroom, I pulled him in with me, locking the door behind. I think he thought it was going to be a repeat of the club in Texas, and while the idea crossed my mind, what I did do was wrap my arms around him, hugging him tight in a silent reminder that I have his back, just like he has mine.

"Where are we going anyway?" I ask.

Being outdoors is great, to an extent, but sloshing around in the muck and mire of the woods is not.

"Just a little further. Promise."

Sighing heavily, I follow behind him. I try to step where he steps, hoping to minimize the amount of mud I'm collecting on my clothes. After a few more minutes, he stops, stepping to the side. While still under the canopy of the trees, what's before us is a tiny clearing with a small, crumbling structure. I stare wide-eyed and completely confused.

"Did you bring me out here to kill me?"

"Fucks sake, no!" Teagan cries indignantly. "It's a...oh, c'mon, I'll just show ya."

Giggling, I let him lead me to the little murder shack. The door is hanging off its hinges, windows are covered with plywood, and the wind is making whistling noises as it blows through the holes in the roof and walls.

Not creepy at all. Nope. Definitely not.

Teagan slowly pushes the door open, revealing a single room covered in dust, twigs, dried leaves, and broken glass. There's a rickety table in the center, and a small hearth on the opposite wall. I hesitantly step over the threshold, casting a wary eye around the space. I'm expecting a jump scare, because that's what my brothers would do. It's not until I squint my eyes that I see what he's wanting to show me.

The wall to my left is covered in chalk drawings and lines of handwriting. I approach slowly, being careful not to step on the broken shards of glass. Teagan is strong, but if I cut my foot, there's no way he's going to be able to carry me all the way back to his parents' house.

Crouching down, I peer at the first drawing. It's a stick figure, carrying a pole over its shoulder with a bundle tied to the end. In crooked lettering under it, it reads: *Step one: leave the farm.* Following the arrow drawn after, the next drawing is the same stick figure on a boat with a large sail. *Step two: go somewhere new* is scrawled below that. The last stick figure is surrounded by other stick figures, all with big smiles drawn on. *Step three: be happy.* Off to the side of that is a list.

What Will Make Me Happy?

-No sheep EVER again.

-My own dog.

-Help people.

-Play football.

-Kiss a pretty girl.

-Eat biscuits at every meal.

Tears have gathered in my eyes, but I laugh at the last two. It breaks my heart to think of a young Teagan feeling so miserable in his own home that all he wanted was to run away. Footsteps crunch behind me.

"I know I had a decent life," Teagan says softly. "I was always fed and cared for, had all the things a lad could want. My Ma was loving and gentle, but she never stood up for us, or herself, where Da was concerned. She always sided with him. He wasn't abusive. We'd get our hides tanned when needed, but he never raised a hand to us otherwise. But I never really felt like I had a father, just an employer. I can't remember a single time that he played with us. He never kicked a ball around with me, pushed Tommy on a swing. He was gentle with Tarrah, but never affectionate. Probably why she's marrying that arsehole."

I stand, pivoting to face him. His hat is pulled down low over his eyes, and his hands are tucked into his pockets again. I don't say anything, just listening as he continues.

"Anyway, this is where I'd come on the bad days. Sometimes Tommy would join me, but he spent most of the time attached to Ma's legs. The day I drew that," he nods toward the wall, "Da had been giving me hell for not doing something properly with the sheep. He was constantly on my arse about something, but never more so than with those fecking sheep. I could have been perfect in every other aspect, but one mistake in the fields or barn made me a disappointment."

"Teagan," I whisper, reaching out to cup his face with both hands, and forcing him to meet my gaze. The light in his eyes has dimmed and it guts me. "I'm so sorry, baby."

He squeezes his eyes shut and inhales a shuddering breath. I've never seen him cry, and I don't want to start now. Not because he shouldn't show emotion—if there's anything he does well, it's share his feelings—but because the idea of someone hurting him so badly that he feels broken leaves me heartbroken and filled with rage. I want to go to battle for him. He's said how he will always be there to block shots taken at me, but who guards him?

In soccer, each position is essential. They all benefit the other. Teagan is a goalie, the last line of defense before the ball hits the net. Before the opposing team even reaches the goalie however, they go through the defender. It's the defender's job to the keep the ball from even getting to the goalie.

Right now, I'm Teagan's defender, and the last thing that I will allow to happen is for one more shot to be fired in his direction.

"We don't have to stay here," I say softly.

"Yeah, let's get back to the house." He starts to pull away, but I hold him firmly.

"No, babe. I don't mean *here*." I pin him with my eyes. "I mean with your family. You didn't come all the way to Ireland just so your dad could make you feel like shit and put you to work. We're here for our friends' wedding. We can spend some time with your mom and then head to Kilkenny. Spend it with people that you know love you."

He gives me a pained expression. "Then I'll feel guilty."

"I know." Stepping closer, I slide my hands from his face, winding them around his neck. "I get it, but that's on them. Not you. If your dad can't even give you a proper greeting without immediately trying to get you to fill some role he thinks you belong in, then you aren't obligated to stay."

* * *

The moment we return from our walk, Teagan's dad immediately requests his help. I don't get a chance to object before he agrees, kissing my temple before following his father outside. He looks so defeated, like a dog with his tail tucked between his legs.

That's enough. I won't stand for this version of the other half of my heart.

While the men do whatever they need to do with the sheep, I offer to help Siobhán and Tarrah with dinner preparations, with the single goal of telling them we won't be staying with them. And I won't be subtle about why.

"I hope you don't mind bunking with Tarrah tonight," Teagan's mother says warmly as she stirs something on the stove. "With Gerard staying as well, I'm afraid the guest room is already spoken for. I don't know how things are done where you're from, but unmarried couples don't share a bed in our house. I'm sure you understand."

Gerard. That's Dickhead's name!

I want to roll my eyes so hard, but instead, I paste a regretful smile on my face. "Of course. My family is the same way. However, Teagan and I won't be staying the night. So there's no need to make any extra fuss."

The spoon clatters onto the stove. "I'm sorry? You're not staying? But I thought..."

Tarrah has paused peeling potatoes, and stares at me with wide eyes.

"We were going to, but I think it's best if Teagan and I stay elsewhere. We'd like for our visit to be pleasant, but I don't think that can happen while there's so much tension between Teagan and Mr. O'Brien."

Siobhan, slowly wipes her hands on a dishtowel, not meeting my eyes. Tarrah is full on gaping at me.

"My dear, some things are what they are. Martin is...very dedicated to the farm, but he's...getting older, you see, and it's becoming more and more difficult for him to manage on his own. He always hoped that Teagan would follow in his footsteps, so when the lad left for the States, it was quite the blow."

I nod. "I understand what you're saying. My family also had certain expectations of me, but they recently realized that I'm my own woman who has dreams of my own. The same is true for your son. Teagan is the most wonderful and caring person I've ever met. He wants to do what he can to help everyone he knows, but he also needs to be able to pursue his dreams without the guilt hanging over him."

"Ach, we don't guilt him!" Teagan's mom cries. "We just remind him of his responsibility as the oldest son. It's his familial duty to take over when Martin is no longer able."

"Mrs. O'Brien," I say carefully. "I mean you no disrespect. It's obvious that Teagan gets his caring nature from you. I saw that the moment I met you. However, we no longer live in the age where everything passes to the oldest son. You have other, very capable children that not only live here, but I'm sure know just as much about the farm as Teagan does. Probably more at this point." I pause, letting the weight of my words fall.

"Teagan has made a life for himself in another country. It's unfair and unrealistic to expect him to change that."

Siobhán's eyes fill with tears, hands twisting together in front of her. "I know you're right, I do. I want nothing more than for him to be happy, but oh how I miss the lad. He's always been this ray of sunshine, even as a wee wan. The only time I ever saw him not smiling was when he was helping with...*oh.*"

In a moment of clarity, her eyes meet mine and I nod sadly.

"Is when he was helping with the sheep," I finish for her.

There's a stretch of silence as I let the words permeate the air.

"I always loved the sheep," Tarrah declares suddenly.

Teagan's mom and I jerk our heads in her direction.

"What's that, dear?"

"I love the sheep. I was always so jealous when Da made Teag go with." She resumes peeling potatoes, not meeting our eyes. The pompous tone gone, she now just sounds sad. "It never made sense to me that Da would have him check the lambs when he knew that I loved it. I'd ask, and he'd tell me it was men's work and to go back inside with you, Ma." Her hands never stop moving across the potato.

"I thought if maybe I acted more like Da, he'd see that I was just as capable as either of the boys. But he didn't notice, so I stopped asking. I started to pretend I wasn't interested, but every chance I got, I'd listen in while he instructed Teag. If you told me I had to take over the farm today, I'm confident I could do it. I even have ideas to make it more efficient."

I'm speechless. Who knew that under that frigid persona was a girl that just really loves…sheep.

"I think I'd like to hear those ideas, Tarrah." A gruff voice sounds behind me and we all shriek, not realizing that Martin was standing just outside the kitchen.

"Jaysus fecking Christ, Martin! Ya scared the ever lovin' shite out of me!" Siobhán yells, then slaps her hands over her mouth like she can't believe she just swore in her own home.

"Bravo, Ma!" Tommy calls from the other room, Teagan's warm laugh following.

Chapter Thirty-Nine

Teagan

I'm not entirely certain what universe I stepped into, but it feels like an alternate reality. My Ma not only swore, but she yelled at Da, who is laughing, actually laughing! I've never heard the man laugh, let alone seen a smile on his face. Tommy is crowin' like a feckin' rooster. I abandon him to his fit, hoping I can get a closer look at this phenomenon that's happening in my parents' kitchen.

I must be dreamin'. Tarrah is giggling with a pile of potato skins in front of her, while Ma is absolutely scarlet, laughing so hard that tears are pourin' down her cheeks. Da is bent at the waist, hands on his knees trying to catch a breath. In the middle of it all is Layla, who looks like a stag caught in the headlights, her eyes are so wide. It's mostly confusion, but there's a spark of mischief in there too, and I wonder what she's been at while I've been mucking out sheep pens.

"You alright, mo chroi?" I ask, maneuvering around the man that looks like my Da, but can't possibly be.

"Yes?" she answers in the form of a question. "I'm not really sure what's happening right now, if I'm being honest."

"Well, that makes two of us. Seems like we both had an interesting time apart, yeah?"

Giving me a curious look, she asks, "What happened while you were away?"

The clones of my family members have finally pulled themselves together enough that the laughter has died down and they're now staring at us.

Tommy strides in, points at me and says, "Teagan grew a pair and told Da he feckin hates sheep, that he loves you, lass, and doesn't plan on leaving the States anytime soon."

I cringe. "That's not exactly how that happened."

What did happen is that my Da wouldn't let up, so I did something I've never done before. I lost my temper.

The hammer I'd been using went flying over Da's head into the wall, leaving a nice hole, and I raged at him. I poured all of the years of suppressed anger out onto the dirt floor of the barn, then followed it up with my dreams, which *did* include loving Layla and staying in the States. I told him that I resented him for how he made me feel as a lad. How he was a shite father to all of us. In that moment, I honestly thought he was going to haul back and hit me his face was so red, but he did something so unexpected that I actually thought I'd died.

He hugged me. Hard.

I'm not ashamed to say that I wept like a babe in his arms, wrapping my arms around his sturdy form to return the embrace. Not to be left out, Tommy jumped in, covering both of us with his spindly arms.

When we finally broke apart, Da's eyes were suspiciously red as he clasped my shoulder firmly. "I'm sorry, son. Not just for being a right shite to ya, but for taking so long to have this conversation. I never wanted to be this kind of father, but I felt like I was failing all of you wans by not being able to provide the way a man should. I poured myself into work and it got the better of me."

After twenty-seven years of hardly speaking at all, we will have to learn how to talk to each other properly. It will be a process, but for once, I'm actually looking forward to spending time with him. If healing can be found, I'd love nothing more than to start fresh with my family and forge new relationships with them. I'm not naive enough to believe it will be all leprechauns and rainbows from now on, but it's a start.

* * *

We stayed at my parents' house for several hours, eating the dinner Ma prepared with Layla and Tarrah, and catching up. Conversation was stilted at times as we navigated this new territory, but eventually we found a good rhythm. There was more laughter in that sitting room than I think there's ever been.

Tarrah and Gerard disappeared for a while, and only my sister returned.

"Tarrah, love, are you alright?" Ma asked as she craned her neck. "Where'd Gerard run off to?"

"Erm, actually, he left. We, uh, broke off the engagement."

A collective gasp fills the room, followed by a shout of joy from Tommy that makes all of us chuckle, even Da.

"Sorry, Tar, but he was a bleedin' melter, that one. You'll be better off." My brother tells her decidedly, conviction lacing his tone

Tarrah glares at him. "Don't hold back now, Thomas. Tell us what you really think!" Turning her attention to our parents, she says, "I'm sorry. I know you liked him, but I just couldn't take the way he talked to me like I was an absolute eejit all the time. And," she stops briefly, color rising on her cheeks, "I know you probably don't want to hear this, but he's an awful ride."

Da chokes on his beer while Ma turns scarlet, fanning her face with her hand.

"Jaysus, Tarrah!" Tommy cries. "No one wants to hear about you and

Gerard's bedroom activities! Fecking hell."

Layla and I chuckle quietly as Tarrah begins to read him the Riot Act.

When it's time to say our goodbyes, Ma begs us to stay, but right now? I need my lass all to myself. The tension and subsequent explosion have left me drained, and nothing sounds better than curling up with her in my arms. That wouldn't be happening at my parents'. There's a quaint little B&B above a local pub that was all too happy to rent out a room when I called them earlier.

The drive is short, and check-in is simple enough. The older woman at the front desk leads us to our room, giving us a saucy wink before scurrying back to her station. A sigh of relief leaves both of us as soon as the door clicks shut. The space is cozy and tidy. There's a queen sized bed to the right of the door covered in fluffy blankets and pillows. Past that, there's a small sitting area with two overstuffed chairs facing the window. To our left is a simple bathroom housing the jacks, a sink and vanity, and a surprisingly large Jacuzzi tub.

Leaving our bags by the door, we shed our jackets and shoes. Layla sinks onto the bed, laying on her back, and closing her eyes. That dark curtain of hair fans across the blankets and all I can do is stare. She's so fucking beautiful.

"You're staring, guapo."

"Aye, it's true. Can't help it," I tell her as I crawl over her, trapping that luscious body between my arms and legs. I lean down, brushing my lips across hers.

"You're beautiful." I kiss her cheek.

"And sexy." A kiss to the spot below her ear has her giggling.

"And stunning." My lips meet her throat.

"Mmm," she moans.

"And I need you naked right this fecking minute, Cailín."

"Okay," she breathes.

"That's a good lass."

It takes less than a minute for us to shed our clothes before we fall back on the bed. Our movements are hurried, full of searching hands and frenzied kisses, like we've been waiting ages for this moment and can't get to each other fast enough. Layla's fingers dive into my hair as I grip her thigh, looping it over my hip. In one swift thrust, I'm inside her. We both groan, our kisses settle into deep, languid strokes of our tongues. I thrust leisurely, savoring the way her lips part with every gasp. Rolling us, I'm graced with the incredible view of Layla riding me, her body undulating with each rock of her hips. She cups both of her breasts, squeezing them and pinching her nipples. One of her hands slips down her soft stomach where her fingers find her clit. I'm simultaneously turned on and jealous. Watching her take her own pleasure is nearly as hot as giving it to her. When her breath starts to come out in short pants, I've reached my limit, no longer willing to share.

"That's my job, Cailín," I growl. Grabbing her fingers, I suck them into my mouth, tasting the sweetness of her arousal.

"Then hurry up and get to work, Papí."

I clutch her hip in one hand, pinching her clit between the fingers of my other.

"Fuck!" She cries out, her body jerking at the contact.

"That's right, baby." I grunt as I punch my hips up harder. "The only one who makes you come is me. If you use your fingers, it's because I'm guiding them. If you use a toy, my hand will be wielding it. Your. Pleasure. Is. Mine."

I emphasize each word with a hard thrust, never pausing my assault on her clit. She's babbling in Spanish, head thrown back far enough that the ends of her hair tickle my thighs. The sensation brings me closer to the edge.

"Papí," the whispered plea falls from her lips, and I refuse to deny her.

"Come for me, Layla."

She shatters, calling out my name as the waves of her orgasm roll through her. When I feel her pussy clamp around my cock, my head falls back and presses into the pillow. I spill into her with a strangled cry. I pull Layla down to me, wrapping my arms around her tightly, while air saws in and out of our lungs. Soft and full lips kiss my chest while her fingertips trace the pattern of the tattoo on my bicep.

"I love you, mo chroi."

CHAPTER THIRTY-NINE

Layla sighs happily. "Tú eres mi todo."

I'm internally berating myself for not knowing Spanish when I ask, "What does that mean?"

"You are my everything."

I'm already gone for this lass, but when she says things like that? It feels like my heart is going to burst inside my chest.

"Tú eres mi todo." The words feel awkward in my mouth, but I want to say them back to her.

Layla carefully slides off of me to nestle into my side.

"I didn't get to tell you about the conversation I had with your mom and sister."

I grimace, considering all the things that could have come up. "Do I even want to know?"

"Yes," she says, kissing my chest. "I think you do."

She relays everything that was said, and once I got past the part where my sister loves sheep, I reach across the nearly nonexistent space between us. I draw her close, holding her flush against me. She snuggles into me, tucking her head under my chin, and I'm overwhelmed with gratitude for the woman who loves me enough to face my family *and* fight for my happiness.

"Thank you, Lovely," I murmur, swallowing the lump in my throat.

Layla raises her head, and just like the day I met her, I'm lost in those brown eyes. She kisses me softly before she speaks. "I'm on your team, Teagan. Even the goalie needs defending."

Epilogue

One Year Later

Layla

"Baila conmigo hermosa."

I look up from the book I'm reading to see Teagan leaning against the door frame of our bedroom, arms folded across his chest, and a lopsided grin on his face. His beard is a little longer these days, and I don't hate it. Makes him look more rugged—like a lumberjack or mountain man.

He's been taking an online Spanish class for the last six months, and has been doing surprisingly well. His accent makes some of the words and phrases sound off at times, but he doesn't let that stop him. Lately, he insists that if he addresses me in Spanish, then I need to respond in kind to help with his conversation skills. If I answer in English, he pouts.

Just now he said, "Dance with me, beautiful" and my stomach did a little flip, like it always does when he gives me a Spanish nickname. I love it.

In Spanish, I reply, "I don't hear any music."

I wait patiently while he figures it out. He struggles with one of the words, but holds up a hand when I try to give him a hint.

"No, give me a minute. I'll figure it out," he says in English.

His dedication is endearing and I love him all the more for it.

When he finally figures it out his face lights up with excitement and he responds with, "We don't need music."

Salsa dancing has become something he really excels at, much to my mother's delight. And fine...mine too. It's fun when he dances with Mami, but when he dances with me? It's foreplay.

Eventually, he persuades me to join him in the living room where all of the furniture is pushed against a wall, leaving a cleared space. The lights are low, with lit candles placed carefully around the room. And even though he just said we don't need music, there's some playing softly from his phone.

I give him a curious look. "No Salsa tonight?"

"Nah," he says, holding out his hand for me to take. "I just want to slow dance with you, Lovely."

Swoon.

I place my hand in his, letting him pull me into his arms. With as many times as we've danced, my body knows exactly where it fits against his. The song changes to "Speechless" by Dan+Shay, and Teagan begins to sing softly against my hair.

"I love this song," I mutter, laying my head on his chest, feeling the steady beat of his heart under my ear.

"Aye. I heard it for the first time shortly after we met, and immediately knew it was about you."

"Really?"

"Yeah," he whispers, shifting slightly.

His heart starts beating faster and I look up at him in concern. "Are you okay?"

"'Course, love," he answers, kissing the tip of my nose. "Why?"

"Your heart just started racing out of nowhere. Do you need to sit down?" I'm starting to panic, thinking that my boyfriend is on the verge of a heart attack.

"Easy, lass," Teagan says soothingly, like he's trying to calm a wild animal. "I'm fine. Honest. I'm just feeling a little nervous, is all."

"Nervous? Why are you nervous, baby?"

He lifts a hand in front of my face, and pinched between his thumb and index finger is a ring. A beautiful oval diamond solitaire sitting on a white gold band.

"Teagan," I choke out, pulling away from his chest.

"Don't freak out. Just listen, yeah?" He places his palm on the side of my neck.

I nod, because all words are stuck in my throat.

"I know marriage isn't something you want to rush into, so I'm not going to pressure you in any way. However, I want you wearing my ring, even if it's just to show the world that you're mine and mine alone. I want the other blokes out there to glance down at your hand, see this rock sitting there, and know you already have someone. I want them to know *I'm* warming your bed, guarding your heart, and loving you unconditionally. If someday you decide you want to get married, then I'll propose properly. But for tonight, I'm only asking if you'll wear this ring as a symbol of how much I love you, Layla."

I'm at a complete loss for words. My heart is telling me to scream from the rooftops that I'll marry him right now, but that's not what he's asking of me. He's communicating his desires while also respecting mine. He wants the world to know that he's a permanent fixture in my life and that I choose him.

And I do. I will choose him every time.

"Yes, Teagan. I'll wear your ring."

Teagan

One Year Later

It's late when I walk in the door. I've been out of town for work all week, and I'm ready to get my hands on my lass. The way I miss her when I have to travel is nearly debilitating. Especially at the end of the day, when I'm stuck in a hotel room alone.

I made an exception to the "all of your pleasure will be at my hands" rule. Now, when I'm away, Layla can use a toy or her hands, but only if we're on the phone together or FaceTiming. She can't go any longer without me than I can go without her. Even after the three years we've been together, our chemistry is still just as strong.

Quietly, I set my keys down on the table by the door, freezing when I see a folded piece of paper. My name is scrawled in familiar handwriting...and Layla's ring next to it. My heart sinks, and I think I might vomit.

With shaky hands, I unfold the paper.

Teagan,
   I'm giving the ring back. You can give it back to me when you ask properly. I'm ready when you are.

xoxo,
   Layla

A bark of laughter bursts from my mouth as the panic leaves my body. Then, I feel like a fecking eejit for even thinking Layla would leave me. We're solid. The next time I laugh, it's in victory because I can finally do what I've been waiting years for. I stalk to our bedroom, opening the door to find her asleep, the lamp on the bedside table still on, and a book face up next to her. She's curled on her side, facing the lamp. Removing my shirt and pants, I crawl in next to her, reaching over to turn the light off before tucking my arm under her. She stirs when I kiss her on the top of her head.

"Teagan?" Layla's voice is thick with sleep.

"Shhh, mo chroi. Go back to sleep. I'm home."

She turns over, eyes barely open, and says, "I missed you, baby."

"Missed you more."

Her answer is to kiss me. I should let her go back to sleep, but I've missed these lips. The feel of her skin under my palms. I don't have to deny myself any longer, and I deepen the kiss, letting my hands travel over her arse. Her responding whimper, and the way she pushes her hips forward, is enough for me to forget letting her sleep.

When we've both found our release, I curl around her, my chest pressing into her back.

"How was your trip?" Layla whispers into the dark.

"Grand. Boring at times, and the nights were brutal, but I made some new contacts."

"That's good," she says around a yawn, wiggling her arse in an attempt to snuggle as close as possible, effectively putting my cock on high alert again.

"Layla?"

"Hmm?"

I kiss her shoulder and inhale her scent.

"Marry me, Lovely."

The End.

What happens next?

Enjoy this sneak peak of book 3 in the Love On Tap series!

Alicia

"I'd love to see the tattoos *under* your clothes."

Wow...that's original. I roll my eyes even though this idiot can't see me. I toss back a shot of whiskey, then whirl to face my nasal-voiced admirer, full of the intention to tell him exactly what he can do with his lame pickup line.

Only, it's not a stranger. "Goddammit, Ro! You just about got throat punched!"

"So the accent worked?"

The fact that Rowan Gallagher—a six-foot-five, ginger-haired, Irish soccer player, and royal pain in my ass—was able to hide his thick Irish brogue is pretty impressive. "Are you saying your goal was to be throat punched?" I quirk an eyebrow at him. I know what he's asking, but I like to give him as much shit as he gives me.

"No! 'Course not! I've been working on my American accent so I can better blend in," he says.

I snort a laugh. "You wouldn't blend in if you were wrapped up in an American flag. Everything about you screams *Irish*."

"Are you stereotyping me, darlin'? Because I take offense to that."

Ignoring him—and the way my body reacts to him calling me *darlin'*—I turn back to signal the bartender for another shot. It's not lost on me that I, the bartender at O'Nelly's Irish Pub, am spending my one night off at a bar. I don't normally drink on my nights off, but it's been a shit day. My rent went up—again—and my little sister was suspended—again.

Two muscled forearms cage me in on both sides as Rowan presses his chest to my back; whispers of his ginger and clove cologne enveloping me. My skin prickles with goosebumps. It's not unusual for Rowan to invade my personal space. However, it's also not unusual for me to lash out when he does.

"Gallagher," I grind out.

"Petersen," he purrs into my ear. The way my name rolls off his tongue has me pressing my thighs together.

"Move your fucking arms before I remove them from your body."

"Ach, no need to get violent, love." He lifts his arms and takes a seat on the bar stool to my right. "What are you drinking tonight?"

I arch an eyebrow at him. "Why do you want to know?"

"So I know what to tell the bartender when I buy your next one," he says, like it's obvious.

"You're not buying me a drink."

"I am, actually. And," he cuts me off when I open my mouth to protest. "as it's not your money, you can't tell me what to do with it."

Damn.

"Fine," I say with a heavy sigh. "Buy me the damn drink."

* * *

He bought me that drink. And then another, and another. When I drink too much, I become flirty and horny; so once the alcohol started working its magic, I pulled him to the dance floor and spun with my back to his chest, grinding my ass against his quickly stiffening cock. He's not shy, so his hands immediately grab my hips roughly while mirroring my movements. One song turns to two, that then turns to three, which leads to us locked in the bathroom, making out like a couple of teenagers. The moment we fall through the door, he slams me against the wall, shoving his hand down the front of my leather pants.

"Fuck me, you're soaked," he growls, licking up the column of my neck. It has me panting and riding the heel of his hand harder.

"If you tell anyone about this, I'll kill you."

"For someone so ashamed, you don't seem to be too upset about what I'm doing with my finger at the moment." Rowan chuckles darkly against my clavicle, curling that finger and massaging my G-spot. The pad of his finger grazes deep within me, making heat pool in my pussy.

"Fuck…" I hiss, then bite down on his neck.

The groan he releases as my teeth sink into his skin is so animalistic, I almost come on the spot just from the sound.

"Christ, woman. You're not just all bark, are you?"

"Shut up, Gallagher." I grip his hair with one hand and pull his head back, silencing him with my tongue down his throat.

My hand that was digging into his shoulder snakes down to his belt buckle. Once it's loosened, I reach in to wrap my hand around his cock and gasp.

He. Is. Huge. What do they feed them in Ireland?

"Like what you feel, love?" he murmurs against my mouth.

I'll stroke his dick, but I won't stroke his already swollen ego.

"Just surprised I found it. Now I wonder if it can do what your fingers can do. *Oh…God,*" I choke out. "Don't stop doing that." He sinks another finger inside, thrusting roughly as the heel of his palm brushes my clit.

"I'm going to give that smart mouth of yours a new job, hen, if you keep talking. Now shut up, and come on my hand like the good girl I know you can be."

And I do.

"Rowan!" I scream, my body shattering.

"Fucking perfect," he whispers against my ear. It's a tone I'm not familiar with, especially coming from him. It's too intense, too expectant, and I can't handle it.

So, I pull his hand out of my pants, making sure he's watching before wrapping my lips around his fingers, sucking them hard. His warm, caramel eyes blaze with the spark of challenge I'm used to seeing, and it riles me up all over again. It may not be the cleanest place, but I'm pretty certain I'm going to let Rowan Gallagher fuck me in this bathroom. He's your typical player. All charm and sex appeal, making you feel like you're the only one he sees, but as soon as he's nailed you? He ghosts. I'm fully aware of this. I don't expect—or want—a relationship or declaration of love. I just want to have this one night of pure, sexual bliss. And after what I felt in my hand, I know Rowan will deliver.

"Do you have a condom?" I ask hurriedly, my hands moving to his zipper.

Long, freckled fingers grasp my wrist, stopping my progress. "No."

"It's fine. I'm on the pill and I'm clean," I mutter, trying to pull free of his grip. "I get checked regularly."

"Alicia, stop."

The finality in his voice stops me in my tracks and my eyes whip to his. "What's wrong?"

His normally smirking and roguish face looks pained. "We can't do this."

I pause a beat, trying to discern why he hit the brakes on a sure thing. "Gallagher, I was kidding about the size of your dick. I'm confident I won't be unsatisfied."

He scrubs a free hand over his eyes before moving his hand down, stroking his beard. "It's not that. I just...I don't want you..."

A cold rage fills my veins. He doesn't want me? "Wow. If that," I gesture towards his still hard cock, "is what you look like when you don't want me, I can't even imagine what you look like if you did want me."

"No...fuck," he groans, pinching the bridge of his nose. "That's not what I was saying. You didn't let me—"

"Oh, I think I let you do enough." I dart around him to leave the bathroom, but he steps in front of me, blocking the way.

"Alicia, would you stop for one fucking minute and listen to me?"

I glare at him, crossing my arms over my chest.

"We're drunk. We're in the jacks. It's a recipe for regret, yeah? I don't want you waking up tomorrow, wishing you'd never met the likes of me."

At this point, I'm completely mortified. I just want to slink away to lick my wounded pride.

"Whatever, Gallagher. You and your excuses can fuck right off. Now," I seethe, fury coursing through me. "Get out of my way and let me leave."

"Li," he starts.

"Don't. Just move."

He sighs heavily and steps aside. I shoulder-check him as I storm out of the bathroom and head for the exit, vowing to never let my guard down with Rowan Gallagher again.

Acknowledgments

A second book?! How is this possible? I have so many people who helped make this happen. I can't possibly list them all so here it is in a nutshell.

First and foremost will always be my husband. In the midst of life, me going back to work, publishing His Ringsend Rose, writing His Spanish Rose, and everything in between, you never wavered. You're the first person I think of when I need to tell someone something. I'd love for every moment in life to be good, but if we have to have bad moments, I'm glad they're with you. You're my rock. I love you.

To my girls, you're growing so fast. I know it seemed like I was ignoring you while I was in the thick of writing, but I hope that someday you'll look back and see your mom chasing her dreams and making them come to life. I hope that you'll both do the same - pursue the things that bring you joy. I miss when you were both little, but I love watching you become confident little women. Don't stop standing up for what is right, even if those around you tell you it's wrong. Trust your hearts and minds. I love you both more than words can say.

Jordan and Andi, two of my biggest supporters, even if you haven't read my books! You listen to me prattle on and share in all of my achievements like they're your own. I love you both so much!

Mom and Linda, my girls have the best grandmas. Thanks for always being available and loving them so hard. Thank you for every single form of support you've provided. Love you!!

Rachel, I'm confident this book wouldn't have happened without you. The amount of times I bugged you about ALL THE THINGS! Thanks for that. And for helping me get Layla and Teagan out of the bedroom so that every chapter wasn't pure smut. I have a long list of things to thank you for, but it would turn into a novel.

My Alpha readers (Rach, Kris, Kim, and Lyra), thank you for constantly being there with tips, unhinged commentary, and so much support! This book is really yours.

Beta readers, why are you guys so awesome? Seriously, before I entered the world of BookTok and Bookstagram, I had no idea beta readers were a thing, and now I realize just how vital you are to the community. Thank you!!!

ARC readers, the last line of defense before books are released into the wild, thank you for catching whatever has slipped through the cracks and building up reviews.

To my Street Team, every time someone tells me they saw my book on social media, I immediately think of all of you and am so freaking thankful. I love the way you love these characters.

Cheyenne, my work wife, I love you. You're still not paying for a book.

Mitch and Kristin, thank you for supporting me and selling my books in the coffee shop. The way you've promoted them on my behalf means the world to me.

Hey besties (you know who you are). Thanks for coming on this journey with me. One day when I'm rich and famous (ha!), I'll pay for us all to go on a besties-only vacation. Love you!

Last, but certainly not least, my readers. There aren't words to properly express how amazing you all are. The way you've fallen in love with the characters on the pages and brought them to life leaves me in awe. Never in a million years did I think I'd write a book and have people that go feral for it! I wish I could thank every single one of you in person.

www.ingramcontent.com/pod-product-compliance
Lightning Source LLC
Chambersburg PA
CBHW020603110726
47899CB00002B/353